Tommie Lee shouted out, almost with glee, "Well, I be doggoned. Look a-there. That's where it must've happened."

Mavis looked out the window. Following Tommie Lee's pointing finger, she saw beside the road pushed-down stalks of corn, already browning, and earth churned up where people had walked. This was where they had found Theda; she recognized the spot from the photographs.

"Oh, Lord," she prayed aloud, afraid that she might see Theda's stretched-out foot, her gloved hand. For the first time, it became real for her, the woman's death . . . and hit her like a fist in her stomach. Those cornstalks had been brushed aside by frightened hands, felled by heavy feet following a woman who must have cried out in fear with no one in that sea of waving leaves to hear her. Mavis felt tears coming to her eyes.

Also by Robert Nordan
Published by Fawcett Books:

RITUALS

ALL DRESSED UP TO DIE

Robert Nordan

FAWCETT GOLD MEDAL • NEW YORK

A Fawcett Gold Medal Book
Published by Ballantine Books
Copyright © 1989 by Robert Nordan

Grateful acknowledgment is made to Century Hutchinson Limited for permission to reprint an excerpt from ''To a Fat Woman Seen from a Train'' from COLLECTED POEMS of Frances Cornford. Reprinted by permission of the publisher, Century Hutchinson Limited.

Library of Congress Catalog Card Number: 89-91414

ISBN 0-449-14576-X

Manufactured in the United States of America

In Memory of My Parents

and for Allen Schuh

O why do you walk through the fields in gloves,
    Missing so much and so much?
O fat white woman whom nobody loves,
    Why do you walk through the fields in gloves,
When the grass is soft as the breast of doves
    And shivering-sweet to the touch?
O why do you walk through the fields in gloves,
    Missing so much and so much.

—Frances Cornford

Chapter One

"Mavis Lashley, I do know those apples are the best thing I ever put in my mouth." That's what people down at the church said about her special dish whenever Mavis brought it to a church supper. She bent down now and looked at the casserole in the oven—brown sugar bubbling with butter on the top and giving off a warm scent of cinnamon that wafted up to her. She smiled. Sometimes people said, "I've just got to have that recipe. How in the world do you make them so good?" But she would only look at them and say, "A little of this, a little of that; nothing to it."

She turned off the oven and stood up, pain slicing at her knees like a knife. She rested a moment, bracing herself against the wall. Lord, she was getting old, older than her own mother when she first taught Mavis how to make the apple dish. Give others that recipe? Well, they could just hold their breath, she'd never do it. So many memories caught in those sights and smells: her mother in that country kitchen, nose shiny with sweat from heat blasting from the old iron wood stove that stood in a dark corner of the room, and her voice (Mavis could almost hear it still in her ears), telling her how to mix in the spices, layer the bread crumbs, dot the butter on top. That memory was more real to Mavis now after—oh, how many years!—than any picture in a frame sitting on a living room table.

The apples could cool down in the oven; she'd want them still to be warm when she took them up to Miss Hattie's house wrapped in newspaper. Death again (the thought struck

1

her almost as hard as the pain of her arthritis), Miss Hattie
Davis gone now, not many of the old neighbors left. Still,
the ones that were there observed the old ways. Mavis would
take her dish of apples up to the house, and there would be
other dishes waiting in the kitchen for family and visitors to
sample during the long day before the funeral, with people
hushed in the living room, talking quietly about Miss Hattie,
what a long, hard fight she made against the cancer that
finally took her. But they were a comfort, those rules, for
what people did when death occurred. Mavis knew—hadn't
they helped her through her own times of sorrow?

She turned away from the stove and looked at the clock
on the wall. Time she should go. In the corner, by the breakfast table where she ate all her meals now—no need to set a
place just for herself in the dining room—the television set
stood, silent, but with the picture flashing. Mavis didn't really watch the stories like some of the other ladies who refused to do anything while their favorite show was on and
talked about the characters as if they were real people living
down the street. But she did like the familiar faces; somehow,
they made her feel less lonely, even though their actions did
not interest her. She knew little of such places, such goings-
on.

Turning off the set as she passed, Mavis went into her
bedroom to change. From the closet, she took a dark voile
dress, with small whirling flowers in lighter colors, the collar
brilliantly white. Maybe the style was a little out of date now,
but it was a good material and not worn at all. Mavis never
was one for changing her wardrobe just because they showed
something new in magazines every month. "I've got my
style," she would say if talk among the ladies at church
turned to clothes. "I'm too old to change now. And anyway,
I don't have the money to throw away on something new
every year."

The same was true for her hair, Mavis thought as she
smoothed a net, thin as a whisper, over the curls that ringed
the back of her neck. Each week, when she went downtown
to the beauty parlor to have her hair washed and set, Shirlee,
the operator, would say to her, "Mavis, honey, why don't

you let me put one of those lavender rinses on to pep up your hair? All the other ladies have 'em.''

"Not me," she would answer back. "If the Lord had intended for me to walk around with a purple head, I reckon He'd have made it that color instead of white." That would shut Shirlee up for at least two seconds before she went on to something else that wasn't worth a hill of beans, but Mavis would close out the voice, feeling the cool water run over her head and Shirlee's strong fingers scrubbing her scalp, half-asleep, as if she drifted on a stream.

She returned to the kitchen, wrapped the dish of apples in the morning's newspaper that she had finished reading while she drank a second cup of coffee, and looked around, trying to remember if she was forgetting anything before going out the door. Used to, she would have put on a hat and worn gloves if she were going to pay her respects where somebody had died, but that custom *had* gone. People didn't even wear hats to church anymore. And it was more comfortable, she had to agree, as she closed the door behind her and locked it, sudden heat weighing down upon her even though she still stood under the aluminum awning that covered the small stoop of her house.

Inside, till late afternoon, the house was cool; she hardly ever even needed a fan. But the heavy air clung to you as soon as you went out the door, and already Mavis could feel moisture forming around the neck of her dress. She checked to see if she had tucked a handkerchief scented with toilet water under the edge of her sleeve. Just a dab always made her feel fresher.

Still she did not go down the steps to the walk, pausing to enjoy the yard. So neat, almost as perfect as it was when John was alive and cut the grass every week, tending it as if it had been a child. Now, she hired one of the Wilson boys from over on the next street, and though he was regular, mowing in straight lines up and down while he had a radio plugged into his ears (she didn't know how he could think, much less cut grass), it lacked John's particular touch. She cared for the marigolds and ajuga along the walk herself. "Mavis, one of these days you're going to get down there and not be able to get up if you insist on bending like that in the yard." Her doctor told her that when she complained about the pain in her knees. But it was something she could still do, and she wasn't about to stop until they laid her out cold.

"Hey there, how're *you*?"

Mavis was startled by the voice. Looking down across the yard she saw Odessa Bailey walking her dogs. Ugly little things that sometimes raised their legs on Mavis's crab apple trees in the corner of the yard, she thought they looked like large white rats. But Odessa loved them like children, talked to them in baby talk that was enough to make a normal person sick. "Just fine," Mavis called back and started down the walk. Thank the Lord Odessa was walking the other way and she wouldn't tag along with Mavis on her way up to Miss Hattie's.

"I bet anything in the world you've made your apples, Mavis Lashley. I can smell them way out here." Odessa smiled up at Mavis.

"That's right. I'm going up to Miss Hattie's with them."

"What a shame. She was so brave." Odessa's mouth turned down. One of the dogs was pulling on its leash and almost threw her off balance. "I've got to take something up myself. I don't know where the time goes."

Mavis didn't say anything. Probably Odessa's time went cleaning up after those little ratty things. Still and all (Mavis's heart softened), Mavis knew what loneliness was. Wasn't she just thinking of John and the yard, even though it had been nine years last April since he passed away? There were worse things than baby-talking a pair of creatures, she supposed. Others she knew turned to drink, or worse.

"Miss Hattie was a good neighbor," Odessa said. "She'll be missed around here. Always visiting the sick and shut-ins till she couldn't get about herself. She lingered on so long, and must have been in pain with the cancer nearly eating her up, but she never complained. So brave." Odessa's eyes were watery. Mavis wanted to get away.

"That's what I heard, too," Mavis said. She walked down the two steps to the sidewalk; one of the dogs came up to sniff her feet, and she moved away. "I better get going," she said. "I want the apples to be warm."

" 'Bye now," Odessa said. "Maybe I'll see you later. Come on, honey," she said to the dog that was pulling toward Mavis. "Mama gonna make you a goody treat when we get home."

Mavis turned and quickly forgot Odessa. Summer sounds came to her and she smiled in enjoyment: the *whirr* of a lawn mower somewhere unseen, the caw of a blue jay as it whirled and swooped near the pear tree next door, a buzz of insects. The one thing not right was the emptiness of children's voices. When she and John first moved into the neighborhood so many years ago, you could hear the lilt and laughter of children as they played up and down the street, free as the birds. Now, they all seemed to be grown up and gone away, except maybe for a brief visit on a Sunday afternoon. . . . Mavis would see their cars out in front of other houses, and a drift of sadness would fall upon her. People on the street were old, dying off like Miss Hattie. She would like to hear the voices of children again.

Mavis was at the corner now, at the intersection of several streets where the old Hedrick house stood on a large V of land. Built by the speculator who developed the neighborhood in the twenties, it stood on the highest point, bigger than all the other houses, with turrets and towers frilly as a wedding cake, though dark red in color, near to blood. Trees hemmed it in and gave it a closed, secret look. The windows, it seemed, were never opened, unless they were raised on the back side of the house, but you couldn't see there because of high hedges. The garage behind held apartments for servants, but only one lived there now. Sadness ruled in that house, Mavis thought. How many years had it been since a child had run across the yard and you could hear the sound of laughter inside?

Cars surrounded Miss Hattie's place, strange on a slow summer afternoon; Miss Hattie almost never had visitors while she was alive, unless one of the neighbors walked up or the preacher came. Mavis turned slowly up the walk, wishing somehow it wasn't her duty to go. But she gripped her dish tightly and went up the front steps, noticing that the wreath of white carnations nailed to the porch post was already wilting in the heavy heat of the day.

"How're you?" a voice said before Mavis could open the screen door. A woman she didn't know pushed it open and motioned for her to enter, and Mavis went inside the small darkened living room. "I'm Paula Murdock, Miss Hattie's niece," the woman said. Mavis peered at her through the low light, a thin woman with a pinched face and dyed curls piled high on her head, sprayed hard to stay. Mavis knew from the flatness of her voice that she came from the country.

"I'm a neighbor," Mavis said, setting down her dish on the small table by the door. "I've known Miss Hattie for years."

"Probably better than we did," the woman said, perhaps with embarrassment in her voice. She moved her hand in a slow gesture to include the rest of the people murmuring in the darkened room. Then she pointed to the leather-bound book on the table. "Won't you sign in?" she said.

Mavis took the pen she offered and bent over the book. She recognized other names, neighbors, as she wrote her own neatly in the rolling cursive she had been taught as a child. "Apple dish," she wrote in slightly smaller letters in the column headed "Gift." "I'll just take this to the kitchen," she said to the woman who still stood near her. "I know the way, you don't need to bother."

"Well, that's real nice of you," the woman said, turning as if relieved. Mavis must have interrupted her whispered conversation with the others, strangers to Mavis, who sat about the room on rented funeral home fold-up chairs.

Of course she knew the women in the kitchen. As soon as she went through the door, Zeena Campbell's voice gushed out, "Mavis, I knew you'd be here. I just told the others, 'If that isn't Mavis Lashley with those apples of hers, I'll eat my hat.' "

The others laughed, then put their hands over their mouths in embarrassment, remembering someone was dead. Zeena took Mavis's dish before Mavis could put it down and carried it over to the table and began to unwrap the newspaper. A dozen other dishes sat there, waiting; no doubt Zeena had arranged them all. Anywhere she went, she took over—and nobody had a chance to do anything different. Zeena read all the women's magazines and seemed to take it upon herself to be the social arbiter of any situation—and though no one said a word to her face, they talked about her behind her back: "Did you ever see the likes of that hair? Black as a crow—and Zeena's got to be sixty-five if she's a day. And you never see her that she isn't wearing a pants suit, unless it's to church." Whatever dish Zeena might bring, it always seemed to have lime jello in it and some foreign ingredient she bought out at the gourmet shop in the mall. Nobody ever touched a thing she made.

"Would you look at this food," Zeena said. "Enough to feed an army. But those apples will go quick"—she smiled at Mavis—"and I may just have a bite myself."

The other women laughed again and Mavis smiled. She noticed that the newspaper had left a dark smudge of ink on her fingers, and she went to the sink to wash her hands. While the water ran, she looked at the shelves on either side of the window where Miss Hattie had kept her little treasures: a ceramic duck with a hole in its back for a plant but vacant now; a small artificial flower arrangement with plastic petals too bright for any living thing; three bottles of medicine that were empty; a small plaque with a Bible verse imprinted in flowery letters. How sad they seemed at that moment, small traces of someone's life, gone as quick as the water washing down the drain of the sink.

"Hey, everybody!" The enveloping voice careened over the sound of the water and Mavis almost jumped. She didn't need to turn; she recognized the voice immediately—Iva Mae Johnson, Zeena's only rival for taking over and running things. Iva Mae knew gossip about people before they knew it themselves, and she spent half her day on the phone talking to anybody who happened to be home and made the mistake of picking up the receiver.

Iva Mae went to the same beauty parlor as Mavis, and Shirlee always had a mouthful of news to tell after Iva Mae had been there. It was Iva Mae that she compared Mavis to:

"She's got the prettiest lavender-rinsed hair you've ever seen," Shirlee would say. "I could make yours just like that." But Mavis would never agree.

"Whew," Iva Mae said, pulling a chair out from the table and flopping down on it. She had put a dish on the table, but no one bothered to look at it. "I thought I'd never get here because I'm just *overwhelmed*." She sat back and looked with her sharp, bright little eyes at the others in the room.

"It *is* a hot day," Zeena Campbell said. She went to the table and slid Iva Mae's dish toward the back, near the salt and pepper.

"That's not what I mean," Iva Mae said, frowning and fanning herself with her hands. She waited again for someone to speak.

"Has there been an accident?" All eyes turned to the woman who stood near the back door—Eunice Fuller. She was new in the neighborhood. She and her husband had moved here a year or so ago when he retired from the railroad. Eunice was quiet as a mouse and never said much of anything, working in her backyard all the time, even in the middle of the day when anybody with a lick of sense would know enough to stay indoors. But she did raise nice vegetables, and when her tomatoes came in, she carried little baskets around to all the neighbors.

"Well that's just it," Iva Mae said, "nobody knows." She bent over, as if to lower her voice, and the others in the room seemed to pull closer. Mavis still stood by the sink.

"I just heard it a while ago. That's why I was later than I expected."

"Heard what?" Nobody noticed where the question came from.

"Why, Miz Hedrick, Theda Hedrick from down on the corner. You mean you hadn't heard?" Iva Mae leaned back and smiled. She knew she had them. Of course they hadn't heard the news before her. She took a deep breath and the ruffles on her blouse trembled. "Theda Hedrick has disappeared. I heard it just a while ago. Been missing since yesterday afternoon."

"You don't mean it," someone said.

"Well I never," said another.

"Whatever could have happened?" It was Zeena, her face white and puffy as biscuit dough under the too-black hair. Her voice rose higher. "Why would she go away?"

"Maybe she didn't go on her own," Iva Mae said. "They have already got a search underway. Nobody knows what happened."

"Where did you hear it?" Zeena had been fumbling at the table, but now she stopped. The room became very quiet as the others waited.

Iva Mae settled back in her chair, her eyes even more intense. "Just wait, honey," she said. "I'll tell you all about it."

Mavis remained at the sink, unable to pull herself away from Iva Mae's portentous voice, though she knew she did not want to hear this bad news, did not want to think about what might have happened in that closed-up, silent house she had passed just a few minutes ago on her way to Miss Hattie's, carrying her special dish of apples.

Chapter Two

"Today was my regular appointment down at Shirlee's Beauty Shoppe," Iva Mae began, fondling the curls on the back of her neck; in the low light of the kitchen her head looked almost purple. "I got home around noon, already wore out from the heat, and knew that I had to fix my dish to bring here. I'd planned to eat something light for lunch—it's too hot to cook more than you have to—and then get the dish ready. Of course I assumed that Pearl was there—it's her day to clean and she has her own key—but when I came in the door, I didn't see hide nor hair of her.

" 'Pearl?' I called out, but got no answer. Pearl is real regular usually, but I thought, Now I suppose she's going to get just like the rest of 'em and I'll probably have to find other help. I went to the kitchen and looked out the window.

"And what do you think I see?" Iva Mae gave no one any time to answer. "There was Pearl talking over the fence to that Charlene Anderson who works for Miz Hedrick. You know how the backs of our houses face each other, though you hardly get a glimpse of Theda Hedrick's backyard, it's so grown up and all, like a woods practically. I didn't even know that Pearl and Charlene knew each other, much less talked. But they all stick together. You know how it is.

"Well, I didn't much like the idea. Pearl was doing her gossiping on *my* time, and Charlene Anderson is not a good influence if you want my opinion. Ever since she got her picture in the paper demonstrating for something down at the courthouse, she acts like I don't know what. I was afraid

10

she'd give Pearl ideas. So I just marched right to the kitchen door and opened the screen and called out, 'Pearl, I'm home. Are you finished with your little conversation?'

"Well, let me tell you, Pearl whipped around like the Devil was after her, but Charlene looked straight at me as pretty as you please, mad, I could tell, because I had interrupted their talk. I looked hard right back, but she still stared.

" 'I'm coming, Miz Johnson,' Pearl said, and she came in then, looking real sheepish. I guess Charlene went back on inside that house. If I'm upstairs and look out the window, I can see the back door, but with that fence and the bushes I couldn't tell what she did."

Iva Mae stopped and shifted in her chair. She looked around. No one moved, and she smiled and began again.

" 'Pearl, you and me have got to talk.' I said. I wanted to cut that little friendship off right in the bud. 'You can have your friends on your own good time, but while you're here, I want you to do your work in this house.'

"Pearl didn't say anything at first, and I thought for a minute she might get real smart after talking with Charlene. Then she came right out with it, and I was shocked to death.

" 'I didn't mean to get tied up like that, Miz Johnson, but I was out beating the dust mop and Charlene poked her head over the fence. She seemed real upset. I don't know her well, but I could tell something was the matter. "Can I talk to you, Pearl?" she asked me, and I said sure thing, she could, and that's how it happened.'

"Then Pearl told me about Miz Hedrick, how she was missing. 'Nobody a-tall knows where she is,' Pearl said. 'She disappeared yesterday afternoon, and the police was called this morning, but they haven't found her yet. The car is gone, too. Miz Hedrick never drove the car, Charlene said. She always had the chauffeur fellow do it. So that made it even more strange. Charlene's scared real bad.' "

"Who is Miz Hedrick?"

The voice intruded like a sudden shot and startled them all. Eunice Fuller looked at the women staring at her, obviously wishing she had not asked her question.

"Don't you *know*?" It was Zeena Campbell. Her red lips were pursed and she almost looked angry at the interruption.

"Now, Zeena," Iva Mae said, "Eunice is new here. She might not know. You hardly ever see Miz Hedrick and Alice Pate out anymore. I guess a lot of folks around town wouldn't know them these days, though if you ever saw that pair, you'd remember."

Mavis knew them, of course. Standing by the sink, she could close her eyes and see those two women riding around in their big car with a chauffeur (hardly anyone else in town had a driver anymore), dressed so peculiarly that they might be strangers passing through from up North somewhere. They lived in that big closed-up house on the corner and never came out—except to shop in their big car.

Dr. Hedrick, when he was alive, was different. You saw him at every banquet in town, and he made a regular run to the snack shop for coffee in the morning, and then to the newsstand to buy himself a cigar, so regular that you could set your watch by him. He shook hands and said, "Good day," whether he knew you or not, and half the women in town were his patients. But Theda, his wife, was different. Stuck up, people said, though others that ought to know reported that she came from way out in the country somewhere and didn't have a pot to piss in—till she came to town to attend business school and then got a job some place where Dr. Hedrick passed by and saw her and was smitten.

Now, you'd never know it. Theda Hedrick looked like something in a magazine, bought clothes in the one exclusive shop in town into which Mavis and her friends would never set foot, it was so expensive. Strange clothes in strange colors, and always wearing a big round hat that looked sharp somehow, for all its curves. Though Mavis remembered once a softer look, for years now, the picture that came to her mind when Theda Hedrick was mentioned was that of a remote figure in the back of a limousine, imperious as a queen.

Alice Pate was not much different. In fact, some people said they couldn't tell the difference. She had been Dr. Hedrick's receptionist till he died. Worked for him for years, and then, all of a sudden, there she was, living with Theda Hedrick and riding around in the car with her. Alice Pate's looks changed, too. She started wearing the strange clothes, the big hats. It was rumored that the two of them went to a men's barbershop to have their hair shingled, and Mrs. Hedrick wouldn't let anybody else come in when they were there.

But they didn't look alike, not to Mavis. Theda was a large woman, dark, with lips that were just a line, hard, as if she bit down. Alice was softer, hair lighter, and she had pale blue eyes that shone even from the backseat of the car. If anything, she looked even more remote than Theda, as if she had turned her back on the office and all the memories there (because the ladies liked her when they went to see Dr. Hedrick; she chatted and acted about as friendly as anybody else), and moved to a different world where she was changed and, ruled by Theda, became a stranger.

"Well, the Hedricks were just about the richest people around here at one time." Iva Mae's voice interrupted Mavis's thoughts and she looked back at the women at the table. Iva Mae leaned toward Eunice Fuller as if she were a child being taught a lesson. "Probably still are, the way they live. Tommie Lee Bagwell has been with them practically as long as anybody can remember and lives up over the garage and drives Theda and Alice Pate around. He's not hurt with sense, but I guess he drives all right. Alice Pate—she's the doctor's former assistant—she lives there, too, don't ask me why. And Charlene works for Miz Hedrick, like I said. Her mama did before, when the doctor was still living, and now Charlene takes care of the place. Her mama passed."

"Whatever do you reckon happened?" It was Zeena Campbell.

"Charlene said they just don't know," Iva Mae answered. "From what I got from Pearl, yesterday, about two o'clock, Theda took the car and drove off without saying a fare you well to anybody, and nobody's seen her since. Charlene stayed all night, and she told Pearl that Miss Alice didn't get a wink of sleep, just walked up and down the floor, smoking cigarettes and drinking whiskey."

"You know not." Zeena's voice was scandalized.

"Well after all they *are* Episcopalian and they do drink."
Iva Mae looked worldly. "Even the preacher."

"I know, but you'd think at a time like that she'd want all
her senses about her."

"Anyway, Theda didn't come home all night and Miss
Alice didn't have a way to get Tommie Lee to go out looking
for her without a car, so she called the police. They're checking everywhere."

Iva Mae sat back, Her recitation was finished, and she
waited for the applause of the ladies like a child who has said
a piece. Zeena started to speak, but before she got a word
in, Mavis blurted out, "Her daughter went off, too. Disappeared in a way. Nobody has heard of her in years."

There was a sudden intake of breath. "Law, I just plumb
forgot that," Zeena said. Her mouth was a little red O.
"Reckon there's any connection?"

Before Mavis could answer, Iva Mae sat up primly and
said, "Well, I should *hope* not. That girl went off in disgrace
and I'm not surprised she was never heard of again. Killed
Dr. Hedrick—that's what they said. He just grieved himself
to death . . . and was in the ground before you knew it.
Theda changed then, too, became even more remote and
closed off. You hardly saw a light in that big house after that.
No, I don't think there's any connection. Probably it's just
some meanness that's happened to Theda. You see it all the
time on TV. Why, you can't go downtown after dark anymore, and sometimes I wonder if it's safe in the daytime.
Lord, I hope nothing has happened to Theda, but you've got
to expect the worst."

"Do you think we could serve now?" Miss Hattie's niece
poked her head through the doorway from the dining room.
"Some of these folks have been here a long time." She stood
waiting; her high hair trembled just a bit.

"Upon my soul," Zeena cried out. "Here we've been
talking and not paying any attention to what we're doing."
She began pushing bowls and plates around the kitchen table.
"We'll have things warmed up in just a minute. Tell 'em to
wait." She turned to Mavis. "Come on over here and help
me," she said. "Let's get things organized."

Mavis moved slowly from the sink, a heavy feeling in her body. In her eyes wavered Theda's face and, vaguely, as if underwater, the sad face of that lonely child who used to roller skate in front of Mavis's house and then was gone, suddenly, never to return again as far as anyone ever knew.

Chapter Three

Mavis checked one last time to be sure she had everything. The smock to protect her dress, the kerchief for her hair, the plain white cotton gloves—they were all in the needlepoint bag she had worked on during dark winter evenings while she watched TV.

Wednesday was her day at the Mission. She had volunteered there once a week quite faithfully for nearly two years; once she had given her word, she had never missed a day. Her job was not particularly attractive, sorting out the donations of clothing people had dropped off the past week, but she gained some satisfaction from it, separating the clothes into piles—dresses here, shirts there, belts in a bin. Some things had to be discarded because they were too worn (funny, wasn't it, how people thought the poor would want just any old thing they wouldn't touch themselves). Sometimes, she became sad as she went through those cast-off clothes, thinking of the people who would wear them again and never know the joy of shopping for something new and fresh, special for themselves.

She closed the front door and locked it, and went down the steps to the walk. Already, the air was heavy with moisture, and she knew it would be another hot day. When she returned home later, she would have to water the grass unless there was a shower—but there was no sign of one at this point, the sky pale blue and not a cloud in sight. It would be close in the room at the Mission. She hoped they had an electric fan.

Walking up the street, she remembered her journey of the day before, and when the Hedrick's house suddenly came into view above the trees, she was startled; she had forgotten all about the news—Theda Hedrick missing. Had anything more happened? No one had called Mavis, and surely Iva Mae Johnson would have been on the phone right away if she had heard anything at all. Mavis saw no sign of life at the house, no cars in front as she would have expected if the news had been bad. On TV shows, when someone was missing, you saw flashing lights and TV cameras and people running in and out importantly. But perhaps it was different in real life. No one Mavis had ever known had really disappeared; there had been no mysteries in her life. People she knew got up and went to work or whatever they did, came to church on Sunday, and then (more and more now, it seemed) grew older and just sat home as long as they were able. If strange things went on behind closed doors, Mavis did not know about them, and she never felt that she should look too close, afraid that she might not like what she saw.

But she *had* been into the Hedrick mansion on the corner. Wouldn't the other ladies be in a state if they knew? Purposely, she had never told them. She kept that one secret to herself, though it had been a temptation so many times just to say, "Oh, yes, I was there. I had tea with Miz Hedrick and Miss Alice." She could just *see* Iva Mae Johnson's face at those words.

That was years ago, but she still remembered the time as if it were yesterday, going up to the house. If she really looked at her feelings carefully, she would have to admit she had been afraid, Mavis Lashley walking as pretty as you please up to the Hedrick's front door and saying, "I'd like to talk to you ladies about the magazines you read. I represent every major publisher, and I've got some specials I'm sure you'll be interested in."

She had no trouble knocking on anybody else's door. Mavis had been selling subscriptions since before her husband died, made quite a little bit of money at it, too, enough to buy her clothes and something now and then for the house. John hadn't complained. "You go right ahead," he said. "I don't mind a-tall.'' But Mavis was reluctant to go visit those two women she had seen only in their big car, in their big hats, as remote as two statues sitting in a museum, roped off so no one could touch them.

Still, she had decided it was just too good an opportunity to miss, and, dressing carefully, wondering even if she should wear gloves but deciding against it, she set out one summer evening—after a breeze had come and the heat had died down—to go to that house just a few steps up the street. So near, yet she felt as if she might be walking to Africa or some other foreign place.

Charlene Anderson opened the door for her. Mavis knew who she was. Most everybody in the neighborhood knew the girl, young then, still in her teens, long before all that mess downtown at the courthouse when she got her picture in the paper at the demonstration. She was a pretty thing, dusty in the lowering light, skin full and smooth as a melon, and so light (much lighter than her mother) that you just had to wonder who her father had been. "Good evening," Charlene said, her voice low and still, like something that had settled down to rest for the night.

"I'd like to see the ladies," Mavis said. "I sell magazines. I'm sure they'd like to hear about some of the special offers I can get them."

Charlene looked her right straight in the eye, and for a moment Mavis was disconcerted. "Maybe," the girl said. "I'll go ask. You wait here."

Like she owned the place, Mavis would have said if she ever told, confident, didn't even invite her in to sit down. Later, when Mavis heard about the demonstration, she wasn't surprised that Charlene had been a part of it.

But Mavis had a chance to look around. No lights were lit, but she could see the gleam of the marble floor in the foyer, the dark mahogany of the stairs spiraling up (where Charlene had disappeared), flowers strangely luminous on a chest nearby, their scent strong in the heaviness of early evening. Except for the call of birds outside, there was no sound, and Mavis did not hear Charlene when she returned down the stairs until there was a swish of her skirts and the brush of her feet on the smooth floor. "They'll be right down," she said. "Would you have a seat in the living room?"

Mavis followed the girl without a word, and Charlene led her into a long room with French doors opening onto a terrace that ran along the back of the house. It was dark, cool, the furniture, covered in summer cotton slipcovers, like ghostly figures. A chandelier sparkled palely, and there was a gleam of silver on the mantel at the end of the room. At the moment that Mavis sat down on one of the smothered chairs, rays from the sun just setting flashed on the glass of the doors and looked like fire burning; she almost caught her breath.

Charlene disappeared again and Mavis was alone. She wondered if she should have come; perhaps she had been too bold. But then she heard sounds from the foyer and the two women came in: Theda Hedrick, big even in a dark dress, darker than the shadows in the corner of the room, her face more severe now than when seen in the car without the round hat to soften her appearance, and beside her, Alice Pate, in a pale dress that the fading light drained of color, short hair like a child's cap upon her head.

"How are you?" Mavis said to the two of them, hearing her voice spiraling upward in the dim room like the whistle of some bird trapped from flight.

"We're fine," Alice Pate said, and her voice was reassuring to Mavis. In the growing darkness, it contained light and sparkle, a genuineness of welcome. Theda Hedrick's lips twitched, but she said nothing. Undaunted, Mavis went on.

"I wanted to stop by," she said, beginning to reach into her satchel where the brochures were neatly arranged in separate pockets, "and tell you about some special offers I have on magazines. I've told several other people in the neighborhood, and I didn't want you to miss out on the chance to subscribe. Here now"—she pulled out a bright folder—"look at that price. I'm sure you'll agree it's a real savings."

Mavis talked on, showing the ladies her other brochures, telling them of the money they would save, though at some point she realized it was ludicrous—they could afford to take any magazine without a thought of price. But she said her speech to the end and then sat back, knowing that they would give her an order.

They chose several magazines, clothing and beauty tips, glossy, expensive publications on home furnishings. Mavis wrote up her order blanks with a smile, and the ladies smiled back at her, almost relaxed. "Well now," she said, closing her order book, "I'm sure you're going to enjoy your reading."

"Yes," Theda Hedrick said, "I think we will." She sat up straighter in her chair. "Won't you have something now that we've finished? We don't have many visitors and we've enjoyed your call."

You could have knocked Mavis over with a feather. To think that she was in the Hedrick's fine house and was being offered refreshments just like an old friend. That's when she decided not to tell the others. They would be so jealous they wouldn't know what to do—but more important, Mavis wanted the memory herself, closed up and special, something that she could turn to in later days and open up like a treasure in her hands.

"Charlene," Theda Hedrick called. The girl appeared at the doorway immediately, as if she had hovered there the whole time. In the near darkness, her face looked as if it were illumined by a small flame.

"Yes, ma'am?" Charlene said, her voice even.

"Can you give us some iced tea? And there are some wafers, you know the ones, bring us some of those, too." Charlene disappeared without answering. Theda Hedrick turned back to the others in the room. "That will be refreshing," she said. "Hasn't this been a hot summer?"

"It sure has," Mavis said. She took the handkerchief daubed with eau de cologne from her sleeve and wiped her upper lip. "You take a bath and five minutes later, you're just as hot as ever."

"Sometimes I go and just run water over my wrists. That seems to help." Alice Pate leaned forward, as if she were trying to see Mavis in the darkness. Her voice was low; Mavis had almost forgotten she was in the room. "We don't go out much in such weather," Theda Hedrick said, as if the conversation was becoming a little personal. "It's cooler in the house."

"Yes," said Alice, with a tone of disappointment in her voice. Mavis wondered if Alice liked being shut up in that house, alone with Theda and Charlene, and Tommie Lee Bagwell living out there over the garage.

They talked on. About nothing really; changes in the weather, gardening, flowers in the yard. Charlene came back and without asking turned on a lamp on a low table and set down a tray of glasses filled with iced tea, a sprig of mint on the side of each. Mavis breathed in the scent and thought of the soft, dark earth behind the house of her childhood where mint grew in summer; when she picked it for her mother the stems left their sharp scent on her hands. Theda passed a plate thin as eggshells and Mavis took two wafers that melted on her tongue like communion bread when she put them in her mouth. The light fled outside, and they sat in the little circle of brightness from the lamp that seemed as feeble as the glow of lightning bugs, binding them close, almost friends, it seemed. Why, Mavis thought to herself, it's just like me and the ladies down at the church when we get together, no difference a-tall.

Then she knew it was time to go. Theda Hedrick cleared her throat and set down her glass of tea, offered no more cookies, though there were still three left on the plate. "Well, this has been just the nicest visit," Mavis said, standing. "But I must go, it's getting late. I do thank you for the order. I know you'll just love those magazines."

Alice Pate spoke before Theda got a chance. "We've enjoyed it, too," she said. "It's good to know your neighbors. We don't see enough of them. You come back, you hear?"

Mavis said nothing more, but she saw that Theda Hedrick was a little upset with Alice's words, too forward it seemed. Theda would not tolerate visits from other neighbors, even though she had welcomed Mavis. "Good night," she said to Mavis and held out her hand. Mavis touched her fingers, cool from the iced tea glass but dry as a bone.

They turned on the porch light for Mavis, and she walked down the walk in its glow to the street. Turning left, she started her way homeward. Such a nice time she had had. Those two weren't stuck up the way everybody said; they had treated her perfectly fine. And she had seen the inside of that house, which had always seemed so closed off and tight. Wouldn't the others be surprised if they knew.

But then she realized a strangeness that had not struck her before: there was no picture of Ruth Anne, Theda's daughter, anywhere around. Nothing to indicate that a child had ever lived in that house. Who could imagine a little girl running around those ghostly chairs and dark tables with laughter trailing behind her? Perhaps there was a nursery upstairs somewhere with fairy-tale pictures on the wall and ruffles at the window, but somehow Mavis doubted it. Ruth Anne must have led a lonely life in that big house; perhaps that was why she had never returned after she went away . . . at least, as far as anyone knew.

Mavis remembered her, that girl; she would see Theda and her child riding by in the backseat of the car. Ruth Anne had dark, long hair with just a bit of curl at the end, her one distinguishing feature, and pale eyes that looked watery, as if she were about to cry. Always she was dressed in dark clothes, perhaps with a white collar edged in lace at the neck, and she must have been told a dozen times a day, "Now don't you get dirty, don't wrinkle your dress." A few times Ruth Anne roller skated past Mavis's house, gawky as a young animal, and surely she did not wear those party clothes on such occasions, though Mavis could not remember. Later, when all the gossip came out and people talked about Ruth Anne, Mavis could not think of her as a teenager. The picture that remained in her head was that of a lonely-looking child in a dark dress, glimpsed from afar, then gone. They said that Dr. Hedrick grieved himself to death after Ruth Anne went away. He died in less than a year, and Alice Pate moved into the house as Theda's companion. That's when the Hedrick house seemed to close up; the front door never opened that anyone saw, and the only view of the two ladies was in the long car driven by Tommie Lee on one of their shopping expeditions to the few small shops they patronized downtown.

* * *

"How're you today?" The bus driver tipped his hat and smiled at Mavis. He was one of the Judd boys from out Apex way; Mavis knew his mother. She climbed up onto the bus and dropped in her fare, showing her senior citizen's card. She had been startled when the bus pulled up beside her at the stop, so lost in thought she had become, her mind still on that evening visit to the Hedrick house those years ago.

"Why, I'm just fine," she said. "Though I could do without some of this heat."

"Me, too," the driver said. "We need rain. My little garden is about to dry up."

"Don't see a sign of any now," Mavis said. The driver closed the doors, and she moved quickly toward a seat so that she would not fall when the bus started up. She took the front seat, near the driver, for protection, even though the only other person on the bus was a teenager with plugs in his ears jerking around to music like he was having some kind of fit. He'd be deaf before he was grown. He did not look up at Mavis.

"Well, the Lord will provide," Mavis said, taking out her handkerchief and wiping the seat before she sat. You never knew who might have been sitting there before. "We just have to wait on Him."

Chapter Four

The bus stop was just a block from the Mission. As they approached the corner, Mavis got up carefully and held on to the back of the seat until the bus had stopped. She didn't ring the bell; the driver knew when it was her stop since she made this same trip every week. "You have a nice day now," she said as she started out the front door. "It's going to be another hot one."

"Yes, ma'am, you, too." He waited until she was down the steps and out on the curb before closing the door, not like some of the other drivers around town who closed the door so quickly the wind blew the hairs on the back of your neck. Mavis smiled at him and he smiled back, then she turned and started down the sidewalk, clutching her purse close under her arm the way they told you to these days; you couldn't be too careful.

Especially in this neighborhood. The Mission sat across the street from a park. When the city's founding fathers had laid out its plan, they designated a large central square for the original courthouse and four smaller squares, one in each direction, for parks. Two were gone now, land taken for drab public buildings, and the two that were left were neglected, bare ground under the old trees where no grass grew, leaves and garbage blowing across them with the wind. The only pretty sight that remained was the large bed of cannas planted there in the summer, the brilliant plants standing like wild exotic birds until the blooms faded and finally dried and rustled in the cold.

Nobody of any account sat in the square. Used to be, people met there and talked on their way to the city market across the way; children played. But that was all gone now, the buildings empty and run-down, though every once in a while Mavis saw an article in the evening paper about making the market into some kind of fancy shopping mall, with boutiques and such, filled with expensive things that nobody really needed. These days, only a few old men sat in the square, looking as dried up as the dead plants, silent, waiting all the day long, for what Mavis didn't know. Some of them came over to the Mission for the food they gave out each evening, and once she thought she recognized one of them wearing a suit she had sorted out the week before in the clothing room, the sight quite startling to her. She had never connected those clothes to real people, never actually saw anyone pick up a garment and try it on and go away with it, theirs now, a part of themselves. She felt embarrassed, as if suddenly forced to be intimate with a stranger.

The Mission was a small building made of stone, the walls thick as a fortress, with small square windows set high in the walls. It had been a church of some sort once, but people stopped coming when that part of town went down, and it had sat empty for a long time before the Mission had found a home there. The sanctuary remained, and there were services in it for the few weary men, and once in a while a woman or two, who trudged over from the square, having heard, Lord knows from whom, about the free food and clothes the Mission gave out. Most came once and were never seen again, moving on, hitchhiking, perhaps, out on the highway. There were offices at the side of the building and a kitchen in back where other volunteers made food and served it in tin trays that clanked against the counter and made Mavis think, somehow, of a jail, heavy doors closing over people's lives.

She turned to the left of the building, walking toward the rear to the side entrance. The door was unlocked; sometimes she worried about that—anybody could get in. But nothing had ever happened. No real meanness around; she supposed people were simply too tired out and hopeless in that part of town to do much of anything. She opened the door and went inside, and had to stand very still for a moment; the small foyer was dark and cool, and coming from the sunshine outside, Mavis could not see for a moment. But the scent was familiar, depressing—the musty smell of old clothes and heavy, dull food mingled together. It never faded, and Mavis felt that the clothes they gave out to the poor people who came there would never be free of that smell, no matter how many times they might be washed and hung out in the sun to dry.

"That you, Miz Lashley?"

The voice came from just inside the next room, an office opening from the hallway that ran to the back of the building.

"Sure is," she answered, her lips already forming a smile. She turned, then walked down the hall and stopped in front of an open doorway. "How'd you know it was me? I didn't think I made a sound."

"I heard the door, and I said to myself right then, 'There's Miz Lashley. Right on time. I could set the clock right there on the desk by her every week.' "

The girl sitting at the desk laughed and Mavis smiled at her. Sue Dillon. She was there every week when Mavis came in, as faithful as Mavis herself, and had been working there almost as long. Volunteering really, like Mavis, but Sue spent so many hours there, and did so much work in the office, that she seemed like a permanent part of the place. But then, Mavis supposed, it was part of her training, or something she was required to do. Sue attended that little Bible college out on the old fairgrounds road, though you had to admit it hardly looked like a school at all, just one old, big house they had bought and a couple of newer buildings, dull as chicken houses, built of gray cement blocks. Riding by, you could see small groups of young men and women hurrying from one building to the other, all of them pale, as if the color had drained out of them and seeped into those gray walls, leaving them faded and lifeless.

But they were good folks. Sue was going to be a missionary, and when she talked about it to Mavis, talked about saving souls for Jesus in darkest Africa or wherever it was she hoped to go, her face almost shone, and you could forget that Sue's eyes were too small and too close together behind the plain glasses she wore, and that her dull hair lay flat on the back of her neck, as if it never held any life at all. It was hard to think of Sue Dillon out in the middle of a jungle with natives dancing around in wildly feathered costumes or whatever they might wear, her trying to tell them how Christ died on the cross for their sins. Mavis had an image of her being swept up and brushed away, she was so light, a wisp that would never be seen again.

"Well, you got your work cut out for you," Sue Dillon said. "A lot of donations this week. Seems like everybody cleaned out their closets at once."

"That's what we need, isn't it? We've been getting short of some things. More and more folks must be coming in here to get themselves something to wear. It is a shame . . . some have so much and some so little."

"It's God's will," Sue Dillon said and looked upward. Mavis could think of nothing else to say, though in her heart she wondered why God would want things that way, so she turned and started down the hall toward the room at the back of the building where they put the clothing donations.

"Good day, Miz Lashley."

The voice startled her, coming from the next office, just across from Sue Dillon's, Reverend Simms's room, though Mavis hadn't expected him to be there. She stopped before she reached the doorway and brushed back her hair, feeling that somehow she should be prepared to meet him and disliking herself for the thought. He was just another man, a preacher, but he had such a formal way about him, as if there were a circle of space around him that must be kept clear so that you could not come too close. Mavis cleared her throat and said, "How're you, Reverend? I didn't expect to see *you* here today." She looked through the doorway into the room.

Reverend Simms smiled up at her from his desk. "The Lord's work must be done. It never seems to end."

"I guess that's right, but I know you have a service tonight, and the other ladies tell me you're here every night for

the evening meal for all those that come. You need some
rest, too.''

He laughed, and the solemn face broke into wrinkles and
Mavis relaxed; the space between the two of them was de-
creased, and he did not seem so remote. ''You ladies worry
about me too much, but I appreciate your kind thoughts. I
give thanks for that.'' His look became serious again. He
motioned to the papers on his desk. ''There's even more to
do right now, with the dedication coming up next week.
There'll be all sorts of people here—maybe even from the
TV channel—and we need the publicity to get more donations.''

''Why, that's right,'' Mavis said. ''I almost forgot.'' Her
own special invitation had come in the mail, and she had put
it on the kitchen table to remind her when the time came to
go.

''Don't you forget.'' It was almost a command. ''We want
to honor all our volunteers, and you're an important one.''

''Well, that's real nice of you,'' Mavis said, a sudden feeling of warmth for Reverend Simms seeping into her breast.
She looked straight into his eyes. He wasn't such a bad-
looking man, she thought. Hair thinning on the sides and
touched with gray, a face too thin, nearly sharp, that made
you want to offer him a second helping of food, dark clothes
always slightly rumpled, as if he had taken them from a pile
in the back room and never bought anything new for himself—that was Reverend Lonnie Simms. He had started the
Mission in a run-down storefront just a few years ago—with
a handful of people to help and hardly any money at all—
and built it up until it provided services for goodness knows
how many poor and homeless people, and he had been able
to buy the stone church and remodel it to provide a nicer
place for them to worship. Now it was all going to be on TV.
She smiled at him again and drew back.

''I'd better be getting my work done,'' she said. Reverend
Simms did not answer, and Mavis turned and went further
down the hall.

In the back room where the clothes were kept, Mavis laid
down her purse and satchel. The room was stuffy, closed up

with the musty scent of clothes, like some huge closet. She opened a window and a faint breeze struggled in, already warm. There had been a lot of donations since last week. Shopping bags stood stacked against the wall, and there were boxes of shoes and other items scattered around. Mavis sighed, fumbled in her satchel for the white cotton gloves she wore to sort the clothes, and put on the smock that would keep her own clothes from getting soiled. She began with the names. Most people included them with their donations so that, later, they could take a tax deduction. Once in a while they complained about the valuation Mavis had made, but that wasn't often. Most people realized how little those scraps were worth, old things that nobody wanted anymore and cast aside. Still, she supposed the poor were glad to get them, though she thought again how sad it would be always having to dress in someone else's unwanted clothing, never to have anything new for your own.

Then her heart almost stopped. On top of a shopping bag Mavis saw a child's dress, not ragtag at all but a pretty pink dress with a ruffled collar and a satin bow at the waist. She pulled it out. Surely it was for a girl just budding, barely a child but not yet teenage. In spite of herself, Mavis clutched that dress to her breast and closed her eyes to quell the tears she could feel forming there. Her own child—after all these years the sight of a dress could overwhelm her and bring back a flood of memories. She could never think of her daughter as older than she had been, never see her as a young girl in high school, or a woman now. Her memory was of fair hair still worn long with a ribbon holding it back, black patent leather shoes for Sunday school, a ripple of laughter at the sight of a dog or kitten. And she tried not to think at all of that crumpled, doll-like figure lying on the grass with just a smudge of blood at the lips and the heavy black skid marks from the car just a few feet away on the street, books scattered beside them and papers covered in a child's large round script spread like leaves.

"Miz Lashley, is something the matter?" It was Sue Dillon's tentative voice, the one she would use for missionary babies, Mavis thought suddenly, out in the jungle. She stood in the doorway, and when Mavis opened her eyes and turned, she could see Sue's tiny eyes filled with worry for her.

"No, I'm all right," she said. "It's just so hot today. I guess I'd better rest for a minute." She sat down on a small bench near the window.

"Well, it's a good thing I came in. I was going over to the hot dog stand to get me a Coca-Cola, and I wanted to see if you wanted one. Seems like it might do you good. I'll be right back."

"That would be real nice. Here, let me give you some money." Mavis started to reach for her purse.

"Now you'll do no such thing. How many times have you brought in something for the two of us for lunch and treated me? I sure don't get that kind of home-cooked food out at the college. I'll treat this time. You just rest."

Sue turned and went out, and in a minute Mavis heard the front door close. She was glad to let the girl take over. Maybe that's how Sue would be in her missionary job, and she would survive in the jungle or wherever she went. Mavis sighed and shook her head.

She did want to rest. She kicked aside the bag with the children's clothes in it and tried not to think about them. If only there were some comfort, some way to understand why her child had been taken. The minister said it was part of God's plan, the Lord worked in mysterious ways, but she was never able to accept that. It had finally come down to just chance: her child on her way to school, not twenty feet from the house, and Mavis's own watchful eyes following her, and a car flying down the street at the same time, some skinny boy showing off who stood, later, shaking and white and silent while the ambulance came. "Sue them," somebody said, but Mavis knew from looking at that white body under a T-shirt and the blue tattoo on his arm—of a heart with initials inside—that this boy had nothing, never would, and even if he did have money, a bushel of it, none of that would bring back her child. Strange, she remembered now, she had thought of all that just briefly the day before when she and the ladies were talking about Theda Hedrick and *her* child. Mavis didn't know what was worse—losing your own by death, but at least knowing what became of her, that she knew no more pain—or being aware that you had a child out there somewhere, lost in a way, with no contact as far as anyone knew, no way to help should she need it.

"You do seem a million miles away."

Mavis jumped. The voice came from the doorway almost like an echo. When she turned, she saw Reverend Simms standing there, the corners of his lips turned up. She put her hand up to her hair. "Why, I guess I *was* daydreaming," she said. "You caught me sitting down on the job."

"Don't you worry about that. Everybody around here knows how faithful you are, Miz Lashley. We couldn't do without you."

"Why, it's real nice of you to say that, but I've had my little rest and should be getting back to the clothes." She reached for another bag. Perhaps Reverend Simms could answer her questions, would find comforting words to say in a way no one else had in all the years. But there was still a distance between them, and she knew she could not confide in him. If he had put his hand on her shoulder, she might have pulled away.

They both were startled by the slam of the side door, both jumped. They could hear Sue Dillon's shoes tapping down the hallway almost in a run, and when she stopped in the doorway just behind Reverend Simms, the sound of her breathing filled the room.

"Lordy, what's happened?" Mavis said. "You dropped the Coca-Colas and broke them?" She tried to smile to relieve the look of fear on Sue Dillon's face. The girl's hands were empty, and were moving like something alive, separate from her body. Reverend Simms stepped back and Mavis could not see his face.

"I just heard the news," Sue Dillon said. "Out yonder by the hot dog stand. It came over the radio."

"What is it?" Reverend Simms asked. His voice was as solemn as if he were giving a sermon to the drunkards in the chapel.

"Miz Theda Hedrick . . . you know, the woman that was missing. They found her. She's dead. It was on the news."

"Lordy me," Mavis said. "I had hoped it wouldn't come to this."

"What happened? What else did they say?" Reverend Simms's voice was cool, calm. It seemed to help Sue Dillon. She pushed back her dishrag hair and grabbed her hands together so that they would stop moving.

"It was on the other side of town, not far really, but out in the country. A farmer saw his corn all bent down, like somebody had run a mule through it. He walked into the field—corn's up shoulder high by now—and that's where he found her, sprawled out like she just went in there and fell down and died. Ain't that just awful?"

Sue Dillon looked as if she might cry, and Mavis had the sudden urge to go hug her, enclose her in her arms, but she knew she would be pushed away. Sue Dillon was someone who, already, had given up hope of closeness or comfort, unless it was from some heathen child. "What had happened to her?" Mavis asked.

"They don't know, at least they didn't say over the radio at the stand. They're doing an autopsy. I reckon it'll be on the front page of the paper tonight."

"A pity," Reverend Simms said, still in his formal voice. "There is so much violence in the world. But it's predicted in the Bible. Surely, the end is coming."

Sue Dillon seemed not to have heard his last remarks and, turning to him, she said, "That was the lady who was in here last week to bring some clothes." She looked around the room as if she could find the bag. "You remember, don't you, Reverend? The lady with the funny hat. You spoke to her in the office."

"Just briefly," he said. "So many people come in, it's hard to remember." Reverend Simms shook his head and turned, heading out the door. "We must try to think of the good things," he said. "Let us hope the woman was right with the Lord."

Sue Dillon and Mavis stood in silence in the hot little room, while outside the noon bells rang in a neighboring church, and Mavis thought of flowers, a casket, eyes prying at Theda's face while others wondered, in guarded whispers, "What happened to her? What did she do to bring this upon herself? Wonder if they'll ever catch who did it?"

Chapter Five

Well, there was just no way around it. She couldn't keep her mind on a single thing. Mavis plopped down the pamphlet she had been reading and pushed her Bible away from her. How could she study her Sunday school lesson when all that she had on her mind was Theda Hedrick, dead, lying out in a field amidst the corn all alone? Whatever good thoughts the lesson might have inspired were cut off by that vision, and she could not bring her mind to bear on the dry words of the page.

She had thought about it all the way home on the bus. She wished Sue Dillon and Reverend Simms had said more about Theda Hedrick. If they had, perhaps the thoughts might have gone away so that she could settle down to her usual routine once she got home—study her lesson, so she could take part in the discussion at church next Sunday morning, fix something light for dinner (Mavis could never eat much in this kind of weather), and then go to bed, as content as she ever was these days, thoughts of murder gone.

But Reverend Simms had walked out of the room, heading back to his office, shoulders bent and his shabby clothes pulled around him, dark as some bird, and Sue Dillon just stood there, lost in thought, looking almost as if she might cry—until she realized that Mavis was looking at her, ready to speak, and then she turned and almost ran down the hallway and slammed the door to the front office behind her. Mavis knew that she could work no more that day, even though there were still bags of clothing piled against the wall to be separated and tagged, so she pulled off her gloves and put them into her satchel, along with her smock, and left the building. When the bus driver greeted her (that Judd boy again, with his polite smile), she hardly looked at him, said, "How're you?" so faintly that he might have thought she was half sick with the heat.

Maybe she should go up to the house. That's what she would have done had it been anybody else she had known—fixed her special apple dish and taken it, still warm, to feed all the people who would come to pay a call. But would anybody visit that silent house on the corner? As far as Mavis knew, Theda Hedrick had no kin, except a daughter goodness knows where, and she and Alice Pate hardly ever went out, except to buy those big hats and funny clothes, had no friends. No one from any church would go there since the two of them were strangers at the gate. In fact, Mavis wondered where they would bury Theda from, would any place want her now after all this had happened?

Still, she didn't feel right doing it, going all alone to that house now that Theda was dead. Taking a dish. Perhaps they wouldn't understand and think it intruding. Would the other ladies go? Mavis thought not, even though they would be curious as a cat. Somehow that house was forbidding, closed to them, and they would feel that no matter what dish they took, how well others liked it, their little Pyrex dishes would look strange there amidst fine silver and crystal, a poor offering even in a time of death.

Mavis still brooded about it all while she fixed her supper. She had some vegetables left from the day before that she could heat up; there was a piece of beef from Sunday. That would be enough. Even though the doctor told her to cut down on sweets every time she saw him, she kept a container of ice cream (Chocolate Ripple right now) in the refrigerator, and if she had just a small serving, there was no need to get upset. "If one thing don't get you, something else will," one of the women in her Sunday school class said when they were talking about diets and cholesterol and such, and Mavis felt the same. Getting older was just a slow process of giving everything up, and there were a few things she was going to hang on to, no matter what.

The doorbell startled her. "Now who could that be?" she said aloud to herself before she even thought. She was expecting no one, and it was late for those salesmen who came to the door trying to get her to buy Lord knows what. And it wasn't Sunday, so it wouldn't be the Mormons. She supposed she should be afraid. Other ladies said, "Goodness no, I don't go near the door when somebody comes and I'm not expecting them. I can see out between the venetian blinds and I just let them go right down the walk and away, even if I know 'em." But Mavis didn't want to be so suspicious, so she went to the door and opened it—and smiled as soon as she saw who stood there.

"Well, I declare," she said, and brushed her hand in front of her face as if she had been got away with. "I should have known it was you, showing up here at suppertime without a word of warning. One of these days, you're going to catch me without a speck of food in the house, and then what will you do? Just starve, I guess, and it would serve you right."

"Aunt Mavis, you know I don't come here just to get something to eat. I like the company. Where else could I find such a pretty lady all alone."

Mavis moved her hand in the air again, then opened the screen and held it back, smiling. She gave the man who passed her a pat on the back and he turned to grin at her. Dale Sumner, her nephew, her only sister's boy, almost like her own child (though who could ever replace the one that was lost?). Her sister, Florence, had died so long ago that Mavis sometimes had to stop and wrinkle her forehead to remember what she looked like, and Dale, nearly grown then, but still like a little boy to her, had seemed to take over Mavis for his own.

She never knew when to expect him, just like tonight. She would hear the doorbell ring, and then she would see that tousled head, blond hair fine as a girl's, and those bright blue eyes, him standing there in outrageous clothes, grinning from ear to ear, cute as the kid on the Cracker Jack box. As he passed close to her, she saw that he had an earring in his ear, just a little gold circle, and she almost exclaimed aloud but decided to hold her tongue. She knew it didn't really mean anything, and Dale would just come back with some bright remark, never serious a moment in his life.

"I thought you might be off to some shindig down at the church tonight, but I risked coming around anyway." Dale slunk down in the recliner in the living room and put up his feet. He held a brown envelope close to his chest like some award he had just been given.

"Humph. Not many parties down there these days. The young folks aren't interested."

"Well, maybe you and I could get one going, liven the place up a bit."

Mavis smiled. "We used to have some good parties, didn't we? Do you remember how I'd take you when you were just a little thing, and all the grownups made over you so? We'd play games and have refreshments, so simple it seems now, innocent. But those days are gone, I guess. People gone, too."

Just briefly a shadow seemed to flicker over Dale's face. "Now don't you go talking that way. Those ladies you go around with, when I've heard them, all they talk about is death and dying. . . . You don't have to be that way."

"Well, these days, that's all there seems to be to talk about." Mavis had sat opposite Dale on the sofa, but now she moved closer and sat on a hassock near him. "Have you heard what happened?" she said, her voice almost a whisper. "Miz Hedrick?"

Dale bent near her, the way he had done when he was little and she read him stories. "Yes," he said softly. "We've got our own murder right up the street."

The two of them shared more than a blood relationship. Dale and Mavis exchanged murder mysteries and discussed them each time they met. Mavis had to admit that some of the books Dale left with her were a little rough. When she read them, she kept a pile of church magazines handy in case somebody came to the door by surprise; she didn't want the preacher to catch her looking at anything like that. But she had learned a lot, things she never knew existed before. "Would you *ever*?" she'd say to Dale when he came the next time. "Mavis," he'd answer, "you don't know the half of it," and look mysterious, and she wouldn't know whether he was serious or not.

Dale leaned back in the recliner. "I've even done some investigating," he said. "You know what's in this envelope?" He held it out to show her for the first time. "Pictures," he said, without giving her time to respond. "Of the murder site and the body. What do you think of that?"

"You don't mean it," Mavis said, but she knew it could be true. Ever since he was a little boy, Dale had been busy taking pictures of anything that came into sight, and later, after college, he got a job down at the newspaper photographing highway accidents and the talent night show at the high school and church socials. He got so good at it that the police hired him, too, when they needed pictures taken at the scene of some crime. As soon as they were developed, he would bring the interesting ones over to Mavis's house, and they would imagine the scenes, discuss the crimes, and speculate on guilt, preferring their own versions rather than reality, disappointed later, sometimes, when the real killers came to light.

"You know better. Look at this." Dale pulled a shiny black-and-white photo from his envelope. "That's where it happened."

Mavis took the photograph from him. Looking closely, she saw little at first; the light was low. Then she noticed tall rows of corn just beyond the edge of a road and at one point, as cleanly as if someone had sliced it with a knife, a narrow cut in the leaves leading inward.

"That's where she went in," Dale said. "You can't see in that one, but it's all trampled down there, like someone just went smashing through. Look at these."

Mavis took the sheaf of photographs from him and laid them on her lap. The next view was closer; she could see a path like a tunnel, though this photo, too, was dark. The next one made her catch her breath: the body sprawled there, like some fallen bird, darker than the leaves. Theda Hedrick. Mavis had seen more than her share of the dead, but they were in their coffins—sedate, hands folded neatly, posed for others to observe. (Except for the form of her own child, broken on the sidewalk, and she would not let that picture enter her head.) This sight was almost embarrassing to her, as if she had entered a room unannounced and someone was dressing. She wanted to look away.

"The police think she just ran in there with somebody after her and they caught her with no trouble." Dale shifted his position, moved nearer to Mavis to peer over her shoulder. She looked at another picture, a closer view of the body, Theda resting on her back, one hand flung out as if she reached after her attacker, legs gently bent at the knees. She wore a black-looking dress, very plain, and the white pearls around her neck shone luminously. "Lord, Lord," Mavis said half aloud, shaking her head. "Isn't it a shame? Neat as ever, hardly a hair out of place."

There *was* a difference, though, Mavis noted. Outside her house Theda always wore one of those big round hats half covering her face. But here Mavis could see quite plainly the close-cropped hair, still dark but peppered with gray. Theda was so particular. Didn't she still have her gloves on, one reaching hand terribly white in the picture? Wherever could her hat be?

"You may not like the next one," Dale said, but Mavis was already drawing it near. It showed a close-up of Theda's face, her neck, and Mavis saw the tongue protruding just slightly over the lower teeth. Theda looked as if she might be spitting something distasteful from her mouth. Around her neck was a black line above the pearls, and the flesh seemed swollen, almost goiterlike.

"They think she was strangled to death, but they won't know till after the autopsy. They found no weapon there." Dale sat back again. Mavis did not move, still staring at the last picture. Then she handed the sheets back to him.

"It's such a shame," she said, her voice low. "I didn't know Theda well a-tall, but she never did anybody any harm. She might have been a little funny, stayed by herself except for Miss Alice all those years, but having her girl run off, and then losing her husband—they said over grief—it could affect her a bit. Who'd want to do that to her? Who could hate her so much?"

"The police think she might have picked up somebody on the highway. A stranger. Then he robbed her. Her purse was gone."

Mavis shook her head. "Now who'd think a thing like that? Just look at those pearls—they certainly aren't pop beads. And she has on a watch, too, I noticed. Anybody going to rob her would have taken those."

"I thought so, too, but they're having a hard time coming up with any ideas."

"Well, it couldn't have been a stranger. Theda never would have picked up anybody on the road. Lord, why in the world was she out in the car alone, anyway? I don't think I ever saw her out if Tommie Lee Bagwell wasn't at the wheel. What did he say? Have they questioned him?"

"I don't know. They just got started looking into things. I suppose they'll get to him."

"Not that he's going to be any great help to them. Tommie Lee is just like a child really. If Dr. Hedrick hadn't taken him on years ago and taught him to drive that big car, goodness knows what would have become of him."

"Maybe he did it? Maybe he got mad about something the old lady said. They found the car not far away, parked near the woods. He could have left it there and gone back to town. Wasn't a long walk."

"Tommie Lee?" Mavis heard her voice go high in the air. "Now you should be ashamed of yourself for suggesting such a thing. He wouldn't hurt a flea. And that car, it was the thing he prized most, never got tired of washing and polishing it. You'd think it was new practically. Even if he hurt Theda, he wouldn't have left the car there, I can guarantee you that. No, sir, it wasn't Tommie Lee. Had to be some other man."

"Why man?" Dale was smiling and Mavis knew he was just teasing her. "A woman could have done it, a strong woman. Could have sneaked up and put something around her neck before she knew it."

"And just who would that be? Alice Pate? If she wanted

to kill Theda, why'd she need to go out to a cornfield to do it? What reason would she have anyway?'' Mavis got up and turned away from Dale. She heard the recliner bounce back as he rose.

"I was only trying to get your goat,'' he said. He put his arms around Mavis's shoulders. "I don't think anybody has the slightest clue as to what happened.''

"Well, let's not talk any more about it right now. It's all so sad. I don't even know what to do myself, whether to go up for a visit or not. What do you say to folks when their family has been murdered?''

"I'm sure you'll think of something.'' Dale gave her another squeeze, then pulled away. "What was that I heard about supper?'' he said.

"Aw, you just hush,'' Mavis said, but laughed. "Come on here in the kitchen and talk to me while I see what leftovers I can put together.''

Dale sat at the kitchen table while Mavis warmed up the vegetables and roast beef; she made iced tea and checked the freezer to see how much ice cream was left in the carton. When she got it all on the table, she said a brief prayer of thanks, and they ate, the two of them close in the fading light, quiet except when they chose to talk about small matters, thoughts of death momentarily gone. Dale dried the dishes for her, and then, with a brief kiss, he was gone, sailing off in the flashy red sports car he drove. Mavis stood on the front stoop for a moment until the sound of the motor died away.

Suddenly, the telephone rang, jarring the stillness of the summer evening.

"Hello,'' she said, nearly breathless; she'd had to run inside, through the living room, to the little stand by her bed.

"That you, Mavis?'' Immediately she recognized Ida Mae's scratchy voice. She could hear a note of anticipation.

"Of course, it's me, Ida Mae. Who else?''

"I just wanted to be sure. Sometimes I think I dial perfectly correctly and then get somebody weird on the other end. But never mind that. I just wondered if you had heard the *news*.''

"What news, Ida Mae?" Mavis knew, of course, but why should she spoil Ida Mae's revelation?

"About Theda Hedrick. They found her. It was all over the TV tonight. Murdered. Have you *ever*?"

"Yes, Ida Mae, I heard. It is a terrible shame."

"Well, who do you suppose could have done it? I bet it was some tramp. There's no place a decent woman can go anymore. And the police don't do a thing. It's a disgrace."

"We'll just have to wait and see, I guess." Mavis wanted to say no more. She could feel her eyes drawing and knew that the sight of Theda Hedrick sprawled between the corn rows would be coming back to them if she did not end the conversation. Suddenly she said very fast, "I can't talk anymore right now, Ida Mae. I've got something on the stove and it's going to boil over if I don't go stir. I'll talk to you."

She put down the receiver without waiting for Ida to protest in a pouty voice. "I'm so *sorry*," she would have said. "I didn't know it was an *inconvenient* time, or I *certainly* wouldn't have disturbed you."

She felt a little guilty about the lie. It wasn't like Mavis at all to make up something like that. Usually, she settled down on the side of the bed and listened to Ida's talk, saying, "Is that right? Well, I never," every now and then. Sometimes just quiet was enough to keep Ida Mae going.

But this time, she could not bear talking about the dead woman. The pictures of Theda were wounding enough, exposing her. Mavis needed no more words to pull Theda apart. And the scene was back now, she could not escape it. She would lie awake long into the dark night with it before her eyes. Worse, something began to bother her about the pictures, like a word you have on the tip of your tongue and just can't find, something no one had noticed. It teased her into the night until finally, much later, she drifted off to sleep, the puzzle still unsolved.

Chapter Six

The smell of spice filled the house. Once, when Mavis went out to the garbage can in the backyard and then came in again, the sweet-sharp scent of vinegar and cinnamon and clove almost made her dizzy. (But then, almost anything might have, she had slept so badly—vague, dark dreams swirling through her head all night—surely the result of seeing those pictures, though she did not recognize them in her visions.) She had to get the pickling done. Archie Teason from down the street had brought the box of peaches by on Monday afternoon. "I got you a half bushel," he said, see-sawing back and forth from one foot to the other out on the front stoop after Mavis went to the door. "They looked too good to pass up, and the price was right, too."

"Lord have mercy, that was real neighborly of you," she said, gently touching a peach with her fingertips. "I reckon they'll make right nice pickled peaches."

She couldn't let them go any longer, they would spoil, so she spent the morning scalding the peaches to remove the skins and then making the pickling liquid that she poured, boiling, over the golden fruit, and finally sealing each jar carefully so that the top was tight. Now all she had to do was wait until the jars cooled before she put them down in the basement, ready to bring out on Thanksgiving or some other special occasion. Her pickled peaches were almost as famous as her apple dish at church gatherings.

People asked for that recipe, too, but she never could tell them. She had none herself, putting together the ingredients just by sight, tasting to see if the combination was right. Her mother had showed her, and as Mavis watched the crystal jars with the fruit cooling inside, she remembered summer days when she was a child and her mother and her aunts gathered in the dining room of the farmhouse where the women had grown up and scalded the peaches and other fruits they preserved, sat gossiping while Mavis and her cousins passed in and out of doors, trailing laughter while the adults scolded them for letting in flies. Sometime, during those easy, lost days, her mother must have called her to one side, showed her the boxes of spice she kept in the tin-fronted safe, and then the measures of vinegar and sugar by the handful so that the memory was as much in her fingertips as in her head. All these long years, she had only to reach for the ingredients and, without measuring spoons or cups, make the mixture and prepare the jars of fruit.

Now that the preserving was done, the jars cooling and the bowls and spoons washed and in the drainer to dry, the peels out in the garbage, she would have to go. She had put it off as long as possible, thought perhaps she might not go at all. They are not like the rest of us, she said to herself. Theda and Miss Alice. They moved in a different world. When there were deaths in the neighborhood, sickness, or even the joy of a baby, those two did not visit, did not come bearing platters of food, a favorite dish. But Mavis knew that she had to go up the street to that silent house and make a call, even though no one else in the entire block might visit. Something drew her like a cord and she hoped, prayed, that it was not just her own curiosity.

She washed the sticky peach juice off her hands, powdered her face and patted her hair into place. She decided to wear a dark dress, plain, and she almost would like to have worn a hat; Theda had been so formal. Then, in the small drawer of her dresser where she kept her handkerchiefs, she saw a pair of thin white gloves and decided to take them along as a kind of token. Theda wouldn't be there to notice, but perhaps Miss Alice would appreciate the gesture.

Mavis moved quickly to the door, then almost turned as if she had forgotten something. Any other time, going to visit the home of someone dead, she would be taking a covered dish. But not to that house. She would go with empty hands encased in gloves, and there would be no one to touch, to put an arm around in comfort. She could not imagine that closeness with Alice Pate; it would be as unwelcome as a kiss, a familiarity not permitted.

The day was warm again, no relief, though Mavis had heard on the radio that there might be storms. The grass was drying up and the flowers down the walk looked wilted. Later, she would have to get out the hose and let it run or they would die. No one was about. A dog closed up in a house across the street barked, and a car backfired somewhere in the distance, but no other noises disturbed the morning. Mavis walked slowly, hoping she might meet someone. Even Odessa Bailey would be a relief. Mavis would gladly have reached over and petted one of her dogs just to delay her visit.

A single car was parked in front of the Hedrick house, and as Mavis drew closer to the walk where she would have to turn, someone came out of the front door and started walking toward her, head bowed so that he did not see her at first. She recognized him. It was Charles Morgan, chief of detectives down at the police station; she had known him all his life. He had been in her Sunday school class when she taught in the Junior Department down at the church years ago, a stolid boy with a plain flat face that never seemed surprised or joyous. He had changed little over the years; only his hair was thinner, and deep crevices were etched at each side of his mouth. Mavis didn't know why, since he rarely smiled. "Why, Charles Morgan," she said, "I never expected to see you this morning."

The man looked up suddenly and almost stumbled. He stepped back. "Miz Lashley, I'm really surprised to see you, too." His eyes were pale gray, hardly any color at all, and Mavis felt she could look through them like water.

"You know, I live right down the street. I was just making a visit at this time of sorrow."

"Oh, yes," he said, eyes cast down again. He had looked that way as a child when Mavis would ask him to recite a

Bible verse he was supposed to know but didn't, and just stammered around till she called on somebody else. "It is a sad time. I'm sure you can bring some comfort."

If he had on a straw hat, Mavis thought, he would have tipped it. His hand went up in a half salute, and then he turned and almost ran toward the car. He was probably afraid she would ask him something about the murder and wanted to get away before she did. She wondered if he knew that Dale Sumner was her nephew, that she had already seen the pictures of Theda dead in the cornfield. Charles Morgan probably would hope she had been spared that. He would think it unseemly for his former Sunday school teacher to have viewed such a sight and want to know more about it.

She watched until his car disappeared around the bend in the street, then walked on toward the front door. She could see no one through the windows: The curtains were drawn as tightly as they had been on that long-ago summer evening when she had gone to ask for magazine subscriptions. She sighed, patted her hair one last time, and pushed the doorbell, careful not to stain her gloves.

There was no answer at first. She wondered if someone had peered through a blind somewhere and had seen who it was and decided not to open the door. But then there was a sudden noise, the feathery sound of someone walking, perhaps barefoot, and the door came open, though just a crack. Mavis peered forward, trying to see a face in the gloom.

"What is it?" The voice was tired, low, perhaps suspicious. Mavis recognized it from her other visit, but the face she would hardly have known: Charlene Anderson, so radiant in the last light of evening when she brought in the minted iced tea and set the tray on the table by Theda. Now the face, half-shadowed, was gray as winter, dull, the eyes, almost hidden within half-closed lids, grimacing against the sudden glare.

"It's Miz Lashley, Mavis Lashley from down the street. I came to express my condolences. Is Miss Alice receiving folks?"

Charlene still did not open the door, but Mavis could see that she recognized her.

"I won't stay but a minute if she's busy."

"No, you come on in." Charlene pulled open the heavy door and stood back for Mavis to pass. The girl had a sweet scent, almost of peppermint, and Mavis thought again of the iced tea and wondered if Charlene had been cutting mint from a patch by the back door. "She's upstairs." Charlene pointed upward; a round window of stained glass, a bird sitting on the branch of a tree, glowed on the landing, but everything else was dark. The air seemed cool, though Mavis heard no hiss of air-conditioning. "You wait here. I'll go get her. She's a little bit upset."

"Well, if she's feeling bad, I could come another time."

Charlene spoke almost sharply. "No, wait. It'll probably do her good. She hasn't had anybody else to talk to."

The girl turned and started up the stairs, and Mavis noticed that she was barefooted, the soles of her feet quite white and faintly luminous in the light coming from the window. Mavis stood in the entryway and wondered if she should go sit down. The house was the same as she remembered, the same summer slipcovers on the furniture. But now there was a scent of mustiness, tables looked pale with dust, as if no one had lived there, moved there, in all the years that had passed since Mavis's one visit. She wondered about the rooms above. Did they enclose a sense of warmth, comfortable chairs, snapshots on a dresser, a tumble of clothes carelessly thrown aside when someone undressed? Or were those rooms, too—Alice's and Theda's, even Charlene's—touched with dust and decay, windows never opened, and the scent of faded sachet heavy on the air?

A knocking sound from somewhere in the back of the house startled her. Surely it was the back door, but who would come there? None of the ladies in the neighborhood. Though they might be reluctant about going to the Hedrick home, if they decided to go they would march right up to the front door and ring the bell, chins raised high.

The sound came again, quite plainly, almost alarming, with quick, sharp taps. They wouldn't hear it upstairs. Mavis moved closer to the stairwell and looked upward, but all she could see was a golden blinding light, nothing more. She would just have to go herself.

Mavis could guess the way. Through the living room, brighter now in midday light, and then through the dining room, where silver gleamed on a sideboard, a huge tea service that must have been a wedding gift to the Hedricks years before, never used, and on into the kitchen, friendlier than the rest of the house with old honey-colored oak cabinets, and the remains of a sandwich half-eaten on the counter. For the first time, Mavis had a sense that someone actually lived in this house.

She did not see him at first when she went to the screen door. It was hooked and she started to undo it until she saw the man—tall and black, wearing jeans and a soft shirt patterned like a jungle. But not really black, Mavis thought (she tried to use that word now even though she sometimes forgot), he *was* colored—a dark, almost orange shade, with high cheekbones; perhaps he had Indian blood. Why, he was handsome, she thought; at least he would be if he didn't frown so at the sight of her. Mavis drew back slightly. "Can I help you?" she asked. Then, as if she needed to explain, added, "I'm Miz Lashley from down the block. I'm just visiting."

The man moved slightly away, perhaps shook his head, though Mavis couldn't be sure. She noticed that his hands were balled into fists. "I want to see Charlene. Is she here?"

He could use some manners, Mavis thought, but she said, "Yes, but she's busy right now. Could I give her a message?"

The man stared back at her, so hard that Mavis felt that she would have to lower her eyes. "No," he said, and let out a deep sigh. He started to turn.

"It's all right, Miz Lashley." Charlene's voice came from behind Mavis's shoulder. Mavis had not heard her come in on bare feet. "This is a friend of mine," she said very formally. "Buddy Dean." She paused, then spoke toward the man. "Buddy, have some manners and say hello."

The man peered through the screen door, trying to find Charlene's form there in the dim light. He looked ready to laugh, and Mavis knew she would not like the derisive sound. "Well, ain't this friendly," he said, but did not laugh. He glanced back at Mavis. "Howdy, Miz Lashley," he said in a slow drawl, and Mavis knew he was mocking her.

Charlene turned her face from the doorway and spoke to Mavis. "Why don't you have a seat in the living room. Miss Alice will be down in a minute. She wanted to freshen up a bit."

"Yes, I think I'll do that," Mavis said. She started to turn, then looked at the man in the doorway once again. "Goodbye, Buddy," she said very politely and walked away. Even if he forgot his manners, she didn't have to.

She took the same chair she had occupied before, on that night she had visited with Alice Pate and Theda Hedrick, feeling just as stiff sitting there on the edge of the seat. She listened for a sound from upstairs, but there was silence for a moment until she heard Charlene and Buddy still talking at the back door. In that hollow house sound traveled as if through a tunnel.

"Why did you come here?" Charlene's voice was sharp, angry. "I told you never to come around without me knowing it."

"What difference does it make now? The old lady's dead. She can't scare you no more."

"Oh, ain't that fine. You think I own the place, now she's gone?"

Buddy's laugh was deep and resonant, like some instrument suddenly played. "Maybe," he said, and laughed again. "Maybe it *could* be yours."

"No, not with *her* still around." Mavis could almost see Charlene jerk her head toward the upper part of the house.

"Well, don't worry. It's all over."

"Oh, yes, it's over." Now, Charlene's voice was mocking. "That's why the policeman just left a little while ago. Came here to ask me and Miss Alice a bunch of questions. I was scared to death."

"You know it's all a bunch of bullshit. Big mouths, that's all they've got. Remember the demonstration—you got arrested then, but nothing happened."

"That was different. We was a whole bunch. And there was no murder, nobody died."

Mavis did not hear Buddy's answer because Alice Pate appeared at that moment in the doorway from the hall. Mavis half rose, but Alice waved her hand, slowly, as if she were in pain, indicating that Mavis should remain seated. Mavis was astonished at the sight of her—that plain face drawn now so that it looked all bone with just the skin stretched over, eyes red from weeping. Alice's hair was like a skullcap, tight enough to give pain; her dress hung on her like a sack. Mavis would have reached out and touched Alice Pate had she been any other woman in sorrow, but she felt that her fingers might break that skeletal body.

"I just came by to express my condolences," she said, hoping her voice would drown out whatever ugly words might still come from the kitchen.

In a weary voice, Alice answered, "That's very kind of you. Nobody else has called."

Mavis did not know what else to say. Should she apologize for the others? Alice must have seen them pass all those years on errands to other houses of sorrow, pies and cakes and platters of chicken held out in front of them like an offering.

"Oh, I forgot, someone did come." Alice gave a little laugh, but the turning of her lips did nothing to relieve the deathliness of her face. "A detective. He came to ask questions." She sighed. "I reckon he had to. They have a job to do."

"He's a real nice boy," Mavis said. "I've known him most all his life. He goes to our church. Why, I taught him in Sunday school."

Alice looked at her and half-smiled, this time a softer movement, her face more relaxed. "Sunday school—why, I haven't thought of that in years. I used to go every Sunday, all dressed up and my mama telling me not to get dirty. That was such a long time ago." The smile faded. "I hadn't even thought of the church service. I'll be going to church again, won't I? For the funeral, I mean. Tomorrow at two o'clock. The funeral director called a while ago." She bent her head down and Mavis wondered if there were tears forming in her eyes.

"Sometimes it helps," Mavis said. "Going through the

funeral and all. I don't know why. It makes people closer for a while. Loving. I do believe it's so.'' (And she thought of the small pale pink coffin with deeper pink carnations and lilies flowing over the top, and the child inside, with people all around, hearts extended to share the grief, help bear the pain.)

"Maybe. But I think of everybody staring. They'll come there just because of the murder. You know how people are. They want to see broken bones and blood. They'll want to see me.''

"Some will be that way, but not all. I'll be there.''

Alice looked up. Her eyes were dry. "Yes,'' she said. "I will appreciate that.'' She seemed to relax then, sitting back for the first time in the chair. "I still remember that night you came up to visit and sold us the magazines. It was real pleasant. I had forgotten what it was like to have neighbors.'' She was silent a moment, thinking. Then she began again.

"Theda and I didn't go out much. It wasn't intentional, at least not in the beginning. Theda was so self-conscious—about what happened with her daughter and all—had the idea people were always whispering behind her back. I always wondered if she thought they would see her as a failure, like it was her fault somehow. I don't know that anyone blamed her. I'm not even sure anybody cared anymore—there were other things to gossip about. But Theda wasn't convinced, and we rarely went out except to shop, and then it was always in the car, us separate from everybody else.''

"Yes,'' Mavis said, "I would see you.''

"It got easier and easier just to stay home. Charlene could do the shopping. Tommie Lee took her in the car anytime she wanted to go, and most other errands he could run. He's dependable, even though he may be a little lacking in sense now and then.'' Again, she paused, her face pulled tighter, little wrinkles forming in the pale skin of her forehead. "That's why it's so hard for me to understand what happened. Why would Theda go out without me, driving herself all alone? She never did anything like that before as long as I can remember.''

"She didn't tell you where she was going?''

"Not one bit, and that was unusual, too. Now, we didn't check with each other about every little thing, but if Theda had been going to do something like that, she'd have let me know. No, it's all strange." Alice shook her head. "Now I think about it, there were other strange things, too."

"Like what?" Mavis bent forward, wondering if she seemed too eager.

"Well, giving Tommie Lee the afternoon off, for one. Usually, he gets Mondays, and he could have most any other time if he wanted. But Tommie Lee doesn't go anywhere much—down to the picture show sometimes, or off to buy comic books at the drugstore. Still, Theda wasn't one to let him just wander. I had even mentioned maybe we could take a little ride later on that afternoon. To get out since it's been so hot. But Theda said, 'Let's wait and see. I don't know I'll feel up to it. After my nap we'll talk about it.' She must have slipped out to tell Tommie Lee soon after."

"Charlene—where was she?" Mavis thought about the big black man who had been at the door; he must have gone off by now.

"In and out, I guess. You don't have to keep up with Charlene the way you do with Tommie Lee. She's got her own room upstairs at the back of the house, so she might have been there part of the time."

"You didn't realize Theda was gone right off?"

"No, ma'am. Not one bit." Alice's voice almost seemed angry. "Theda usually lays down for a rest in the afternoon and doesn't want anybody to disturb her, or else she'll be snappy as a snake when she gets up. So, I do chores or read or whatever then. Sometimes, I might lie down, too. With Tommie Lee gone and Charlene quiet, you'd of thought I'd hear her moving about if she was going out. But my room is in the front of the house and Theda's is off on the side, so she must have gone down the back stairs to the kitchen and right on out the back door to the garage . . . and got the car without me hearing a thing. Maybe I did doze off, I just don't remember."

"When did you finally know she was missing?" Mavis felt as if she were being as nosy as Iva Mae Johnson, but she did want to know what happened. And Alice Pate seemed to need to talk. Her face had relaxed just a bit, so that the skin didn't seem so tight, and she sat with her head back against the chair, remembering.

"Not until it was time for supper. I went down to the kitchen, and Charlene was there just finishing up the meal. We eat light in summer, so we were just having something cold. 'Miz Hedrick come down yet?' I asked her. 'No, ma'am,' she said. 'You want me to go call her?' 'That's all right,' I told her. 'I'll go myself.'

"I went up the back way and knocked on Theda's door two or three times, but she didn't answer. I opened it, thinking she must have really been tired to sleep through all that, but she wasn't there at all, the bed smooth as silk. Later, after I called the police and they asked me what she was wearing, I came back and looked in the closet, and I knew she had dressed to go out. Theda was neat as a pin, with everything organized, so I could tell right away which dress and hat she wore, pocketbook and gloves.''

"That must have been a scare," Mavis said, trying not to think of Theda dead, her hands still gloved but her head uncovered.

"Well, you know, I still didn't think too much about it at first. Sometimes Theda would go out and mess around in the yard. Tommie Lee does most of the yard work, tends the flowers the way he tends to that car, but every now and then Theda would turn her hand to a job or two. I thought she was out weeding, though it was awfully hot for that. I went back downstairs and told Charlene, 'Miz Hedrick's not in her room. You go outside and see if she's in the yard and tell her it's suppertime.'

"I had already sat down at the table—we eat in the kitchen when it's just the two of us—and in a minute Charlene came back with Tommie Lee traipsing behind her. He takes his plate out to the apartment over the garage and brings it back for Charlene to wash later. 'She's not there,' Charlene says. I didn't know what to answer, I was so surprised. 'Lord have mercy, where can she be?' I said. 'I don't know. Tommie Lee says the car is gone.'

"That's when I knew something was wrong. Theda hasn't driven that car in years as far as I know. And I've heard her say a dozen times when we'd be out, 'I don't think I could get around in this car by myself, what with all these bypasses and freeways. You can't get anywhere the old way anymore. And people just fly by you on the street like they were up in New York or somewhere.'

"Well, I made Charlene and Tommie Lee go off and look every place they could think of and I ran all over the house, even to the basement, but we couldn't find a trace of Theda. It was then that I thought about the phone call."

"What phone call?"

"Right after lunch. Theda made a phone call, which was kind of unusual, too. As I've said, we didn't get out much, didn't have many close friends, so I wondered who Theda might be calling. She was at the hall phone upstairs and I couldn't hear. Didn't talk but a minute and then went into her room, and I didn't disturb her after that. I forgot about the phone call till later, after she had disappeared."

Alice paused and was silent, then she rubbed her hand over her face as if she were brushing cobwebs. "Maybe there were other strange things and I didn't notice. Now that I look back, I wonder if Theda wasn't a little upset those last few days. You know how it is when you live with somebody"— Alice gave Mavis a questioning look—"well, Theda seemed a little on edge, sharp at Charlene a few times when she didn't need to be. Even to me. I didn't think much about it. We all have our bad days. And I thought maybe something might be worrying her."

"What? What would have been worrying Theda?"

Alice sat up straighter. Her face pulled tight again, and she stared at Mavis a moment before she spoke. "I didn't tell the detective this," she said, still staring. "I didn't think it was any of his business. But maybe I should tell somebody. Maybe it will help."

"You'll have to decide," Mavis said, but she sat looking at Alice Pate expectantly.

Alice leaned back again. "Her daughter," she said hesitantly, as if the word were one not said in polite society. "Ruth Anne. Theda worried about her all the time."

"Well, I declare." Mavis was too astounded to say more at first. She had thought the girl had faded from the face of the earth, and here was Alice Pate talking about her like she'd never been away. "I didn't know Miz Hedrick even knew where she was. Nobody around here had seen hide nor hair of her in all these years."

"No, Theda knew." Alice paused. "I knew. Not at first, not before I moved here. That was long after Ruth Anne left, after Dr. Hedrick died. Then I found out. We'd be at the bank and Theda would make out these money orders and put them in the mail. We'd go shopping, and I'd see her buy things I knew couldn't be for herself, and she'd send packages off. Finally, I just up and asked her, 'Theda, where in the world are you sending all those things to?' And she answered without even halting. 'To Ruth Anne. She needs them. She's having a bad time.' But you know, it was funny; I never saw a single letter come to Theda in all those years, not a word of thanks—and I don't think Theda ever wrote, either. Of course, when Ruth Anne moved nearby, there wasn't any need to write . . . they could see each other."

Mavis knew that her eyeballs must be bulging in surprise. Iva Mae Johnson probably would have fallen on the floor. "You don't mean it!" she said. "Theda's daughter was around here?"

"Not far. Out past Piney Plains on the old Six Forks Road. Way in the country. I guess she wanted it that way. Certainly never said a word about her coming back here." Alice hung her head. "I don't suppose she'd come anyway . . . with me in the house. Theda wouldn't let me come along on visits, just say, 'I think it's better you don't go with me to see Ruth Anne,' so I never did. She'd go out there with Tommie Lee driving her—with a whole bunch of things for Ruth Anne—and then come back later empty-handed and be silent and closed off all the rest of the day. She never told me what they did on those trips, and I never asked. It would only have led to trouble.

"Oh, my goodness!" Alice Pate looked as if she had been

hit. "I bet anything in the world Ruth Anne doesn't know about her mother, that Theda's dead."

"Surely she would have seen it on TV. There's nothing else on."

"She doesn't have one. Theda said she doesn't even listen to the radio, buried out there. She'll have to come to the funeral. She won't have to sit with me, but she *must* come."

"I'm sure you could go out and tell her."

"No, that would never do." Alice looked afraid. Suddenly, she stared at Mavis. "Would you go, Miz Lashley? I don't know anybody else to ask. You must have known Ruth Anne, living here in the neighborhood long as you have. Would you do that for me?"

Mavis crumpled up her gloves. She did not want this task, despite all her curiosity. To see little Ruth Anne Hedrick after all these years—how strange that would be. And then to have to tell her of Theda's death . . . she wondered if she would have the strength. She could feel Alice Pate's bright eyes on her. Finally, she looked up. "If the Lord will give me strength, I guess I can try," she said.

"Oh, *thank* you, Miz Lashley. I do appreciate it. You'll be blessed. When can you go? I'll have Tommie Lee drive you out. He knows the place, how to get there. You just tell me."

"I suppose I should go on ahead if I'm going. Ruth Anne will need time to get ready. I'll just go fix myself a little lunch. You tell Tommie Lee to come by around one-thirty. I'll be ready."

They stood. Mavis moved slowly toward the opening of the door to the foyer. Alice Pate followed her. "Thank you again," Alice said, her voice very soft. She put her hand on Mavis's arm, and Mavis almost drew back, so unexpected was that touch. Mavis took Alice's hand and squeezed it.

"You're welcome," she said. "It's little enough I can do at this sad time."

Chapter
Seven

"You mind if I turn on the radio, Miz Lashley?"

Tommie Lee Bagwell was watching her in the rearview mirror; she could see his eyes there, and the back of his head, a tiny bald spot surrounded by that white hair.

"No, you go right ahead," Mavis said, and smiled, though Tommie Lee couldn't see, already bent over to turn on the radio. The sound blared out, and before he turned it down, Mavis could hear the twang of guitars and a whining voice going on about lost love. She never listened to such music at home. The lyrics were too sad, or worse, about things good Christian people didn't talk about, much less sing, and she had better ways to spend her time.

She settled back into the seat, and it gave a sigh as the air squished out. Against her shoulders the leather was soft as butter. Sitting there, she suddenly thought, What if Ida Mae and the ladies could see me now, what in the world would they think? She smiled to herself, but knew already that she would not tell them of her visit. It was between her and Alice Pate.

She had been upset after returning home from the big house on the corner that morning, wishing she had not made her promise to go see Theda's daughter. Although she fixed herself a little lunch, some soup she found in the freezer and a glass of milk, she could hardly touch a bite; her stomach felt as if it were going in circles, and she ate a Tums to settle it down. Still, when Tommie Lee had pulled up in front of the

house, she was ready; she had given her word, and she would
not go back on it.

But she had called Dale Sumner to tell him where she was
going—why, she wasn't sure. "He's out," a fluttery voice at
the newspaper office said over the telephone and didn't offer
more information. Mavis decided not to leave a message, a
little ashamed of her uneasy feeling. What could happen to
her? She would be safe.

Particularly with Tommie Lee driving. She had known
him for years. Everybody around the neighborhood did. A
few times, when he'd be out polishing Theda's car in the
driveway and Mavis passed by carrying a load of groceries,
he would come out and take the bags from her, even though
she protested, and carry them right up to the front door for
her. Back when she sold subscriptions, she thought she might
give him a little visit sometime in his room over the Hedrick's
garage and try to sell him something, a sports magazine or
whatever. But then she thought that he might not be able to
read a-tall, in fact, would have bet on it, so she didn't go,
not wanting to embarrass him.

Tommie Lee was lucky to have that job driving for Theda
and Alice. His mother never was any account—ran off with
some soldier from down at Camp Anderson during the war
and came back big as a cow with Tommie Lee and nobody
for a daddy anywhere in sight. She did a little bit of this and
a little bit of that, but mostly hung out around the pool hall
and bar behind the bus station, Lord knows who taking care
of Tommie Lee. He never did a thing in school, and all the
other kids teased him people said. When he finally joined
the service, he was back in a couple of weeks, nobody surprised. Mavis guessed that Dr. Hedrick kept up with him
somehow, probably was the one who delivered him, and gave
him the job driving the car. Tommie Lee had never strayed
far from the place since, and you could see him most any
time, working in the yard or washing the screens in the spring.
Strong as an ox, he looked like, but gentle. Mavis never
could think of him as grown up, with that round face and
simple eyes and hair so white it looked silver.

I wonder what will happen to him now? The thought struck

Mavis like a bolt of lightning. She had not thought about the house before, who would get it, what would happen to them all. Surely, Theda had a will, though sometimes you were surprised. People who ought to know better died and left things in a terrible mess. Maybe it would go to Alice Pate. In a way, Alice was just like Tommie Lee: she had been there so long, had no other place to go after all these years, that it would be a shame if she had to leave.

But then, what about Theda's daughter? From the little that Alice had said, it sounded to Mavis as if she could use a little help, though Mavis couldn't imagine her coming back to live in Theda's house. People would still remember and talk, at least the older ones. For young folks, things like that didn't seem to matter much anymore.

She decided to speak to Tommie Lee, wondering if he was worried. Maybe he was too simple even to think about change, what it all meant.

"It's a real shame about what happened," she said, leaning forward, trying to talk above the sound of the radio moaning on.

"What's that?" Tommie Lee turned the knob on the radio, and the sound died. Mavis heard only the smooth *whirring* of the motor of the car.

"I said it was a shame what happened—to Miz Hedrick, I mean."

"Oh, yeah," Tommie Lee answered, but there was nothing in his voice to make Mavis think he grieved. It suddenly occurred to her that Tommie Lee might not have liked the woman he worked for.

"It's sad to think of Miss Alice there all alone. Wonder if she'll stay."

Tommie Lee's shoulders went up slightly in a shrug, but when he spoke his voice was a little warmer. "Reckon she might," he said. "She ain't told me no different."

Mavis decided to ask him a little more. Wouldn't hurt; he'd tell nobody anyway. "This is a real nice car," she said. "Did Miz Hedrick take it out often?"

Tommie Lee shook his head vigorously. "No, *ma'am*. Hardly ever did since I been there. That's what they had me for. I took 'em to the store or to the bank, and I drove it myself on errands, sometimes with Charlene. You could of knocked me over with a feather when I came home and looked in the garage and saw the car wasn't there.''

''She didn't tell you she was going to take it?''

''Not a bit. That morning I was 'round in the back getting up some dead branches and she comes over and says, 'Tommie Lee, why don't you take this afternoon off? It's hot, and you've been working hard.' Now that *was* a surprise. Miz Theda was usually real strict about time. But I said it was fine by me—I'd been wanting to see the picture show down at the Capitol Theater—so I finished up with the branches and then took the bus downtown right after lunch. I didn't know anything had happened till I got back home and Miss Alice was having a conniption fit, running around looking for Miz Theda.''

Tommie Lee stopped speaking, and Mavis thought that they would drop into silence again; she could think of nothing else to ask him. But then, suddenly, slowing down the car so that she lurched forward, Tommie Lee shouted out, almost with glee, ''Well, I be doggone. Look a-there. That's where it must've happened. That policeman told me where they found the car, but I didn't think about we'd pass it till right then.''

Mavis looked out the window. Until that moment she had been oblivious of the houses, streets, people outside the car— as removed, sitting there, as if she had been in a room with half-closed blinds, the light dim, almost watery, dreamlike. But now, following Tommie Lee's pointing finger, she saw beside the road (they were in the country now, fields on either side) pushed-down stalks of corn, already browning, and earth churned up where people had walked. This was where they had found Theda; she recognized the spot from the photographs.

''Oh, Lord,'' she prayed aloud, afraid that she might see Theda's stretched-out foot, her gloved hand. For the first time, it became real for her, the woman's death. Before, when there was only a photograph of a figure like a fallen doll, she had kept the awareness distant from her; the death was something she knew in her mind and could talk about but nothing more. Now, the reality of it hit her like a fist in her stomach. Those corn stalks had been brushed aside by frightened hands, felled by heavy feet following a woman who must have cried out in fear with no one in that sea of waving leaves to hear her. Mavis felt tears coming to her eyes.

"Well, I was right." Tommie Lee started up the car again; his voice sounded like that of a child who has won an argument. "I told that policeman the car had gone only about fifteen, twenty miles, but he acted like I didn't know what I was talking about. I always do. I look at the numbers every time I start out and then when I come back again. I knew how many miles the car had on it before Miz Hedrick took it out, so I could tell just like that how many miles had been put on after the policeman brought the car back. But it's not quite the same on this trip—not as far. She must have gone somewhere else first that day. I wonder where it was."

Mavis could not help but ask, "Where else could she have gone? Did you drive her any place recently that was different?"

"No, ma'am. Like I told you, only shopping and that sort of thing. And then down to the Mission with some clothes."

"Had you been there before?"

"Yeah, mostly by myself. Miz Theda and Miss Alice would get up their old things and put them in bags and I would drop 'em off. This time they were going on another errand, so they told me to stop there first."

"Did Miz Theda go in?"

"Well, not at first. I carried in the bags like usual, but when I came out, Miz Theda asked, 'Tommie Lee, did you get me a receipt? I need it for my taxes.' 'No'm,' I said. 'I forgot.' Miz Theda seemed a little upset, so she jumped out of the car and went inside without saying another word. When she came out again, she was frowning right smart, and she said before even closing the door, 'Go on back home, Tommie Lee. I've got a headache.' Miss Alice didn't say a word, and neither did I. You never did when Miz Theda was in one of her moods. She'd bite your head off if you said a thing."

Chapter Eight

They were further into the country now. The car purred smoothly along, the only other sound was the gentle hiss of the air-conditioning, and once Mavis nearly dozed off, the drop of her head jerking her suddenly back awake.

She knew this road. Further out, where there was a crossing, if you turned left, you came to a small country church, white but mud-splashed at the bottom with red, windows green as the sea. Her parents were buried there. Used to, she would come out and put flowers on the graves for Memorial Day, cleaning off the grass, the weeds. Dale took her the last time. He wandered there reading the names on tombstones, and though he looked with her at the carved letters of his grandparents' names, he seemed unmoved by them, they had no connection. Young people had lost that, the ties with those gone on; they lived such scattered lives, and never knew about their kin.

And here things had changed, too—the road, once just a meandering country lane, hardly more, was now graveled and surfaced, with new homes built all along where once there were fields and orchards. Mavis saw other roads winding up into the hills under signs that said, "Partridge Ridge" or "Quail Hollow." Children with bicycles rode up and down calling to each other; the sound came like the tinkle of bells over the noise of the car. Mavis wanted to call out to them to be careful, not to run out into the highway, they might get hit.

"Did she come out here often? Miz Hedrick, I mean?"

Mavis spoke suddenly, and Tommie Lee jumped, startled, as if she had reached over and touched him on the arm.

"Not a whole lot," he said after a moment. "A few times a year. She brought stuff, presents at Christmas. For the young'uns."

"She had *children*? Ruth Anne?" Mavis's voice sounded very loud in the closed-up car.

"Yessum, two. They're right nice. We'd talk while Miz Theda was inside with Ruth Anne. I always stayed outside in the car, away from them. Those two children seemed like they was hungry to talk to just about anybody, living way out there with no one else around."

Well I never, Mavis thought to herself. Ruth Anne with children. She could hardly imagine such a thing. For the first time, she realized that she had been thinking of Ruth Anne still as an overdressed little girl who, once in a while, got to go out and play like other children, roller-skating down the street. She tried to think of that childish face grown up, aged, but she was no more able to do that than she could form a picture of how her own child might have looked had she lived to become a woman.

But then Mavis remembered another picture of Ruth Anne, not seen, but like a vision that she had formed in her mind, planted there without her wanting it to be, against her efforts.

How old would the girl have been back then? Fifteen maybe, in high school. Mavis hardly saw her at all in those days. Ruth Anne no longer skated past on the sidewalk, and Mavis had only a fleeting glimpse of her a few times when she ran out of the house, up the street, into a waiting car, young voices rising up like birds in early twilight. Mavis heard a few rumors. "Wild," people said about her, but Mavis didn't ask what they meant, didn't want to know, sorrowful then for her own child, perhaps resentful that another's lived.

So, that day, when she was down at the beauty parlor, lying with her head back under the running stream of water, she had not expected Shirlee's words.

"You heard about the *scandal* down at the high school?" Shirlee asked her. Mavis tried to shake her head, hardly listening. This was a soothing time for her, the firm touch of

Shirlee's strong fingers on her scalp, the warmth of water; she almost floated, lying there.

"Well, honey, *everybody* is talking about it." Shirlee turned off the water and pushed Mavis up, swirling a towel around her head. "It was out at Silver Lake State Park where it happened."

"What was it?" Mavis asked. She might as well say something; Shirlee would never stop now.

"Well, seems like at least two cars of boys and girls went out to Silver Lake and broke open a gate—you know it closes at ten o'clock—and then they had this *party* in the picnic grounds. Beer bottles all over the place, though not a one of 'em was old enough to buy it. They're trying to find out who provided them with that, I heard."

Shirlee was a little hard to understand: She had bobby pins in her teeth, and she talked around them as she rolled Mavis's hair in tight little ringlets. Mavis thought of the park where church groups went for summer picnics. The pine trees crowded close in the woods there, and down a small embankment spread the lake, not silver like its name, but black, smooth as glass. Only when children splashed did the water sparkle, scattering in the air like raindrops.

"That wasn't the worst part." Shirlee stopped rolling hair and bent close to Mavis's ear. "They decided they was going to take them a little swim—now you understand it was midnight at least—and not a one of them with a suit to wear." Shirlee moved even closer. "This part may shock you, Miz Lashley, but I think you ought to know. One of your neighbors was involved, their daughter anyway, and I'd think you'd want to be aware. For the sake of the neighborhood."

Mavis wanted to tell her, No, she did not want to hear more, but she felt imprisoned by Shirlee's fingers, unable to move out of the orange plastic chair, bound to it by a plastic sheet.

"So, they just decided they'd go skinny dipping." Shirlee's voice slid up. "Boys and girls together with not a stitch on. Did you ever hear the like? Right out there in a public place, even though it was dark and nobody else was around. They probably would have got away with it if they didn't take pictures."

"Pictures?" Mavis echoed Shirlee's voice before she thought.

"Snapshots. I suppose they wanted to preserve the moment." Shirlee's voice was sarcastic. "They took pictures and they was passing them around at school, and one of the teachers walked by and happened to see them. She got every last one of them and took them to the principal."

"What did he do?"

"Expelled the lot of 'em. I don't know for how long. And of course told all their parents. Lord knows what I would do if it was a child of mine. Your neighbor was one of 'em. The Hedrick girl. Ruth Anne."

It was at that particular moment that Mavis felt as if Shirlee had pressed a picture upon her eyes and she could see the smooth water of Silver Lake, perhaps really silver in the moonlight, and the small form of Ruth Anne standing in the water up to her waist, pathetic little breasts pointed toward the camera. How sad, Mavis thought. Little Ruth Anne Hedrick, trying so hard to claim her body from those heavy velvet dresses she wore as a child, and from her mother, whose own bosom was bound up, draped with cloth, and covered with beads. Without realizing what she was doing, Mavis crossed her own arms over herself, as if she could contain that small body, protect it from probing eyes.

That was her other picture of Ruth Anne, not a sight seen, but a vision in her head she had never been able to chase away.

They sent Ruth Anne to boarding school after that. Most of the others who had been involved ended up in the Catholic school on the outskirts of town (the nuns would take anybody in those days, there were so few Catholics around); but Mavis heard that Ruth Anne had been sent way up north, not a week after it all came out. And she never came back, at least, as far as Mavis knew, even though the incident all blew over, people forgot, and most of those who had participated in that midnight party were back at Central High the next year.

It was Dale who had told her later of Ruth Anne. He had been behind her a few years in school, but must have known her, particularly after all that had happened. Once when he was at Mavis's for supper, he said right out of the blue, "Remember that Hedrick girl, Ruth Anne, the one from up the street that got in all the trouble out at the state park?"

"Yes," Mavis said, slightly ashamed to realize that she hadn't thought of Ruth Anne since, not even when she saw Theda Hedrick and, later, Alice Pate, riding around on their shopping excursions.

"Well, guess what I heard?" He always bent closer when he had something to tell, though no one else was in the house. He lowered his voice when she didn't answer.

"You know how she got sent away to school, to several, I hear. People said she didn't last more than a semester in a single one of them. You know the kind—where they make prissy little girls learn to cross their legs right and do their hair and that's about all, just waiting for the debutante ball and the chance to find a husband. Well, finally, Ruth Anne just ran off, and nobody knew where she was for a long time . . . until they heard she had taken up with some religious group. Not the ones that shave their heads and stand on the corner and chant and carry on like a bunch of fools—more the hippie type. Don't you know Theda Hedrick would have *died* if she had known?"

Mavis didn't ask Dale more about it, didn't want to encourage him in his gossip, but she did wonder about Theda, how she took all that. Poor Dr. Hedrick wouldn't have known; he died soon after Ruth Anne left town—some said because he was so broken up over it all. Strange how things happened. You did your best bringing up a child, and then they were struck down or went away so that you never saw them again. There was no understanding.

Except that Theda *did* see her daughter again, knew where she was and gave her gifts, money perhaps. But why didn't Ruth Anne come back to that big, nearly empty old house, particularly if she had children? Surely Theda would have forgiven her after all that time, and you'd think she'd want to hear the sound of children's voices calling, laughing. Why had Ruth Anne stayed away?

And why, Mavis thought to herself, if she wasn't going to return, would she pick a place like this to live in? She looked out the window of the car. The road had become flat as a plate, and barren woods lined it on either side; there were no houses, and only a few faded advertising signs to indicate anyone had ever been there. When Tommie Lee suddenly turned the car off onto a sandy track, she thought that he had to stop to make some repair—until she saw the mailbox. She could not read the name.

"It's bumpy," Tommie Lee said. "They must of had a downpour, the road's washed." Mavis wondered how Ruth Anne ever found such a godforsaken place. Nothing grew there except scraggly pines and broom straw; nobody around. Garbage littered the track they followed, and Mavis saw a broken toilet, white as bones, sitting on a little hillock. There was such a desolate feeling about the place that she shivered slightly in the air-conditioned car.

She had expected a house, at least some sign of respectability, perhaps flowers planted at the steps in an attempt to soften the ugliness, swings and slides for children's play. But, when they turned a last bend and drove into a cleared space and Tommie Lee stopped the car (at the edge, as if he dared go no closer), she saw only the battered facade of a trailer, once painted white but now spotted as a dog, rusting at the base. Nothing grew near it, not even a weed. The ground was fine sand, tramped down; out back, the ground was blackened from burning trash. To Mavis it looked as if this place had fallen out of time, lost to all that had happened in years. Until she saw the wires, she wondered even if they had electricity.

"I'll stay here," Tommie Lee said. His voice was quite low, as if this place affected him also. "You go ahead, and I'll wait."

Mavis got out of the car without answering him. All at once she thought there might be a dog, some rawboned cur with diseased spots on its back that might come from beneath the trailer and snarl at her, but none appeared. She walked slowly; little wisps of sand stirred around her feet and covered her shoes with a fine powder. She clutched her purse securely under her arm. When she got to the door, she wanted to turn back, and when she finally tapped (the sound as sharp as metal clanging), she prayed no one was home.

The door opened only slightly, and Mavis could not see into the darkened interior. "Is Ruth Anne here?" she asked in a wavering voice. "I need to talk to her."

The door opened wider, and whatever face Mavis might have expected to see there, whatever image she might have formed in her head of Ruth Anne grown up and become a woman, this wasn't it. The woman at the door was slatternly, breasts dragging down the skimpy cotton T-shirt she wore, stretch pants bulging below the waist, imprinted with the cavelike hollow of her navel. The skin of the face was roughened, and the hair, greasy-looking even in the low light, was straight, pulled back with a rubber band. Worst (and Mavis almost cried out when she noticed) was the ear, or what was left of it—a part was missing, as if she had been bitten there by some vicious animal. Only the eyes, dark, probing, edged, it seemed, almost in gold and reflecting the light, marked the face as that of the girl Mavis once knew. They held her in their stare.

"I'm Ruth Anne. What do you want?"

Mavis cleared her throat and pushed her purse higher beneath her arm.

"I was asked to come tell you some news." Mavis saw that Ruth Anne's eyes flicked briefly away from her, out to the car parked at the edge of the clearing. "It's about your mother," she said. "Can I come in?"

Ruth Anne stepped aside and Mavis walked into the trailer but stopped suddenly, half-blinded by the darkness. The only light came in redly through shaded windows. "I'll turn on a light, you wait," Ruth Anne said quickly. "Don't fall." Mavis felt flooded with comfort. At least Ruth Anne showed some little concern. Perhaps it was another sign of that past child, taught manners, no doubt, even if she chose to forget them.

Ruth Anne lit a lamp hanging from the ceiling and it cast a round circle of light inside the trailer. Mavis expected to see dirt, clothes on the floor, half-eaten food on dirty dishes, but the place was spotless. It was as if Ruth Anne were able to cope only with this small space, trying to blot out everything beyond the thin walls of the trailer, living in semidarkness like some small animal beneath the earth. Mavis sat on the edge of a sofa, and Ruth Anne stood across from her, her elbow propped on her other forearm, hand covering her mouth, waiting.

"I'm Miz Mavis Lashley," she said, as if starting over again, trying to forget her first impression.

"I know." Ruth Anne took her hand away and Mavis almost thought she might be smiling.

"I live near your mother's house. You probably don't remember."

"Yes, I do." It *was* a smile. "We used to go skating in front of your house and you never yelled at us. Somebody else down the street—I can't remember her name, we called her a witch—she'd poke her head out the window and carry on like we were raising the dead, and we'd just skate on by and laugh at her."

"Mrs. Eason," Mavis said. "She's gone now. A stroke."

"I'm not surprised," Ruth Anne said. "Lord, how many years has it been? I can't even count." She sat down suddenly, opposite Mavis, crossing her arms across her breasts, as if to cover herself in embarrassment. Perhaps she remembered those snapshots from the party at Silver Lake. "But you didn't come here to talk about old times, did you?" Ruth Anne hugged her arms closer around her. "You mentioned my mother. You came in the car. I almost thought it was her at first, seeing the car stopped out there and then the knock on the door."

Mavis pulled her eyes away from Ruth Anne's staring ones and noticed that her fingers were twisting the handles of her purse. "She won't be coming anymore. She's gone on."

Ruth Anne gave a little gasp, and Mavis looked up suddenly, her hand already out to comfort. But Ruth Anne had pulled away; her face was in shadow outside the circle of light, and Mavis could not see her eyes. She dropped her hand. "I'm sorry to tell you, but I was asked to come."

"Who? Who asked you?"

"Alice Pate. She wanted you to know, said you didn't have a telephone or anything."

Ruth Anne laughed, and the sound startled Mavis. "Of course she wouldn't come herself. I suppose she thought I might shoot her with my shotgun." Ruth Anne slid down slowly again into her chair. Mavis looked for tears in her eyes but saw none; they had only softened and become darker, the reflected light gone.

"What happened?" Ruth Anne asked at last. Mavis wanted to get this over with; she felt very tired. If anyone should be there telling the news of Theda's death, it was Alice; it was she who had been close to Theda all those many years, not Mavis. She leaned back and tried to relax her fingers so that they would stay still.

"I'm sorry," she said. "But it was real bad. They found her out in a field. She'd gone away, left the house, and wasn't discovered till a long time after." Mavis stopped. The picture of Theda's bulging eyes staring came to her mind; she wanted to spare Ruth Anne that look if she could.

"Why out in a field? Did she have a heart attack?"

"No," Mavis answered, knowing she would finally have to say it. "She was killed, murdered, somebody strangled her."

Ruth Anne drew back as if Mavis had slapped her. Before her eyes merged with the shadows again, Mavis saw fear springing up there, the darkness settling into complete blackness. "Oh, Jesus, oh, Jesus," Ruth Anne said, but with no tone of prayer, just words to cover the silence that had formed, rocklike, in that small room. Mavis sat looking down at her hands spread out on her purse, and for a moment they seemed no part of her . . . until she felt the urge in them to reach out and stroke Ruth Anne's arm, to provide in some way comfort to her. But she knew that she could not get through that barrier of space between them; Ruth Anne might have struck her had she tried.

"Who did it?" Ruth Anne's voice was even and dead.

"They don't know yet. The police think it was some robber, somebody she just met up with."

"No," Ruth Anne said, the word slipping out, almost whispered.

"It doesn't seem likely to me, either. She had on jewelry, her watch. What was strange—she drove out herself the other afternoon and didn't have Tommie Lee drive her."

"Where did she go?" Ruth Anne leaned forward again so that Mavis could see her face.

"Nowhere special, out in the country. It was a cornfield."

Mavis picked up her pocketbook and set it upright before her on her knees. She was ready to go. "The funeral is going to be tomorrow. Two o'clock. They'll send a car. They want you to come."

"Do they?" Ruth Anne had a sudden little smile on her lips. "Alice? Did she say that?"

"Yes. She was the one who asked me to come out here, like I said."

Ruth Anne kept smiling her little smile. "Well, wonders will never cease," she said.

Mavis did not know how to respond. "It's at the Episcopal church, with internment at Oakdale Cemetery."

"All nice and proper. God knows, we'd have to be *proper* about it. What would the neighbors think?" Ruth Anne laughed again, louder. "That's all I heard when I was a child: *'What will the neighbors think?'* Any time I did something that wasn't just so, those were the words. I don't know how many years it took me to realize it didn't make any difference. Nobody ever cared. But Theda never knew, never learned that, I bet. I expect she was dressed up to beat the band when she got herself murdered."

"Do you need any help about things?" Mavis tried to sound vague.

"You mean clothes, mourning? No, we've got enough. Theda brought out stuff when she came. Don't worry"—she bent over closer to Mavis—"I'll be proper at the funeral. I suppose I owe her something. After all, she did tolerate us living out here, though she must have been afraid. Think someone would find out and tell and embarrass her. And she gave me money when I needed it, though I would never ask her. It came in envelopes in the mail, with no note. We had so little to talk about. I suppose she could find no words to put on paper, either."

Mavis knew that her face was flushed. She did not want to hear any more of Ruth Anne's words. She was embarrassed by them, had a feeling that she spied on someone without their knowledge. "If you do need anything, you can call," she said. "I'm in the book."

"Will you be there?"

Mavis was surprised at the question. "Well, why certainly. I expect a lot of the neighbors will be going."

"I don't care about them." Ruth Anne moved closer. Mavis stood up. "Maybe I haven't shown it, but I appreciate you coming out here to tell me. It was better." She reached and took Mavis's hand, and squeezed it before letting go. "I'd very much like you to be there."

Mavis smiled, relieved. For the first time since she had got up from the soft backseat of the car, she felt her body relax. "It's a hard thing to bear," she said. "Funerals. But they kind of finish things off, like closing a book. It's strange, but they help."

"There are worse things." Ruth Anne sighed. She looked away from Mavis, and the silence rose up again.

"Well, I'll just be going." Mavis moved to the trailer door and opened it. The sun, lowering behind the thin pines, fell on her face and startled her. She stumbled, then caught herself and moved carefully down the cinder-block steps to the sandy ground. She turned back. Ruth Anne stood in the doorway, sagging against the frame, hand up, shading her eyes.

"Say hello to Tommie Lee," she said, looking toward the car. "Poor boy. I think he's always been a little afraid of me. He never would come any closer when Theda came out."

"I'll do that," Mavis said, trying to make her voice sound as if she were ending just any visit. She said no more, and walked over the dry yard to the car. Tommie Lee turned off the radio and hopped out and held the door for her. Sinking down, she felt as if all the air had rushed out of her; she was deflated, like a balloon. She was thankful for the car—cool, soft, engulfing; in it she was protected from all the ugliness spread around her.

But she could still see Ruth Anne standing in the doorway of the trailer, one hand propped up higher than her head. The dark eyes stared steadily at the car, but she made no gesture of good-bye, just stood there as if she might remain till nightfall. That was the last sight Mavis had of her, such a lonely figure, waiting.

Tommie Lee backed the car around and turned out onto

the rutted road. "Things go all right?" he asked. Mavis wondered if he had been afraid for her.

"Well enough, I suppose. As good as could be expected."

Tommie Lee shook his head and bent forward over the steering wheel.

They had to wait at the exit to the highway. A bus was coming toward them, yellow-painted but with rusty spots, rattles heard even through the padded walls of the car. On the side was painted ANTIOCH BAPTIST CHURCH CAMP BUS, and beneath that a homemade banner saying VACATION BIBLE SCHOOL NOW. She expected to see the bus pass by, but it slowed, then stopped just in front of them. Mavis saw the faces of children pressed against the window glass, distorted, like the faces of fish in an aquarium. On the opposite side, two children got out, turned, and then went around the bus and started across the road, eyes curious (dark eyes, luminous), a boy of seven or eight, the girl a little younger. Ruth Anne's children, of course, though Mavis remembered seeing no toys in the trailer, no lines for hopscotch on the barren ground surrounding it, not even washed clothes on a line between trees.

The children stared at the car but did not seem surprised. Their faces showed nothing except blankness. "Poor little things," Mavis said aloud, a rush of compassion squeezing her heart. She wanted to tell Tommie Lee to wait, let her get out and put her arms around those children. But she knew that if she approached them, even murmuring words of endearment, they would have run off like frightened animals to the bleak protection of that darkened trailer and Ruth Anne's listless arms.

"Go on," she said loudly to Tommie Lee, and she could see the look of surprise in his eyes reflected in the rearview mirror at such a command from her. But he drove off quickly, a trail of dust and pebbles flying up in the air beside the mailbox marking the side road.

Alone in the backseat, Mavis tried very hard not to cry.

Chapter Nine

Mavis called Dale early next morning to ask him if he would take her to the funeral. She could have asked a neighbor; surely some one of them would be going and she could get a ride. But then she would have to hear them talking, speculating about Theda's death. She could almost hear the sharp intake of breath in the church when Ruth Anne and her children came in and people realized, all in a rush, that this was Theda's daughter, long lost, returning now after that small scandal years ago.

Dale's voice was sleepy when he answered the phone, and Mavis knew that she had awakened him. "I'm sorry, honey," she said. "I know you were asleep, but I wanted to get this settled."

"That's all right, Mavis. Time I was up anyway. What time is it?"

"Eight o'clock. You should be dressed already."

"You know I'm never any good in the morning. I never woke up in my life feeling wide awake."

"Just laziness," Mavis said, not scolding. It was always difficult for her to think of Dale as more than just a boy.

"Well, maybe I can move my lips now. What's so important."

"Theda Hedrick's funeral is this afternoon. Reckon you could take me? I mean, if you can get off, of course."

Dale laughed. "They'll never know. Long as I get the pictures they want, nobody cares. Sure, I'll come by whenever you say. After all, it's our own mystery, isn't it? You couldn't keep me away."

He arrived right on time. Mavis was dressed and waiting, sitting by the front window. Dale honked the horn, and she got up, glancing in the mirror as she went toward the front door, pleased with the way she looked in her good dark dress, always appropriate on such occasions, a wispy veil over her hair. She locked the door.

Then she almost turned back, wondering if she should take her umbrella. The day was as hot as ever, hardly a breath of air stirring, but the sky had darkened and there were storm clouds in the west. She didn't want to take the time to open the door again and get her umbrella, so she went ahead, saying a little prayer that it wouldn't rain. Nothing was worse than a funeral in a storm, with everyone huddled together around the grave like a bunch of shuddering birds, watching rivulets of water trickle closer, sliding toward the hole in the ground.

Dale reached over and unlocked the door and Mavis got in. She looked at him carefully. Thank the Lord he was dressed properly in a white shirt and quiet tie; his navy blue jacket hung on the hook over the rear window. She was almost afraid to look at his ear, but finally she did and, with a sigh of relief, noticed that the earring was gone. Well, at least he had some sense left.

"You're looking mighty pretty," Dale said to her.

"Don't need to look pretty for a funeral," she said, trying to be solemn.

"Aw, come on. It's not as bad as all that."

"It's not good," she said, and she felt a little surge of genuine sadness come into her heart as she thought of her visit the day before to Ruth Anne in that tacky trailer out in the middle of nowhere, and those two little children she last saw trudging into the woods as lonely looking as any two figures you might see in a picture book of fairy tales.

Dale's voice lost its teasing tone. "What?" he asked. "What do you mean?"

She told him then, about her visit to the Hedrick house and Alice Pate's urgent plea for her to go tell Ruth Anne of her mother's death. She told him of the ride out into the country in that old fine car with Tommie Lee and the surprise of passing the cornfield where Theda had died. And finally she described the sad little place that Ruth Anne had ended up in, her bitter looks and one last, sad gesture when she touched Mavis's arm. Last she mentioned the children, the two little ones whose faces lingered now in her mind, more familiar than she ever would have expected.

"Well, that was quite a trip," Dale said when she had finished. "Did you ever think you might be in danger? I mean even Tommie Lee, bless his poor soul, could have done it. You might have ended up like Theda Hedrick—spread-eagled in a cornfield."

"He wouldn't hurt a fly," Mavis said very fast, indignant. "You know that."

"Sure I do, but the police apparently are saying all sorts of things. One of the reporters was hanging around down at the police station and heard them."

"What's that?"

"Well, they've just about given up any thought it was a robbery committed by some stranger. They've finally gone back to what everybody knows anyway if they watch the news on TV: it's family or somebody close who usually kills. Not strangers a-tall. They've mentioned Charlene, say she might have gotten mad at Theda and did it with her boy-friend. People still remember that time years ago when they demonstrated. Tommie Lee, too, though it's hard to take such thoughts seriously. And Alice Pate's name has come up . . . Lord knows why since she seems to have been kept up by Theda. I bet they don't know about Ruth Anne, or they'd think she might have done it, too."

"I suppose they'll include me next, since I live down the street."

"Probably," Dale said. "I always did think you'd make a good ax murderess." Mavis smacked him on the arm, and then they both laughed, relaxed, the thought of the service ahead for a moment gone from their minds.

Grace Episcopal Church sat catty-cornered from the central square, the oldest church in town, a historical monument it said on the new-looking metal plaque at the corner of the building. Built of dark brown sandstone weathered to softness, it looked solid and respectable, countrylike in the middle of town, with a covering of shiny green leaves that ruffled up, lighter underneath, when the wind passed by. In all the years Mavis had lived there, she had never been inside that church. "It's too highfalutin for me," she would have said if anyone asked her why. "I'm happy with the Covenant Baptist Church. It was where I was baptized and where they'll send me out when the time comes. I don't need any robes and incense."

Dale parked the car across the street. The sky had darkened more, and when they went inside the vestibule of the church, they could hardly see, only a dim light covered in mottled glass hanging from chains overhead. Carved wood, nearly black, framed the doorways and arched toward the ceiling in support; the only color to be seen was the velvet covers of the cushions, red as communion wine, that lined the pews inside the sanctuary.

Soft organ music was playing, though Mavis did not recognize the tune. She expected heavily spiced air, but the only scent was one of slight mustiness. Surprisingly, it was cool; Mavis felt goose pimples on the back of her neck. She took Dale's arm and was glad he was there with her.

A few people were scattered throughout the church. Some probably came to every funeral, every wedding there, wept in joy or sadness along with everyone else, as if they belonged. Then Mavis made out a few faces, neighbors, Iva Mae Johnson sitting with two other ladies. When Iva Mae spied her, she waved frantically at Mavis and motioned for her to come join them, but Mavis simply nodded her head and held tighter to Dale's arm, pulling him further toward the front.

Thank the Lord the casket wasn't open. It stood at the foot of the altar, dark bronze, covered simply in gold chrysanthemums with no letters spelling out sentiments on satin ribbons. (But then, what would they say? "Beloved Mother"? "Dearest Grandmother"? "Friend"? How sad any of those words would be, since none seemed to apply to Theda.)

Mavis knew that some in the audience would be disappointed
not to view the body, looking for signs of strangulation, or
trying to read something into the line of Theda's lips. But
she was glad that Theda would not have to put up with a
viewing. So afraid all those years of others' eyes, keeping
secrets in that darkened house on the corner, better to let her
keep her face covered now in death.

The others came. Alice Pate, all alone it seemed at first,
until Tommie Lee came stumbling behind her, head lowered,
his pale hair still wet from his comb. Alice looked thin as a
rail in her dull black dress, and her hair seemed to have
grayed. She looked straight ahead, neither at the others assembled there nor at the enormous casket set up in front.
Then Mavis saw Charlene out of the corner of her eye as she
walked down the aisle with Buddy Dean beside her, him in
a suit, Charlene dressed all in white so that in the darkened
interior she almost glowed. Mavis knew what the ladies
would say later on about that. And finally, from a side door
with the minister, came Ruth Anne with her two children
trailing behind her. In the room there was a little rush of
sound, not words but a murmuring and drawing in of breath.
Who is that? if something could be said.

Even to Mavis, Ruth Anne looked like a stranger. Ruth
Anne had been right. She did have clothes, she knew how to
dress. From where Mavis sat she could see the good cut of
the dress Ruth Anne wore, the thin fabric soft and silky. Her
hair was loose, clean, shining around her shoulders (covering
that torn ear), and she had touched pale pink lipstick to her
lips. Her eyes, though, were hard as stones.

The minister stepped into the pulpit and the service began.
From high above, as if some angel lingered in the stained-
glass window there, a thin, sweet voice sang words of comfort and hope, and the minister, boyish, his just-shaved face
glistening, echoed those words in the service he read. You
never would have known he was talking about a perfect
stranger, someone he had never met (for surely Theda had
not been to church in years). In the quiet of the summer
afternoon, the words mesmerized all who sat there in the
sanctuary, except at one point, when there was the word *love*,

Alice Pate sobbed aloud for a moment and the spell was broken.

Well, that was real nice, Mavis thought to herself, as she went outside. It was a sweet funeral, not at all what she had expected in that ponderous old church. If you hadn't known where you were, you might think you were in just any regular church, nothing unusual at all.

There was a police escort to the cemetery. The sound of the siren wavered over the string of cars like a scream, and people in other cars, stopped at intersections, stared with vaguely interested faces, glad, perhaps, they were not in that procession. The hearse came first, then the family car with Ruth Anne and her two children; Alice must have ordered it for them, a kind gesture, Mavis thought. Alice herself rode in the big, old car of Theda's with Tommie Lee driving, poker-faced. The others came straggling behind.

The cemetery was in an older part of town, a little run down. Most people nowadays preferred the new cemetery out on the highway where there was perpetual care, a carillon tower that played tinkling hymns three times a day, and a pond where real swans swayed. A Ponderosa Steakhouse and a Taco Bell were just down the road.

But Mavis preferred Oakdale Cemetery, with its slightly grown-up look, old stones tilted, lone draped figures and marble lambs on little graves worn by the wind and rain until they looked blurred. Her husband was buried there, her child. They shared a single stone, pink granite with lilies carved in a spray across the top. Mavis's name was on it, too; only the dates were not incised.

When the hearse stopped near the gray canopy marking the grave site, the other cars slowly closed in behind it along the curving road, parked, and the passengers got out, stretching, pulling at dresses and shirts. The sky was gray, but no air stirred, and the moisture was like a damp hand on your arm. To Dale, as they were walking toward the tent, Mavis said, "I hope it holds off for a while, the rain."

"Might cool us all off," he said, and winked. Mavis did not answer him, walking with her head down, reading the names on the gravestones. She knew some, though this was not a part of the cemetery she visited when she came to put flowers on her family graves. When they were near the tent, she noticed the tall, gray obelisk of polished granite that stood there, slicing the air, with the one word HEDRICK carved on it in deep letters. It was like a knife, cold and ugly.

The family were seated under the tent, waiting, scattered, with empty chairs between them no one else dared occupy. Ruth Anne was there, with the children who sat wide-eyed and solemn; Alice Pate was at the other end of the row, eyes swollen from weeping. Charlene and Buddy Dean sat in the second row. Tommie Lee must have stayed in the car; Mavis did not see him anywhere.

The minister said a few more words of comfort with hope for eternal salvation, and read a prayer. When he gestured toward the coffin set in the middle of them all, the golden chrysanthemums on top and bright green artificial grass covering the raw earth beneath it, a little whining sound began as the coffin dropped level with the ground. Someone gave a gasp, but Mavis did not know who. Thank goodness they did not lower the casket all the way into the grave any longer, the way they used to. People were spared that. Mavis had been to more than one funeral back in the country where her parents were buried, and some stricken mother, child, tried to jump into the grave and had to be restrained.

It was over. The minister, sweating in his black garments, closed his book and took out a large white handkerchief and wiped his forehead. People began to move away, though some few went to greet Alice Pate. Ruth Anne sat alone, as if she needed to be told this was all, she could go now, take up her children and hide herself away again. The minister touched her on the shoulder and she jumped, a startled look on her face. Mavis turned away and looked up at the sky. The clouds were darker, closer; surely it would rain.

"Well, that's done," she said to Dale in a low voice. He had already taken off his jacket and Mavis noticed that his shirt was wet in back.

"Yes. Kind of sad, wasn't it? All those people sitting alone. You'd have thought death might have brought them closer together somehow."

"Yes," Mavis said, "but maybe there are old reasons keeping them apart. It happens sometimes." She moved on toward the car.

Then she stopped, looking up ahead where Alice stood next to the big car. "I ought to go over and say good-bye," she said to Dale. "You stay here. You don't have to go."

She turned away and walked over the graveled drive, her steps making a loud sound in the quiet afternoon. As she drew near Alice Pate, she suddenly realized she did not know what to say. All the old words, ways that could be counted on as a guide in such times seemed strange now, awkward; the usual formalities no longer held. So instead of saying more, she simply took Alice's hand (gloved, strange on such a hot day, though surely Theda would have approved) and said, "I'm sorry."

Tears spilled from the reddened eyes for a moment, but Alice made no sound. She continued to hold on to Mavis's hand, her grasp hard enough to hurt; her fingers were strong. When she finally let go and fumbled in her purse for a handkerchief, Mavis wanted to flex her hand. "Thank you for coming," Alice said. "You're probably the only one who wasn't just curious, the only one who cared." She took Mavis's hand again, fingers pressuring. In her eyes Mavis saw pleading. "Will you do me one last favor?" she asked. "I would appreciate it so much."

Mavis closed the other hand over Alice's. "Why, of course. You just ask."

"There will be people at the house. I know they'll come, neighbors and such. Some have brought food already. Would you be there, just for a little while? I don't know that I can deal with it all. And there's no one else."

Mavis wanted to say, *What about Ruth Anne? Isn't that house part hers now? She's family, she should be there to carry out the duties.* But she held her tongue and said, "Why, sure I will, honey. Go on and get in the car. We'll get there probably quick as you."

Alice turned and Tommie Lee held the door for her. Mavis went back to where Dale stood beside his car. "We can't go eat now," she said to him. Earlier, he had proposed taking her out to the cafeteria in the mall after the funeral for an early supper. They had a senior citizen's discount till five. "Miss Alice asked me to go to the house for a while and be there for visitors. I have to do it." He did not answer, but raised his eyes upward.

Mavis did not want to go to Theda's house, but somehow she was glad to be asked. Going there was the proper thing to do; it would put the end of the afternoon back into its proper form. Any other time, with another neighbor, she would have gone on to the house and never thought a thing about it. Dale unlocked the door of the car, and Mavis turned and got inside.

Chapter Ten

There was no police escort to lead them back to the house. The hearse pulled away, then Alice Pate in the big car; the others moved slowly behind, leaving a trail of reddish dust hanging over the cemetery drive. Late afternoon traffic was thick, people returning home from work. Mavis envied them, those people who would park in their driveways, go inside to a family meal, watch TV, and then go off to bed. At most, they might see death at a remove on the evening news, no need to be involved.

"You've got to come with me," Mavis said to Dale. "To the house, I mean. I don't think I can stand it if you don't."

"Of course I will," Dale said, reaching over to pat her arm. "We have to observe the suspects, don't we?" He spoke lightly, and she knew he was trying to make her feel better.

"Not likely. Probably, all they'll do is sit around and eat and gossip and then go home. But it may be different. Everything has been so strained. Usually, it's a relief, returning to the house, having it all over. People can relax, even laugh a little, begin to pick up things again and go on. Here, I don't know what will happen. It's just a mess."

The others had arrived when Mavis and Dale pulled up to the house, cars parked all along the curb and in the driveway on the other side of the house. They got out and went slowly up the walk. Above, the sky was still dark. "Surely, it will rain," Mavis said, "though, Lord knows, I'm glad it's held off this long."

Well, wouldn't you know it? Mavis thought as she entered

the front door. Already she could hear Zeena Campbell's voice giving instructions somewhere in the back of the house. Didn't set foot in church, much less go to the graveyard, and here she was taking over the way she always did. Mavis felt a little rush of anger and then thought it unchristian. But after all, Alice Pate *did* ask her to come to the house to help take care of things. "You come on," she said to Dale, and they went into the living room.

People sat there like the survivors of a storm. A small group of neighbors was at the far end, with Iva Mae Johnson talking so hard in a whisper that at first she didn't even see Mavis. The preacher stood alone by a window and looked even more like a boy than before in his loafers and khaki pants and not a sign of a tie. Ruth Anne sat in a corner with her back to the doorway, the children beside her like stiff dolls, perched on tall chairs with their legs straight out in front of them. She seemed drawn in upon herself, as if she existed there all alone.

"Well, Mavis, I declare. I thought you'd never get here." It was Iva Mae, rising up from the group, her arms waving. Her voice was too loud in the room, and she looked embarrassed when the others jumped and turned toward her. She sat back down again.

"You wait here," Mavis told Dale, as if he were a boy in kneepants. "I'm going to the kitchen."

She turned and went into the dining room. A delicate cutwork cloth covered the table, and a large silver coffee urn stood in the middle like some shimmering prize. Napkins, embroidered ones with a large "H" on the edge, were neatly arranged, and in the butler's pantry, between the dining room and the kitchen, cups were set out with monogrammed spoons, real sterling, not the stuff people bought nowadays at the discount store. Charlene must have arranged it all before the funeral. Somehow, Mavis thought, I don't think it would ever occur to Alice Pate to make such preparations.

Zeena Campbell was in the kitchen with Charlene. The counter was piled high with food, though Mavis knew at once that little of it was homemade. There were no casseroles covered in aluminum foil with the owner's name written on a label on the back so that they could be returned later. Mavis saw bags from the market, a box from the bakery, and she knew that Charlene had gone shopping early in the morning and brought in all this food. Poor girl, at least she had some feeling for what was right, the old ways. Her mother must have taught her.

"Mavis, can you just give us a little hand." Zeena's face was flushed, and she stood with her arms raised as if she were about to fly, fingers glistening with grease. "I've got to finish slicing this ham, and there's other things to do."

"That's why I'm here," Mavis said. "Miss Alice asked me to come." (Maybe she shouldn't have said that, but she did anyway.) "Charlene, what can I help you with?"

Charlene looked at Mavis. Her face was sullen, angry, Mavis could see, at Zeena's intrusions. Her eyes thanked Mavis for coming. "We've got some Colonel Sanders in those boxes and rolls to warm up. The coffee's done, and you can use a pitcher to put it in the urn in the dining room. I guess folks won't starve."

Mavis found an apron hanging on the pantry door and put it on over her good dress. Silently, she began to work with the other two women, and a kind of peacefulness settled over the heavy air. This was a routine they could follow, a rightfulness, an order. They sliced and warmed and arranged platters and carried the food to the dining room, actions so familiar that they could have completed them blindfolded. The others murmured in the living room, and that, too, seemed right, though they could hear no words. When Mavis went, finally, to the archway separating the two rooms and announced that they could all have a bite to eat, there were smiles and then outright laughter when Ruth Anne's little boy, hair mussed, his shirt all wrinkled, said quite loudly, "I'm hungry, Mama. I want something to eat."

The people milled around the table, taking food, talking louder now. They, too, seemed relieved to have something ordinary to do. Iva Mae Johnson said, "Isn't this the prettiest tablecloth you ever saw in your whole life?" and the other ladies murmured assent, touching the cloth with reverential fingers. Charlene came out with a silver punch bowl that

Mavis hadn't seen in the kitchen and set it down opposite the coffee urn, and the preacher immediately took the ladle and poured a large cup for himself, then one for Dale. The two had been talking quite animatedly in the living room. Mavis wondered if the punch was spiked and decided not to try it. She'd ask Dale later.

Only Ruth Anne still seemed isolated, space around her solid as a wall. She fixed the children's plates, bending close to ask what they wanted. The children seemed not to notice her distance. They sat on two chairs in the corner, plates balanced on their knees, and Ruth Anne stood by them, eating her own food, watchful.

It was then that Alice Pate appeared, pale in the dark doorway that led out to the entrance hall. Mavis caught her breath, realizing for the first time that she had not even thought of Alice since she had been in the house, perhaps did not want to see her—that slim woman standing there as if pulled taut by strings, the cords in her neck stretched out, veins looping up her arms, fingers clasped tightly, as if she might fall apart should they come undone.

The others must have felt the same way. The easy conversation stopped. People were left with their hands stretched out, empty, as they reached for another roll, the spoon of a dish. Mavis had the sensation that they were all posed for a photograph, waiting for the flash. Instead, there came the piping voice of the little boy who sat by Ruth Anne, his bright face turned up, saying, "Who is that, Mama? Who is that lady?"

The others might have gone on then, finished reaching for the roll, taken another helping of green bean and french fried onion casserole, except that Ruth Anne turned suddenly toward all of them in the room and threw back her head in laughter so startling that someone dropped a fork and it clattered on the floor. "Why, that's *Auntie*, honey. That's what they always told me to call her. Auntie Alice. Isn't that a nice name?"

Mavis was sure Alice would fall. The hands had become unclasped and she reached out as if to find support. Dale was near her, saw her need, and he reached out and put his arm beneath Alice's own. She closed her eyes for a moment, then opened them and smiled a ghastly smile. "Thank you," she said almost in a whisper. "It's been a difficult day." She pulled a little away from Dale. "I would like to thank you all for coming. I appreciate it more than you know."

She turned. Dale followed her to the doorway, but Alice signaled that he need not follow. She did not look up as she passed Ruth Anne, and Ruth Anne said no more, turning back to the children as if she were afraid Alice might strike them.

The mood was broken. The ordinary was gone, and the old fears returned, flitting around the room like trapped birds. People set down their plates and cups and made murmuring sounds about leaving, having to get home to fix supper for others, they'd best be gone. Iva Mae Johnson came over to Mavis and said, "I'd like to stay and help you clean up, but you know how J.T. is. If I'm not there with his supper on the table, he has a fit." The other ladies left with her, heads bent close. Mavis knew that even before she fixed her husband's supper, Iva Mae would be on the phone telling what had happened.

Mavis stood by the door and thanked people for coming. Alice Pate had disappeared back upstairs and Ruth Anne made no motion to take the part. Mavis didn't mind. In fact, she was glad to see the others go. Only Dale and the minister remained, standing in the living room with another cup of punch. They seemed to have struck up quite a conversation.

For the first time, Mavis thought as she stood surveying the room, the house looked as if someone lived there. The dining room chairs that had stood around the room in a rigid order were disarranged, gathered into little groups where people had talked as they bent over plates of food. The perfect white tablecloth was wrinkled now, stained with rings of coffee and crumbs of food. Dipping and lighting, a single fly buzzed in the silence over the remains. It could have been any lazy Sunday afternoon after a family dinner: people scattered for a quiet nap or to watch a game on TV; the children outside in dress-up clothes playing tag, even though they had been told not to get dirty. Mavis would gladly have gone home at that point, that pleasant little daydream in her head, but she knew she would have to stay and help clean. It would be expected.

Sighing, she gathered up cups and saucers and started toward the butler's pantry to the kitchen. Why she stopped before going further (hidden in that small space, glass-fronted shelves on either side of her sparkling with crystal and china), she didn't know; a sense of foreboding perhaps, quiet before a storm. And then, when she heard the voices, she could not move, could not indicate her presence, for surely it would have seemed as if she were listening behind the half-closed door to the two of them, Ruth Anne and Charlene, there in the kitchen together.

"So you knew all the time?" It was Charlene's voice, smooth as syrup, something golden. Mavis could imagine her at the sink, scraping plates, while Ruth Anne stood away from her, at the table perhaps, fumbling with leftovers. She must have sent the children outside to play, releasing them for the first time that day.

"Of course I knew." Ruth Anne's voice almost held laughter.

"How?"

"The two of them arguing. I would be in my bedroom and they would think I was asleep and they would go at each other tooth and nail. 'Where have you been?' my mama would say." (It was the first time Mavis had heard Ruth Anne use that word, *mama*, about Theda.) "Before Daddy had a chance to answer, she would go on. 'With that nigger woman? Is that where you were? Then you expect to come in here and nobody say a word?'

"They'd go on like that for hours, it seemed to me, and though I would cover my head and try to sleep, knowing I had to get up and go to school next day, I could still hear them, hear the hate in their voices. But there was something else in my mama's voice, perhaps an enjoyment in inflicting pain."

"Was she really that mean? Lord knows, she probably never wanted me here, but she's never been evil."

"I think that's why she sent me away after all the mess out

at Silver Lake, to punish him, get even. I was always close to him. *My daddy.* She was always jealous of us, too, maybe more so than him and your mama. I wonder if it was easier to have his other daughter in the house than her own.''

''I don't know. Lord, I don't know.''

Ruth Anne made a laughing sound, or it could have been a sob. ''Funny, isn't it? The two sisters united by death. Strange how things work out.'' There was a pause. ''Think you'll stay on here? Will Alice keep you?''

''I don't know that it will be up to Miss Alice. Maybe she won't get the place.''

''Do you think it will go to me? That would be a joke. I'm sure Theda would never allow that. The daughter that went astray returned to the home place. In her grave she's still probably concerned about what the neighbors think.''

''Maybe she didn't leave a will.''

''Theda? Of course she did. If nothing else, Alice would have seen to that. Don't you know? You've been with them all this time. Alice could get anything she wanted. Twist Theda right around her little finger.''

''Wasn't like that no time recently. They argued some. Tried to keep me and Tommie Lee from hearing, but we knew. Sometimes they wouldn't speak for days.''

''My, that's a change. Alice didn't move in till after I got sent away, but Theda and she were friendly already. Theda would take the car and go down to my daddy's office when Alice was to get off work and pick her up, and the two of them would go off somewhere to eat. Daddy didn't like it. You could tell. They argued about that, too. Funny isn't it? Maybe she did it. Alice Pate. Maybe she just got tired of Theda and wanted to get out.''

''Why would she do that? Alice never did know a thing about keeping house. Miz Theda gave all the orders, planned the meals and saw that things got done. Alice couldn't go out and get a job now. She's too old. Nobody'd want her.''

''Well, maybe *you* killed her, hoping that Theda might have left you a little something.'' Mavis heard a change in Ruth Anne's voice, cutting now. Perhaps it sounded like Theda's voice those years ago when she argued with Dr. Hedrick. Ruth Anne learned from her.

"What do you mean? I'm the last person she'd leave anything to."

"I saw you and that big buck boyfriend of yours. Saw you this afternoon when you ran out to talk to him by the garage. I was in the washroom and happened to look out the window. You two could have done it together."

"You're crazy. You always were a mean child. Miz Theda said that. Said you were hardheaded since you were a little baby, never could make you mind. She said that's why she sent you away. To teach you some sense. I see it didn't work. You're as bad as ever."

The door next to Mavis's hiding place suddenly was swept open as Charlene rushed past. She looked neither right nor left, and Mavis hoped she had not seen her standing there in the low light. She wondered if Ruth Anne would follow.

But then, sweet as sugar, Ruth Anne called out, "Hey, you kids, we've got to go home. It'll be dark soon. Come on now. Mama's getting your things together."

Lord, how changeable she is, Mavis thought. Never could predict a thing she might do.

Chapter
Eleven

It had been an exhausting day. Mavis could hardly put up
her hair, she was so tired. She sat before the mirror of her
bureau with her hands up, twining the thin white strands on
the special rollers Shirlee had told her to buy, thinking she
would have to get a new permanent soon, this was too much
trouble.

Other times, she might have felt relieved, at peace, after
a funeral. Miss Hattie Davis—with her everything went just
fine. They had the service, people gathered at the house afterward, ate, even joked a little as they left, order restored.
But this afternoon had ended in discord, with Ruth Anne's
jarring laughter and the others hurrying out, eager to escape
the uneasiness in the air.

And then there was the conversation Mavis had overheard,
revelations she never would have dreamed of: Dr. Hedrick
the father of Charlene, who would have thought it? After
Charlene had rushed past her, disappearing through the darkened doorway and running up the stairs, Mavis made two
trips to the kitchen and then decided to leave. She didn't even
say good-bye to Ruth Anne, avoided her really, glad that she
was outside calling to the children. Lord knows who locked
up for the night and turned out the lights.

I should sleep well tonight, Mavis thought to herself. Often she lay awake for hours, thoughts buzzing in her head,
images on her eyelids. Those times, she probably should get
up and read or watch TV, but the loneliness of the dark night
upset her, no other lights visible anywhere, as if she were

the only person alive, and she would rather stay in bed until she fell, finally, asleep.

She was nearly finished with her hair when the doorbell rang. Who could that be this time of night? Fear clutched at her, and she saw in her mind Theda Hedrick with her bulging eyes, a knot around her neck. Perhaps someone had come after Mavis, was waiting now at the door.

But that was silly as could be. Murderers didn't come and ring your doorbell, and it wasn't all that late anyway. Mavis got up and pulled her old rose-colored chenille robe around her and went into the living room; a lamp glowed there, lit all night, and she turned it up so that the gloom disappeared. She clicked on the porch light and looked out the diamond-shaped window to see who was standing there.

Charlene Anderson, and that boyfriend of hers. What was his name? Buddy Dean. Again, Mavis was slightly afraid. What in the world did they want? Maybe something else had happened—Miss Alice sick, or Ruth Anne and her children in an accident on the way home. Mavis knew she had to open the door. She undid the lock and, leaning on the frame, she opened it slightly so that she could poke her nose through and see Charlene's face, distorted, wavering through the screen wire. "What is it?" she asked, trying to keep a tremor out of her voice. "Is something the matter?"

Charlene bent closer. Mavis could see her dark eyes quite plainly now. For the first time, she saw fear in them and thought how different Charlene looked when she got her picture in the paper at the courthouse with the others, her eyes, even smudged by newsprint, blazing. "I'm sorry," Charlene said. "I know it's late, Miz Lashley, but I wanted to talk to you. There ain't nobody else." She paused, then gestured toward the tall, black man behind her. "He wanted to come with me," she said. "He don't mean no harm."

Mavis opened the door wider and reached out to undo the hook on the screen door. "All right, I suppose you can come on in. I was just getting ready to go to bed, so you'll have to excuse the way I look."

Charlene and Buddy came in, him so tall that Mavis had to look up high to see his face. She saw nothing there that would give away what he might be thinking. He was as impassive as a picture on a wall.

"Sit down," Mavis said, pointing to two chairs. She herself sat on the sofa, plumping up a pillow beside her. Charlene perched awkwardly on the edge of her seat and Buddy reared back like he owned the place, surveying the room. Well, you won't find anything amiss, Mavis thought to herself, following his eyes and wondering if they were critical. The crocheted doilies on the arms of the sofa and chairs were crisply white, washed and starched stiff not a week ago, and Mavis had just replanted the dish garden that sat on the coffee table with slick, dark-leaved plants; a china castle with a tiny tower sat right in the middle, like some fairy-tale kingdom. Mavis smiled and sat back against the back of the sofa, her arms folded, waiting for what the two of them might have to say.

Charlene began. "I know you heard us talking this afternoon, me and Ruth Anne." Mavis bowed her head a moment, embarrassed. "Oh, that's all right. I was actually glad you were there. I'm tired of keeping secrets. It didn't matter to me, but Miz Hedrick would have a fit if anybody ever found out. I was just surprised that Ruth Anne knew. I thought they might of kept things like that from her. But I want someone to really know what happened. Buddy said, 'What for?' when I told him I aimed to talk to you. 'The police will probably find out sooner or later,' I said to him, 'about Dr. Hedrick and my mama, and I want somebody to know the truth, not hear rumors and tales.' "

"Why pick me?" Mavis asked. She couldn't keep back her surprise.

"I don't have anybody else. It's nothing I could talk to Miss Alice about, and I don't have no other relatives now that my mama is gone. Buddy knows, but nobody'd ever believe what he said."

Buddy Dean looked at her, his smooth dark brow wrinkled; in a moment he would be angry. "How come you say that?" he asked.

Charlene dismissed him with a gesture. "You been arrested. Not just the demonstration. That time you got caught with dope. They think, 'Here's just another nigger boy, who cares what he says?' " Buddy sat back, his forehead still wrinkled, bent over with his long hands hanging in front of him between his legs.

"I didn't kill her. That's mainly what I want to say." Charlene's eyes had a pleading look. "Miz Theda just tolerated me because she had to in a way. But she never was mean to me. *Resigned* maybe is the word. Miss Alice always was a lot nicer, but then, she had no reason not to be. And *I* had no reason to kill Miz Theda. I knew I'd never get anything from her, not in a million years."

"You said 'tolerated.' 'Had to.' What do you mean?"

"What my mama did." Charlene looked down at her thumb and pushed at it with another finger. "You won't think it's so nice, but I guess Mama thought she had no other choice. She's gone now, so I can't apologize. It's just something that happened."

"*What* happened?"

Charlene sighed, then looked up. "She didn't go after him. Dr. Hedrick, I mean. I know what others would say. 'Nigger woman go after a white man, tempt him.' But it was the other way around. My mama was a good woman, went to church long as she could before the cancer began to work on her and she didn't have the strength. But she was younger then, a long time ago when things were different from what they are now. She cleaned up in the building where Dr. Hedrick had his office. Miss Alice worked there then and she knew my mother.

"Sometimes he stayed late at the office, writing up his notes, things like that. My mama told me he would be sitting there at his desk illumined in a little circle of light from the lamp on the desk, and she would creep in real quiet so as not to disturb him and empty the wastepaper basket. He was always nice and polite, she said. Would say, 'You go right ahead, don't mind me,' and thank her when she finished.

"Then he started talking more, asking her about little things, the weather and what time did she finish up, nothing important. She thought he was right nice to be so friendly, and she began to look forward to seeing him there, seemed like, more and more. When he put his hand, lightly, slowly, over hers as she held on to the desk to bend over and pick up the basket, she was so startled she didn't know what to do, and I guess she didn't do anything. After that, it was too late.''

"Too late?" Mavis knew that her voice sounded angry. "That poor woman. It wasn't fair."

"Well, who'd believe her? She going out and say that Dr. Hedrick's been flirting with her? And maybe she loved him by then. She did, no matter what happened later. But she felt guilty, I think. That's one reason why she went to church every Sunday, though she never told me that. Maybe Miz The'da made her feel that way. I don't know.''

"What a shame," Mavis said, more to herself than to the other two. Charlene hardly seemed to hear her.

"Anyway, he started seeing her there at the office, waiting almost every night till she came in. He would take the mop from her hand, and undo her apron and lay it on a chair, and they would lie together on that red leather sofa in his office, the cushions squeaking so loud as they moved together that they were afraid somebody in another office might hear, resting finally in their sweat, the wet cushions dark as blood.

"My mama was afraid to tell him about me, and she kept it a secret long as she could. When she did finally let it out, he didn't seem to care much, was only a little put out that they couldn't do it on the sofa anymore because she got so big, wanting her to do other things then that my mama refused. After I was born, I guess they continued, and he gave my mama some money along. Just left it on the edge of the desk by the wastepaper basket and never said a word about it.

"Then he died. I don't think he told my mama about Ruth Anne getting sent away, but she said all the joy seemed just to drain right out of him. Sometimes, he'd just talk to her and not do anything else—they had hardly said a word to each other before. 'He looked lost,' my mama told me, 'and I would want to give him comfort, but I was afraid, scairt he take it the wrong way.' When he died—at home, somewhere in that big old house, his heart gave out—my mama didn't know it until she saw it in the paper, and she said she fell on the floor crying, a hole in her heart with him gone.

"She had come to depend on the money, and now there was no more. It paid for me. My school clothes, books, extras she liked to give me, and I guess she felt she couldn't give that up, even if it meant going begging, pride stuck in her throat enough to make her gag. But she did it, went to Miz Theda and talked to her. Marched right up to the front door like anybody else, and Miz Theda invited her in, 'not even surprised,' my mama said, like she was expecting it.

"Of course Miz Theda knew, maybe not that it was *my mama* he was seeing, but you can't keep something like that hushed up for long. My mama and she sat there in the living room, talking like two ladies at tea, except they were talking about the man that gave each one of them a daughter. 'I don't mean you no harm,' my mama told her—she told me about it all long after, before the cancer got her and she couldn't speak no more. 'I know I'm to blame a little, too, but I just can't make it on what I got now. I need some help.' "

" 'Why should I give it?' " Miss Theda said.

" 'Because you don't want people to know, do you? Even if he be dead and gone. People will still point at you and talk behind your back.' "

"Miss Theda turned white then, my mama said, whiter than anybody she had ever seen. Mama probably could have got anything she wanted right then if she asked, but that's not what she did. She didn't want any gift. Maybe she felt she had had enough from Dr. Hedrick. I don't know.

" 'You wouldn't do that,' " Miz Theda said in a kind of pleading voice.

" 'No, ma'am,' Mama said. 'But I need some work. You pay me and I'll come here and do your cleaning and washing and ironing. I can still do the cleaning downtown at the building at night. You won't regret it, I'll see to that.' "

"So that's how it started, my mama working for Miz Theda and Miss Alice in that big old house. Sometimes, she would take me with her, and I'd wander around the house looking at all the pretty things until Miz Theda came down. When she saw me, she would look so hard, so hateful, that I'd go back to the kitchen and stick close to my mama's skirts, or go outside to play by the garage. If Tommie Lee was there, he'd play games with me, younger even than I was, it seemed, till it was time to go home.

"Later, when I finally found out who my daddy was—I pestered the life out of my mama, asking her again and again until she finally whispered to me the words—I would look at pictures sitting in the house, of the doctor and Miz Theda and Ruth Anne, and try to trace my face in theirs, but I could find nothing there, and I even wondered if my mama was lying to me, though I couldn't think why in the world she would make up such a story.

"Things went on that way a long time. My mama went to the Hedrick house two or three times a week to work, and Miz Theda wasn't mean or anything like that, though my mama said she stayed in her room most of the time she was there. Miss Alice was always friendly. I guess she had known my mama from the time she was the receptionist down at the office, but she didn't lord it over my mama, now that she was living with Miz Theda and had all those fancy clothes. My mama said something funny once about Miss Alice: 'She look like she just wearing those clothes like they some kind of finery, like on Halloween. Don't look like they belong to her at all, like she wanna be wearing something else.'

"Then my mama got sick. I wasn't even through high school yet. That was the one thing my mama wanted to see— me up there on the stage in a gown getting my diploma, and she never did. The cancer worked fast, and she had to stop work at the Hedrick's and at the office building. We went on welfare, and I think that hurt her more than the cancer. 'I took care of us all these years,' she'd say. 'Now we be like trash.' 'Hush,' I'd tell her, 'we can't help it,' but that didn't seem to make no difference with her.

"One last thing she did, though—got me on at Miz Theda's to work. 'After I'm gone,' she said, 'you'll get some money from the welfare, but you can earn some there, too— go to school, go to college, be something.' Miz Theda must have agreed, even though my mama won't in no shape to go out telling stories to anybody at that point, just skin and bones and could hardly walk. And nobody would have cared then, anyway, those old tales. Lord, a lot worse goes on now, and nobody ever notices.

"I been there ever since. Work all the time now and have a room. Take some courses down at the college. Everything was going along fine until this happened. Now, they're gonna try to blame me, maybe Buddy, too. It ain't fair."

Charlene leaned back in her chair; to Mavis she looked like a tired child, nearly exhausted and ready to sleep. Buddy Dean reached over to Charlene and touched her arm. His sullen look was gone. He looked sad. Perhaps he had never heard that story before, or all of it, and he shared Charlene's loss and grief at that moment. Charlene, responding to his touch, almost smiled, and sat up a little straighter.

"I'm so sorry," Mavis said, and felt how little this was. How could you really understand another's sorrow? You could only compare your own and it might not be the same at all.

"You reckon they'll arrest us?" Buddy Dean's voice was light in the air, small, it seemed, coming from such a big body.

"Course not," Mavis said. "What have they got to go on? Maybe some old gossip. Where were you that afternoon? When Miz Theda was killed, I mean."

Buddy Dean looked at Charlene and she flushed, her blooming skin suffusing rose. After a few moments she said, "We were up in my room, Miz Lashley. I didn't have any jobs to do, and Buddy was off. I know you won't think that's proper, but it was the only place we could be private. Nobody would ever come there. We were . . . involved. I didn't hear nothing a-tall. Miz Theda leaving or anything. It would just be our word, though. No one else could testify."

"Well, don't you worry, honey." Mavis sat up very straight. She did not want to know more about Charlene and Buddy's afternoons upstairs in the house on the corner. "You have no reason to want Miz Theda dead far as I can see. Even if you told you were Dr. Hedrick's own kin, there'd be no way to prove it. Unless somebody tells them, the police never will know." She reached over and grasped Charlene's hand. "My lips are sealed," she said. "Nobody'll ever hear from me."

Charlene smiled full out for the first time since she had entered Mavis's living room. "Thank you, ma'am," she said. "I felt I could trust you. Buddy was afraid, but I've seen you all these years, been around, and I never heard a bad word against you."

"I'm sorry," Buddy Dean said. He touched Mavis's hand. "I should have taken Charlene's word. Now I know she was right."

"Well, I've got to go to bed." Mavis stood up and pulled her robe tighter around her. The other two scrambled up. "You get a good night's sleep," she said to Charlene. "It's been a tiring day for everybody."

She turned and Charlene and Buddy accompanied her to the door. They said good night one more time, and Mavis watched until the two of them were out of sight down the front walk. Then she turned off the porch light, leaving the yard in darkness.

Chapter Twelve

"How would you like to fix breakfast for your favorite nephew?"

"Hey, how're you? Come on in."

Mavis stepped aside and let Dale come into the house. She was wearing her robe, and her hair was still up in curlers. In the kitchen, she had just got the coffee on, enough for her; now she would have to make another pot.

Dale did that sometimes, came by early without a word of warning, carrying a big bag of Krispy Kreme donuts from the place up at the intersection, a surprise every time. She would pretend to be annoyed with him—why hadn't he called so she could have something special?—but she really didn't mind. In fact, she looked forward to those times, the two of them sitting at the kitchen table, drinking coffee, gossiping about nothing at all important, sometimes watching a silly game show on TV. Then, suddenly Dale would look at the clock high on the wall and rush up. "Lord, it's time for me to go. I've got to take pictures of a bunch of ladies at the Daughters of the Confederacy meeting, and they'll kill me if I'm late. They've probably been primping for hours."

Today, she said to him. "Good thing you didn't come any later. It's my day at the Mission, and I wanted to get down early, before it's too hot. Sit down now, and I'll do the eggs." Sure enough, he had the donuts, and Mavis got a plate out of the cabinet to put them on. It was then that she noticed the envelope that he had carried along with the donut bag. "What's that?" she asked.

"What?" Dale put the envelope behind his back, a teasing grin on his face.

"Don't play games with me. I'll whip your *be*-hind the way I did when you were a little boy and didn't mind me when I told you to do something."

"Such talk." Dale made clucking sounds with his tongue. Then his face changed and he looked serious for a moment. "I'll show you later. Pictures. You don't really want to see them right now, not if we're going to eat."

She didn't push him, busying herself with the food. She cooked bacon, not too crisp, the way they both liked it, and soft-scrambled eggs. At the grocery store the last time she was there, they had a special on English muffins, and she bought a bag; they would be good with her homemade blackberry preserves. The donuts would be dessert. Dale sat silently smoking at the table, watching her (she fussed at him about that habit, but he would not stop). It was a warm time for her, relaxed and easy, and she thought of times past when she had cooked for her own family, so unknowing then of what was to come. She would have treasured those times so if she had been aware of how quickly they would end.

"Let's say the blessing," Mavis said as she sat down at the table, noting that Dale had already eaten half a donut. They bowed their heads. "Dear Lord, we thank Thee for this food for the nourishment of our bodies. Bless us as we go through this day and keep us safe from all evil. Amen."

They ate in silence, enjoying the food. The preserves, newly opened, gave up a scent of hot dry fruit ripening in the sun, and Mavis remembered going blackberry picking as a child, a metal bucket grasped in her hand, legs smelling of kerosene to keep chiggers away.

"That was good." Dale sat back and wiped his mouth with a paper napkin, then reached for another donut. Mavis got up and refilled their coffee cups. When she was seated again, he leaned over and put his curved hand up to his mouth as if telling secrets. "I've got something to tell you," he said. His eyes gleamed the way they did when he was a little boy and had gotten into some mischief. "About the *murder*."

"Dale Earl Sumner, don't you tease me. Murder is nothing to joke about."

"Oh, Lord," he said, and put his hands up to cover his ears. "Do you have to use that name. *Earl* just about murders *me*. I don't know where my mama got that white trash name. Must have been one of her old boyfriends."

"It's as good a name as any. Don't be stuck-up." Mavis tried to look stern and had planned to be silent, but her curiosity got the best of her. "What's the news? Are you making it all up?"

"No, not a bit. I was hanging around down at the police station—it's a good way to get pictures sometimes, you never know what might happen, who they'll drag in—and I heard that detective, Charles Morgan, talking. Since I'm there sometimes on 'official business,' they don't mind me, so I overhear a lot. He had heard from Theda Hedrick's lawyer. He knew about the will."

"Well?" Mavis said, her voice lingering in the air.

"You may be surprised," he said. "Ruth Anne got just five dollars, not a nickel for those two children, Theda's grandchildren. Makes you wonder why Theda ever bothered about Ruth Anne and the children at all. Maybe Alice Pate got her to send out the clothes and gifts. Or maybe there was another reason—like she just wanted Ruth Anne to stay out there in the country, more or less invisible, and not come into town and bother her."

"Just a lot of maybes," Mavis said. "Come on, tell me who she left it to."

"Charlene and Tommie Lee both got a small gift, five thousand apiece."

"I bet it doesn't seem small to them. Like a fortune really. That Tommie Lee'll spend it on comic books. Be gone in a week. He hasn't got sense enough to keep it."

"The rest went to Alice Pate." Dale sat back, waiting, as if he had dropped a bomb.

"Well I never," Mavis said. Certainly she might have thought that Theda would give Alice something, perhaps even the house to live in during her lifetime. But not the whole estate. She would have thought Ruth Anne would get it. Blood ties were strong, even though there might be bad feelings in a family for years; in the end, people usually did the expected thing. For once, Mavis thought, Theda must not have cared what the neighbors might think.

"That means any one of them could have done it, would have a reason."

"Who?"

"Alice. Charlene. Tommie Lee. They seem to be thinking that down at the police station."

"It doesn't mean any such a thing. And if Charles Morgan is going around accusing people, he should be ashamed of himself."

"That's just talk. They aren't about to arrest anybody."

"Well, it's silly. Tommie Lee wouldn't hurt a fly, and he'd never know, anyway—not about the will."

"What about the other two? Maybe Charlene thought she would get some money so she could run away with her boyfriend, and I bet anything Alice knew she'd get all the rest of it."

"But why would she need more? Alice had it all already, didn't have to worry about a thing, no responsibilities. They had gone on living there together all those years, why change?"

"Maybe she just got tired of kowtowing to Theda. She wanted to be the queen of the house."

"I never will believe it. You were at the funeral. You saw how Alice grieved."

"Could have been just put on."

Mavis shook her head. "No, I know what grief is, loss. It was genuine what Alice felt. You're too young to know."

Dale was quiet for a moment. Then he said very quietly, "Maybe not."

Mavis might have asked him what he meant, but she decided not to pursue the subject. She decided to talk about Charlene, and she told Dale of the visit the night before, the sad story of secret love that no one back then would have allowed, and all the unhappiness it led to. When she finished, she said, "I know that Charlene couldn't have done it, either. Why in the world would she tell me all that if she had something to hide? No, you're thinking wrong. So is Charles Morgan.''

"Well, I suppose it'll all come out. It seems easier when you read about it in novels. But here, I didn't show you these.'' Dale wiped his fingers on the paper napkin again and slid out the brown envelope he had brought in with the donuts. Mavis had forgotten all about it. "More pictures,'' he said. "I got them from the coroner's office. Not ones I took. These pictures were made when they first brought in Theda's body, before the autopsy. That's the way Alice Pate saw her. When she identified the body, I mean.''

"Lord, I never thought of that,'' Mavis said. "I suppose she'd have to. They wouldn't have known about Ruth Anne, and there was no one else.''

Dale did not answer, but took the pictures out of the envelope and handed them to Mavis; in spite of herself, she gasped. There was Theda, lying on a table, dull metal, her head pulled back so that you could see the deep indentation on her neck (only a shadow before in the other pictures). Mavis peered closer, expecting to see a cord pulled tight, but she saw instead a belt, obviously from a woman's dress, the fabric an old-fashioned pattern of curling leaves. Mavis looked down at Theda's waist and saw that she was still wearing her own belt, so it must have been from another dress. Had the police looked at her closet at home?

"Not a very nice sight, is it? Kind of a strange expression she has when you see her from this angle. Fear, maybe, but more, like she has some sort of grim satisfaction.''

Mavis looked at the face. "I don't know. It's just sad. To see her there in one of her fancy dresses, still with her gloves on and hardly a hair out of place. She was so private before; now here she is lying out ready to be violated. Poor Alice, having to see Theda like that, when the last time they were together Theda would have been walking around, talking, no expectation of dying. It must have torn Alice's heart right out.''

Mavis handed the photographs back to Dale. "I don't want to see any more. That's enough.'' She stopped and frowned. "Still, there *is* something else.'' She took the pictures back for one last look. "Something that bothers me about it, something not right." Dale craned his neck to see.

"I don't see anything unusual, except, of course, she's dead."

"I know. It's probably silly." Mavis jumped up. "Lord, will you look at the time." She had glimpsed the clock. "Half the morning gone and me still in my bathrobe. What if somebody came to the door? The neighbors would think I'd gone right off, lying around all day with no clothes on. And I'll be late down at the Mission. They won't know what happened to me."

Dale laughed. "They won't worry. They'll know nobody would ever dare do you in."

"The very idea. That's not anything to tease about."

"I'm sorry. Just running off at the mouth. I've got to go, too. I need to get these pictures back before anybody notices they're missing." Dale slid the photographs back into the envelope and stood up. "Thank you, ma'am for the good breakfast. Mind if I come again?"

Mavis couldn't help but smile. She patted Dale's arm as they walked to the front door. "Any time you want, long as you bring the donuts."

Dale went down the walk, and Mavis stood by the door until the red sports car had pulled away. Then she turned and went to the kitchen and quickly cleared off the table. Though she hated to do it, she decided to leave the dishes soaking in the sink; she would wash them later when she returned from the Mission. She dressed hurriedly and only half combed out her hair. With any luck, nobody she knew would see her and notice how scraggly she looked.

Did she have everything? Pocketbook, the needlework bag, the cotton gloves she used to handle the clothing? No, the gloves were still in the drawer where she had put them after washing and drying them the last time. She pulled out a pair and put them in her bag, then turned to go.

She stopped, standing stock-still right there in the middle of the bedroom floor. That was it—that was what had been bothering her. In her head she saw again the picture of Theda and realized what was wrong. She would tell the police, though maybe they had already noticed themselves. She would have to find out.

Hurrying, she went to the front door, opened it and stepped outside. The Mission would just have to wait. She knew something that might help find a murderer.

Chapter Thirteen

Mavis got off the bus at the south end of the mall that ran all the way up Main Street to the central square. She hardly ever ventured downtown anymore (there were purse snatchings in broad daylight), but still she thought, *foolish*, whenever she saw the mall, though it had been ten years or more since the city council had voted to put it in when the downtown stores started closing and moved to the shopping center on the outskirts of town.

Mavis could have told them it wouldn't make a bit of difference, cutting off traffic with island beds of flowers, trees, and benches for people to sit on. Who would sit there? Not shoppers—no one ever went into the few trashy stores that were left. Not even people who worked in the office buildings and banks who might have their lunch there in good weather. No, those benches were left for drunks and a few strange old people, dressed in layers of dirty clothing even in the hottest weather, who brought crumbs to feed the pigeons that gathered around their feet making rumbling sounds.

Mavis remembered when the street was filled with people most any time of the day, actually crowded on Saturdays when country people came to town to tend to business or sell their produce at the city market. Shops lined the street, some of them fine ones, like the expensive dress shop, so quiet and hushed, with only a single dress displayed in the window beside a vase of fresh flowers, where Theda Hedrick and later Miss Alice bought their clothes. Even at night the streets were lively. Mavis, with her family, would drive downtown on a summer evening after supper, park on the street and watch people stroll past. The picture show would let out with a burst of light, and they would almost always recognize someone they knew who would come over and stand by the car and talk for a minute. Later, they would stop by the drugstore for ice cream and then go on home, content, in the last reddish light of day.

Mavis crossed the street, watching for cars. Half the time, people went right through a red light, and you could get killed in a minute. The post office was there, and then the county courthouse, unchanged, still solid and tall, with heavy columns across the front and a wide spread of steps leading up to the main entrance encrusted with black ironwork. The building had a sense of strength, protection; its presence seemed to indicate that here order would prevail, no matter how much other things might change. Mavis suddenly remembered it was there on the steps that Charlene had been photographed with a bunch of students who had protested the trial of a black man accused of attacking a white woman—that everybody knew was sorry as anything and probably led him on—though the jury seemed to think differently.

City jail was across the way, a small building, but no less substantial, made of granite, stained now and weathered, with deep-set windows and a doorway that seemed like a cave. Mavis went inside and walked to the rear of the main hallway where a double staircase wound upward. She knew where Charles Morgan's office was located. She had been in that building often and passed the mottled glass door with his name on it on her way to city court.

After John died, attending sessions had become a habit for Mavis. Better than watching TV, she thought, though the sad little lives of some of the people who passed through the courtroom could be upsetting, a string of lost souls, most of them, petty thieves, and a few bad women whom she could hardly look at in the face, thinking what they had done. She made friends there, people who had no more to do than she, and they would greet each other with small signs of recognition, a nod of the head or a slight smile, before settling into their seats (always the same ones) to watch that passing parade. Eventually, Mavis began to work down at the Mission, and she stopped coming to the court, preferring to help in some small way those who were downtrodden, rather than sitting back and peering into their lives at their most unfortunate times.

"Come in," a voice said when she knocked on Charles Morgan's door. She opened it and went inside. He was sitting in a swivel chair with his long legs stretched out, his feet up on the desk, and he almost turned over, trying to jump up. "Why, Miz Mavis, I didn't expect to see *you* here." He pushed together papers on his desk and Mavis thought she saw a corner of *Playboy* beneath a file folder. "Here, let me clean off a place for you to sit."

Charles started around the desk to the only other chair in the room, piled high with books and papers and a greasy Colonel Sanders box, a jacket thrown across the back. "Don't you mind," Mavis said to him. "I can do it." She picked up the whole mess and put it on a filing cabinet, then carefully brushed her hand over the fake leather seat before she sat down. Noticing that she looked at the pile of cigarette butts in the top of a coffee can used as an ashtray, Charles took it from the desk and clinked it loudly against the wastepaper basket behind him. Still, the room smelled stale, and Mavis wondered why he had the window only open a crack; he'd suffocate in this little space on a really hot day.

"What can I do for you?" Charles asked, crossing his hands in front of him on the desk and leaning toward Mavis. Then suddenly he smiled his forlorn smile. "Somebody out your way been taking your paper? Somebody got on a radio too loud?"

"Now don't get smart with me. I remember you from my Sunday school class. Sugar wouldn't melt in your mouth, you looked so sweet, but if there was any mischief behind my back, I knew who to look at first."

"Yes, and you always caught me. We were all scared to death of you. I'm not sure even now how I'd react if you gave me one of those long, hard looks of yours."

"It was all put on. I liked every one of you boys." Mavis sighed, her smile was gone. "They've all scattered now, seems like, one or two gone from us altogether, I guess. In Vietnam. Who would have thought it back in those days? I had such high hopes for you all.''

"You never know," Charles said. "Never can tell what will happen.''

Mavis didn't answer at first, wondering if Charles was thinking of his own life. He had grown up to be such a fine young man—finished high school, joined the police force after he got back from service, went to night school and got promoted. Any mother would have been proud to have him for a son (though his own mother died and his father went into a home soon after, lost, his mind wandering). He taught Sunday school class, and he was one of the leaders of the Royal Ambassadors, going camping with the group of boys in summer and helping them memorize Bible verses so that they could win prizes at Youth Recognition Night at the church each year. When he became engaged to Arlene Coleman (a retiring girl, she sang in the choir in a high, sweet voice that some of the older ladies compared to that of an angel), everyone smiled approval, it seemed like such a perfect match.

But then, just a few days before the wedding, with dresses bought and the cake ordered for the reception in the church dining room, it was all off. "Ran away," Iva Mae Johnson told Mavis over the phone, her voice quivering with excitement. "With some man she met down at the restaurant where she was cashier. He was just passing through, said he was in the music business and could get her a singing job, and she took off with him to California before you could bat an eye. Her mama's in the bed, and five girls have cherry pink taffeta bridesmaids' dresses they'll never wear. Have you ever heard of such a thing?'' Charles Morgan never said a word to anybody and went on about his business the same as before. But his face seemed to become longer, more solemn almost overnight, and except for a few flashes of humor and scattered laughter, brief as fireworks, he became a silent and remote man whom no one could draw out.

"I suppose there is no way of knowing," Mavis said finally. "Why, look at Theda Hedrick—who ever would have thought she'd be murdered like that? Lord knows how many years she's been riding around in that big car with Alice Pate, and folks probably thought it would go on like that forever. She hardly seemed to age." Mavis sat up straighter in the chair and leaned toward Charles. "That's why I came to-day—Theda Hedrick, I mean."

Charles scratched his head. "That's right, I did see you coming up to Miz Hedrick's house the day I was there talking to them." He smiled a little. "I just thought you were bring-ing up something for people to have after the funeral. Didn't know you were investigating a murder. I'd of thought you'd leave it to us."

"I would," Mavis snapped, "if you were doing a decent job." She raised her chin. "Suspecting that poor Tommie Lee Bagwell. You know as well as I do he wouldn't do a thing like that in a million years. Nor any of the rest of them. What did anybody have to gain?"

"Sounds like you know an awful lot. More than was in the paper."

"Well, maybe I do. But maybe I just use my head and figure things out."

"Now I know. That Dale Sumner, I forgot he's some kin. He's always hanging around discussing theories with people, trying to get something out of us. I bet he told you."

"That's for me to know and you to find out." Mavis laughed then, couldn't help herself. "I guess you are pretty good at figuring out things, too," she said. "It *was* Dale. I don't suppose I should tell you, but he showed me pictures, too—ones he took, and then another from the coroner's of-fice."

Charles's face sank back into its solemn, remote look. Mavis began speaking again very quickly before he could reprimand her. "Now don't you get on your high horse," she said. "If he hadn't, I wouldn't have thought about what was wrong in the picture. I wouldn't be able to tell you my clue."

"What? What's missing in the picture?"

Mavis leaned closer to the desk and rested her hands there on top of her pocketbook. "I said *wrong*, not missing, though

Theda's hat *was* gone; anybody with half a mind could see that right away. Theda Hedrick never set foot outside her door unless she was dressed to the hilt, and she and Alice Pate were known for those big hats they wore, no matter what the style was. Folks wondered sometimes how they found them; must have ordered them from New York or somewhere through one of the stores. But that's not what I'm talking about.''

''Well, what is it?'' Charles seemed to be a little irritated. Mavis saw that his eyes were red-rimmed, and she wondered if he got enough sleep.

''The gloves,'' Mavis said, and she knew there was a note of triumph in her voice.

''The gloves were there, she still had them on.''

''I know she did, but it's the *way* they looked that's important.''

Charles let out a deep sigh. ''All right, how did they look?'' he asked in a flat voice.

''Clean,'' Mavis said. ''Too clean. Far as I can tell in the picture, they looked like they just came out of the wash, not a speck of dirt on them.''

''That's right, but I don't see what's so important. There didn't seem to be any struggle. Her hair was hardly mussed, and the only dirt was a little on the back of her dress where she was lying.''

''That only makes me think it more: Theda Hedrick wasn't killed there. She didn't go running through a field knocking down cornrows with those gloves on. They'd be stained with green, torn. You know how corn leaves cut. She must have been killed somewhere else and then brought there. Just dumped.''

Charles Morgan was silent, his eyes avoiding Mavis's face. His thin, long fingers twisted around each other. ''Well, maybe you're right. I'm sure the coroner will find all that out. We wouldn't have missed it.''

Mavis gave a little snort and sat back. ''Don't tell me that. Doc Parnell? Why, you know if he wasn't the police chief's brother-in-law, he never would have been appointed to that job. Drunker than a skunk most of the time. You'll never find out a thing from him.''

Charles looked back at Mavis. He was actually smirking, a look she remembered from the time he was a boy. "Now is that Christian, Miz Lashley, talking about somebody in such a way?"

"It's Christian to tell the truth. Once he got that job and stopped doctoring folks around town, the death rate went down overnight. He can't do any further damage to the dead, but he won't be able to tell you much that's helpful, either, at least in my opinion."

"What about the car?" Charles seemed to want to change the subject.

"Well, what about it? Theda drove it off herself. Surely you must have got that out of Tommie Lee. He couldn't hide a thing, even if he wanted to."

"It's just his word. Nobody else in the house saw her."

"He was at the picture show. All you've got to do is check."

"I've got somebody on it. But even if he was seen going in, who's to say that he didn't go right through the exit into the alley out back. Nobody would have noticed."

"So then he goes back to the house and for no reason anybody can think of kills Theda and hauls her away in the car, with people in the house, even though they might be occupied." (Mavis thought of Charlene and Buddy Dean up in her bedroom together and she didn't want to say more.) "Did you check out the car?" she asked.

"The doors." Charles looked a little sheepish. "I can't say we looked at the trunk or backseat. But there wouldn't be any blood, anyway."

"What did you find on the doors?"

"Nothing. They were wiped clean."

"Well, if that doesn't convince you, I don't know what will. Can't you just see Theda getting out of the car and wiping off her fingerprints before she goes to meet whoever murdered her. It doesn't make a bit of sense. Somebody else had to do it. I bet they just got into a panic and didn't think.

Had to get rid of the body as quick as they could and dumped it off at the first place they came to."

Charles absentmindedly picked up a pack of cigarettes from the side of the desk, drew one out and started to put it to his lips when he saw Mavis frowning at him. He sighed and put it back inside the package and laid it on the desk. "Well, Miz Lashley, I've got to admit you've made a pretty good case. We'll look into it more. Maybe I should hire you. Ever thought you'd like to be a policewoman?"

"Not for one minute. I can't even look at a gun without getting scared." Mavis pulled her purse from the desk and started to stand up; her back hurt and she frowned in pain.

"Sit for a minute," Charles said. Mavis thought he had caught her look and just wanted her to rest. Then he said, "Maybe you could help us in another way. I *was* going to ask one of the women on the force to do it, but you'd be better. It would seem more natural. Lord knows, you know everything anyway. No reason for you not to learn a little more."

"What?" Mavis said. She forgot about the pain; her heart was beating quite quickly.

"I'm not sure. Just whatever you can find out. We want someone to go out to Theda's daughter's place with the lawyer. He's got some papers for Ruth Anne to sign, not that she's going to get anything." He looked hard at Mavis, one eyebrow slightly raised. "I suppose you know all about that, too?"

Mavis shook her head in affirmation.

"Well, that's why we want somebody there, just to observe. How does she take being left out of Theda's will? Was she expecting anything? Will she give something away?"

"What's there to give away?"

"I don't know. Maybe she thought she would inherit, and she killed Theda. Maybe she had it done."

Mavis made a brushing movement with her hand to dismiss the thought. "Not very likely. I've already been out there and seen her, and she was at the funeral." Charles raised his eyebrows again, but Mavis went on. "Why would she wait till now? Lord knows, as poor as she is, she could use something, though I guess Theda did provide them with clothes and maybe a little spending money. If she was going to do it, she would have done it long ago. But I don't believe she could carry out something like that, anyway."

"Women's intuition?"

"Call it that if you want to. It's almost like she's too beat down to try, just accepts things as they come along—with no idea she might have a choice."

"Did she? Didn't Theda send her away when she was a young girl?"

"She did, but Ruth Anne still had choices later, down the road. She chose to do what got her sent away in the first place, didn't she?"

"I suppose. Sometimes it seems, though, that no matter how hard you try, things go wrong, like it was intended. But I don't think we can settle that issue." Charles looked hard at her again. "Will you do it? Will you go?"

Mavis did not wait one moment. "Of course I will," she said. "I'm as curious as the next person. Why do you think I've stuck my nose into it this far? You just tell me when, and I'll be ready."

"I'll tell Owen Luther to pick you up around two o'clock tomorrow afternoon. That's the lawyer."

"I'll be waiting." She got up, this time to go. "You remember what I said about the gloves," she called back as she was walking out the door. "Tell Doc Parnell what I said. Maybe he'll have sense enough to confirm it."

She let the door close slowly behind her and it made a wheezing sound. Charles Morgan was still standing there, blurred by the rippled glass, as she turned the corner and headed for the staircase down.

Chapter
Fourteen

Mavis decided to walk down to the Mission. It was only a few blocks away, no need to take the bus. It was more trouble than it was worth to have to wait—and anyway, she would have to pay another fare, even with her senior citizen's card. When she came down the stairs of the city court building and went outside, the heat hit her like a hand, and she quickly turned the corner to get on the shady side of the street. People were about, a surprise to her until she remembered it was lunchtime and office workers were out strolling (though she couldn't think why in the world they didn't stay in their nice air-conditioned offices), on their way to lunch.

Lunch. She realized that she hadn't eaten and she was hungry. Usually, on her days at the Mission, she went early and finished by lunchtime, returning home to eat a sandwich and a piece of fruit or whatever else she might find in the icebox. But with Dale coming for breakfast and then her meeting with Charles Morgan, the morning had fled and now, quite clearly, she heard her stomach make a rumbling sound.

She looked about. She did not know whether any restaurants had survived downtown; it was all steak houses and Chinese restaurants out in the mall, and she seldom went there. At the corner, where she would turn, there was a small luncheonette, and she peered through the window. It looked all right, clean. Several other people were in there and they didn't seem a rowdy type. Checking one more time through the window, she opened the door and went into the coolness. That was enough to make her stay.

"Hey, how're you?" A girl with a bored-looking face and a mouth distorted by a wad of pink bubble gum stared at Mavis from the counter.

"I'm just fine," Mavis said, looking at the other people there. They did not notice her.

"Get you something?"

Mavis looked at the acne spots on the girl's face and then at her hands. As best she could tell, they were clean. "I think I'll have a hot dog," she said after looking up at the menu on the wall behind the counter. "With a lemonade."

"Everything on it?"

"Why, I suppose so." Mavis knew that she would regret eating the onions; they would repeat on her all afternoon. But a hot dog wasn't fit to eat without onions, she thought. That used to be a favorite treat. She and her daughter would come downtown on a late afternoon to meet John when he got off work and they would go around behind his office building—not far from here, actually—and get hot dogs at a Greek place no longer there. So different from what they served up now. (Mavis looked down at the thin bun and skinny hot dog, with a little onion and piccalilli on top that the girl had plopped down in front of her, and almost wished she had ignored her stomach pains.) The other place had a smell of warm, fat buns, and there was plenty of homemade chili and all the onions you wanted, cut up quite nicely. They would pick up the hot dogs in napkins already transparent with grease and laugh, trying to get the whole thing in their mouths to take a bite.

She ate quickly. The other customers went out and the girl turned on a glittering silver radio behind the counter and began to jerk around like someone having an epileptic fit in time to the music. Mavis got up and took her handkerchief out to wipe her lips. She left just a dime for a tip, even though she knew the girl would give her a mean look behind her back. No need to pretend the service was anything special, she thought to herself, though that girl would never learn anything from such a gesture.

The stores she passed were quiet, most people back at work now. Mavis walked slowly, trying to avoid the heat, looking into the windows. She would never shop here. The clothing was cheap, flashy as fireworks, and at the furniture store on the corner there was a display of waterbeds, vaguely distasteful to her, though she was unable to think why. When she hurried past a pool hall, the *clack* of the wooden balls shot from the doorway and startled her. Surely not a respectable place—who would be there in the early afternoon on a workday if they were any account a-tall? The place gave her an uneasy feeling, even though it was broad daylight. Not a soul was anywhere on the street and, goodness knows, even if she saw someone, she might not want to call on them for help should she need it.

She breathed a little sigh of relief when she arrived at the Mission. It looked solid, that building, safe, and the stone face was warm and strong. When she went through the door, it was like entering a friend's house, and she paused a moment in the vestibule, waiting for her heart to slow down. She had been walking too fast in the heat.

"Who's that?" It was Sue Dillon calling from the next room. Her voice sounded a little fearful, and Mavis wondered why Sue did not keep the doors locked, anybody might walk in. She became slightly apprehensive again and felt less safe.

"It's Mavis Lashley." She walked down the hallway to the door of the office, her heels clicking on the tile floor.

Sue Dillon made a sighing sound. Mavis looked at the pale face and the mousey hair, pulled back with bright pink barrettes shaped like a pair of hearts on each side, like a little girl. They were the only bright, pretty things Mavis had ever seen Sue wear, and she wondered what they would think of them out at the Bible college. Sue gave her a nervous little smile.

"I just must be jumpy today. When I heard the door close, it scared me half to death."

"Why don't you keep that door locked?" Mavis said. "With all those loafers lying around the square across the street, you don't know who might come in. You read about all sorts of things in the paper.''

Sue's face flushed slightly; she looked down, fumbling with some papers on the desk. "Reverend Simms says we shouldn't do that. 'This is the Lord's house,' he told me. 'The doors should always be open to any or all who come. He will protect us. We will abide by His will.' ''

Mavis thought to herself that those were perfectly nice things to say, but you had to use your common sense. She couldn't say that to Sue Dillon, though; just take one look at the girl when Reverend Simms was around and you knew she worshipped the ground he walked on, like he was one of the apostles or something. Lord knows how many hours she put in at the Mission for practically no pay, but Mavis had never heard the girl say a word of complaint. She supposed it was part of her training, getting ready for the missionary life. In the jungle, she'd have it even worse.

Sue looked up and smiled. Mavis knew she was going to change the subject. "Well, how have you been this week? I was getting a little worried about you, you're so faithful. When you didn't come in early, I was beginning to wonder if you were sick or something.''

"No," Mavis said. "I had some business to attend to downtown.''

This time Sue giggled nervously. Her face softened and the childish barrettes did not look so strange in her hair. "I thought maybe the killer might have got you. That's all you see on the TV.'' Sue looked very hard at Mavis, almost as if she were asking a question.

"Who'd want to murder me?" Mavis laughed, though to say those words were a little frightening.

"I shouldn't make jokes about such things," Sue said, ducking down her head. "It's just been so upsetting. I dreamed about her last night, that lady I mean, Miz Hedrick. Can't get her out of my mind. The police came yesterday to talk to us, and I was so nervous I could hardly speak. Asking us all sorts of questions.''

"What did they want to know?''

"Oh, just said they were going over Miz Hedrick's actions

on the days prior to her death. They wanted to know what happened here. I told them how that man who drives her car came in with some bags of clothing and I showed him where to put them in the back room. 'He was real nice and polite,' I said, 'not stuck-up at all the way they show chauffeurs on TV. I thanked him when he left and he smiled at me.'

" 'What else?' " the policeman asked.

" 'Well, nothing much,' " I said. " 'I went back to work. Lately I've been busier than ever getting the invitations out for the dedication service for the Mission. Before I knew it, though, the door opened again and Miz Hedrick came in. Now, I had never seen her before, but I knew somehow right away it was her. Those strange clothes and a hat looking like a flying saucer or something. Nobody I ever knew dressed like that. 'Can you give me a receipt?' she said, not saying 'how are you?' or anything else like a normal person would. Grabby, sort of, her hand already out.''

"I said we didn't give out receipts for gifts right away. The stuff had to be gone through first and sorted out and some valuation made. 'That's most inconvenient,' she said, but I didn't answer, just told her to leave her name on a piece of paper and I'd send her a receipt later on, the way we do for everybody else. I started to give her a notepad, but she fumbled around in her pocketbook and brought out a card and handed it to me, like she didn't want to touch anything here or she might get some disease. She still had her gloves on, even though it was a hot day. 'Thank you,' I said, pretty as you please, but I have to tell the truth, I didn't feel it one bit. I prayed long and hard that night for the Lord to forgive me my bad thoughts.''

"Theda Hedrick was just that way, I guess.'' Mavis felt sorry for Sue Dillon; the girl had such a guilty look. She probably never knew one night of peace, always wondering if she had sinned. "She didn't mean anything by it. I wonder if Theda wasn't just shy of folks, put on that way of hers just to cover it all up. Like the clothes she wore.''

"Maybe so,'' Sue said, but she didn't sound convinced. "Anyway, she just turned and walked out the door, and I waited for the outer door to close, but then I heard voices.

Miz Theda and Reverend Simms. Just a few words that I couldn't understand and finally the outside door did slam shut. Reverend Simms came in then and asked me what that woman said. I told him, and he asked me for the card. 'I'll answer her myself,' he said, 'a personal letter. She's got a lot of money and could help us with the Lord's work here. I'll invite her to the dedication.' "

"Lord, I doubt she'd ever have come. Theda Hedrick hardly ever left that house—certainly not to come to a big gathering."

"Maybe, but Reverend Simms is powerful persuasive." Sue shuffled the papers again. "But you'll be here, won't you, Miz Lashley? It's going to be real special, the dedication, and we hope to raise a lot of money for the work. The volunteers will all be honored."

"Well, I suppose so," Mavis said, though she did not know if she really wanted to take part in the festivities. Speeches and some gospel quartet singing through their noses, and warm Kool-Aid punch with store-bought cookies—that's what they would have, and a large box for contributions. She'd rather give them the money and just stay home. She almost laughed out loud: she'd have to pray tonight about her own bad thoughts.

"Certainly, we'll want Miz Lashley to come. She's part of our faithful little family here."

Reverend Simms's voice boomed out behind Mavis. Neither of them had heard him come in and both jumped. Mavis turned and saw him standing in the doorway smiling his remote smile, his skin pure white next to the dark jacket he wore, as if he had never been in the sun. "Miz Lashley is an important part of this community," he said, and smiled.

Mavis should have felt flattered, but the only feeling she could identify was a vague sense of irritation. Reverend Simms had never talked to her in such a way before, hardly even noticed when she was there working on clothes in the back room except to say, "Good day." "I'm not all that important," she said, and looked back at Sue Dillon, hoping he would go away.

"That's not what I hear." Reverend Simms almost had a

smirk on his face. "They tell me you've been investigating that sad occurrence, Miz Hedrick's death."

"Who told you?" Mavis was even more irritated.

"Never you mind." Reverend Simms almost laughed. "A man in my position hears a lot. From the grapevine."

"Just gossip," Mavis said, but wondered inside if it was Christian for a minister to listen to such talk.

"Well, let us know what you find out."

"That won't be much." Mavis closed her lips into a little line. Whatever she knew, she wasn't going around telling just anybody. It was none of Reverend Simms's business, knowing about the photographs, about Ruth Anne and all the others. If her thoughts were bad, then she'd just have to ask the Lord to forgive them.

Mavis stood up, gathering her bag to her. She wanted to put an end to the conversation. "I've got to get to work. It's already late." She turned to Sue, ignoring the reverend. "I'll be in the back. Let me know if you're going to leave."

"Whew, I've got a pile more of invitations to get out. I'll be here till dark."

"Such dedication," Reverend Simms said, and turned.

They both looked after him, unable to tell from his voice whether his words were in praise—or possibly derision.

Chapter
Fifteen

Owen Luther, Theda Hedrick's lawyer, pulled up in front of Mavis's house at two o'clock on the dot in his long, burgundy-colored Cadillac. Mavis was ready and waiting, and she quickly got up from the sofa where she had sat watching for him and went outside. She had dressed carefully, something dark with no frills, feeling that she was going on a professional journey; she was a part of the law.

As soon as he saw her, Owen scrambled out of the car and was standing beside it by the time she got to the sidewalk. "Hey, how're you?" he said, his hand proffered, smiling as broadly as he would have on a social occasion. He was a small man, rotund, dressed in a gray suit, even though it was hot as blazes; a film of moisture covered his face. When he helped Mavis into the car, hurrying just in front of her over to the other side, his breath came in little short gasps. Mavis thought his wife should put him on a diet or she wasn't going to have him with her much longer.

Inside the car the air-conditioning hummed and blew cold air onto Mavis's face. She sat far over on her side of the car, feeling a little awkward alone there with Owen Luther, though they had met a few times before, at a banquet when John was still alive or some other civic occasion. He sat beside her, short in the seat—he could hardly see over the steering wheel—still smiling, making careful little movements with the steering wheel, which pulled the car from side to side just slightly, so that the ride seemed jerky, despite the car's weight and size.

"Glad you could come with me today," Owen said. "I dreaded going out to see Theda's daughter alone."

"She won't bite," Mavis said before she thought. "I mean, I was there and she was perfectly nice to me."

Owen glanced at her briefly sideways. "You didn't have bad news for her the way I do."

"I'm not so sure she'll think it's bad news. I don't think she was expecting anything from her mother. They were estranged."

"Well, you'd be surprised." Owen was talking in a lawyerlike voice now, wise, as if he had to explain the facts of life patiently to her. "Folks get real strange after a death. May not have seen the person in forty years and be a cousin three times removed, but they expect to be remembered in the will and get real upset when they aren't. They seem to think sending a Christmas card once a year is enough concern shown for them to inherit something."

"Never count chickens, I always say." Mavis looked straight ahead through the front window. "It's better, I think, not to depend on anything—then if it comes, it's a real surprise."

"Well, that's a right good attitude. Sometimes it does happen that way, somebody getting an inheritance when they didn't expect it a-tall. That's when my duties are a real pleasure, like Christmas almost, particularly when the people are needy."

Lord, Mavis thought to herself, Ruth Anne and those children are sure needy. She almost dreaded seeing them again in that forsaken place in the woods. Ruth Anne had gotten herself together for the funeral, and the children looked real cute everybody thought, but Mavis knew it wouldn't last. They would find Ruth Anne unawares again, closed up in that trailer, back into her own small world.

And am I making it worse for her? she wondered. Going out there like a spy, pretending I'm just along for the ride. The thought had kept her awake last night, and she still had no answer. Perhaps it *was* just curiosity, and if so, certainly it was unchristian. But then, maybe she could help Ruth Anne bear it all (that final slap from Theda, giving her nothing), provide comfort. She only hoped so.

They rode along in silence after that, Mavis remembering her first trip with Tommie Lee Bagwell. That trip had seemed so long, she unaware of their destination, riding along lost in her own thoughts. Now, in what seemed like no time at all, they were at the turnoff point in the woods. "It's here," she shouted out suddenly, pointing at the tracks between the trees. "Turn!" Owen Luther put on the brakes with a loud screeching sound and turned much too fast off onto the side road.

"Have mercy," he said, trying to control the bouncing car. "I didn't expect that a-tall. I had directions from Charles Morgan down at the police station, but I'm not sure I'd of ever found it without you."

Once again Mavis was surprised by the barrenness of the place when it came into view around a small curve: the dilapidated trailer, the ground around it scratched dry as if chickens had vainly looked there for food. If only Ruth Anne had planted a few flowers around the door, Mavis thought, done something to make things better. It was as if all hope of any beauty had gone from Ruth Anne's life, all joy. Or was it perhaps a gesture of defiance, saying, *Leave me alone, I am abandoned, I want no help from you*?

Owen Luther parked the car in the same spot where Theda's big car had sat the day Mavis had come out with Tommie Lee, a set of rutted tracks at the edge of the bare yard. They got out and noticed the silence. Not a bird sang and there was no traffic on the road; only the *whirr* of a small plane could be heard from somewhere far above, small as the buzz of an insect, then disappearing. It was hot. Mavis could see that Owen was sweating again as he straightened the jacket of his suit.

Then they saw the children. At the edge of the trailer, they peeped out. "How're y'all?" Owen called in a hearty voice. When they didn't answer, still stood staring at him, his face fell, as if he had nothing else to say to young children. Mavis walked over to them, but stopped before she was too close.

"Your mama here?" she asked the boy. He was older, looked bright.

He scratched his stomach where the washed-out shrunken shirt showed skin. "Yeah," he said, not smiling, but added nothing more.

The girl poked her head around. Mavis noticed a smudge on her face, dark beneath the eye. She wondered whether it was dirt or a bruise. "My mama's asleep," she said in a tinkling voice, the one bit of beauty in that ugly space. "She told us to go outside and play."

Mavis looked around, wondering what any child would find to do there. She saw no space beneath tree branches where a playhouse had been set up, with old boxes for furniture and empty canning jars containing wildflowers to make it pretty. There were no hopscotch lines in the dirt. Ruth Anne said that Theda had sent toys, but Mavis saw no sign of them. Perhaps Ruth Anne kept them inside, put away so that the children wouldn't damage them, or perhaps she had destroyed them all in some moment of fury against Theda. Mavis gave a little shudder as she looked down at the child again.

"Won't you tell your mama we've come to see her?"

The boy looked at Mavis with something like fear in his eyes. "She'll be mad if she wakes up. She told us to be quiet."

"Well, we've got business, come all the way from town." Mavis moved and both children seemed startled. "But never you mind," she said, "I'll just knock on the door. You go on and play."

She walked to the door of the trailer, knowing that the children had not moved, their eyes following her, waiting. She reached up to knock, but before she touched the screen door, it opened and Ruth Anne stood there. No change, though Mavis realized that she was hoping for one. The hair lank and dull, held back with a piece of yarn. Clothes that should have been thrown away, they were so old—one sleeve torn, polyester stretch pants, and a man's old shirt. Barefoot probably, if Mavis could see.

For the first time, Mavis felt anger against Ruth Anne.

The girl knew better—she hadn't been brought up trash—and no matter what had happened to her, she could have made some effort to take better care of herself, of the children. Hadn't she dressed up for the funeral? She had made a choice to live this way. No one said she had to.

"What do you want?" Ruth Anne did not open the screen. She looked at Mavis as if she were a total stranger.

"It's me, Mavis Lashley," she said. "You remember."

Ruth Anne sighed. "Yes. What is it this time?"

"It's not me that wants to see you. I was asked to come along. It's him." She pointed to Owen Luther, still standing by the car. "He's your mama's lawyer. He has some things to discuss with you."

Because of the screen, she could not see the expression on Ruth Anne's face, though she wondered if interest might have quickened there, the eyes caught life. Mavis motioned to Owen, and he came running over in short little hops, panting as he reached the steps. "How do you do, Miz Hedrick?" he said, and Mavis nearly caught her breath, realizing for the first time she did not know what name Ruth Anne used. Whether she had a husband, whether those two young'uns who still stared at them had any last name that was different. They waited for Ruth Anne to respond.

"Come on in," she said flatly. She stood aside to let them enter. The inside of the trailer was as dark as before, but cool, and there was no clutter, no scent of mustiness. Ruth Anne gestured for them to sit, and Mavis took the same place on the sofa where she had sat before. Owen Luther went over to the fold-out table where a Coca-Cola can sat. Ruth Anne whisked it up with a quick movement. Then she stood waiting.

Owen sat down and cleared his throat. He opened his briefcase and took out a sheaf of papers, looking, it seemed to Mavis, as if he felt right at home, as if he sat at a big mahogany desk in an office rather than in this tacky trailer out in the middle of nowhere. When he had the papers assembled, he put on half-glasses that made his face look rounder and looked over them at Ruth Anne.

"This won't take long," he said. "I just need you to sign

some things. I asked Miz Lashley here to come along as a witness. Seems like you and she know each other already.''

Ruth Anne tilted her head slightly to the side; it was hard to tell what she acknowledged, what she believed. ''It's your mama's will,'' Owen said. ''Real simple. I made it out for her years ago and she never changed it.'' He paused, looked down at the top paper, and then peered back up at Ruth Anne. He sighed once before he finally spoke. ''I'm sorry, but she didn't leave anything to you. Just five dollars. That's all there is to it.''

Mavis expected Ruth Anne to laugh or scream, do anything rather than just stand there like she had been hit by a bolt of lightning. But there was utter silence in the little room, as if they all held their breaths. Ruth Anne half turned, and Mavis had the sudden fear that she might walk out the door and leave, going down that piney road out of sight. Then she turned back, her face a mask.

''Well,'' she said in a very low voice, ''I suppose that's no big surprise to anybody. What did she ever give me, anyway? Birth, but I don't suppose she could help herself. Sometimes I used to wonder if she wouldn't rather have had an abortion, then she wouldn't have had to bother with me. But nobody got them back then, not like now.''

''Oh, Ruth Anne, honey, don't say such a thing.'' Mavis held out her hand in the air as if she could stop the words.

''Why not? She's dead, isn't she? It doesn't matter.''

''She sent you clothes, things for the children. You said so yourself.''

''What of it? Cheap things from the discount mall. Old dresses of hers and Alice's that never were in style anyway. A few toys that broke the day after. She never forgave me, never let me forget that she was *embarrassed* by my behavior so long ago nobody else even remembered.''

''Why did she do it then?''

''I always wondered. To punish me? To help feel better about herself? Or maybe—and I never wanted to admit this, not for the world—it was Alice that got her to do it. She'd do anything for Alice, just name it. Alice could twist her around her little finger. So maybe that's why she came out once a year with her gifts. Alice told her to.'' Ruth Anne laughed, a dry sound almost like a cough. "Shouldn't that be pretty obvious now? You aren't going to tell me Alice didn't get the house, everything else. I'd faint dead away if you did.''

Owen looked slightly embarrassed. "I don't see any reason why I shouldn't tell you. There were small amounts for Charlene Anderson and Tommie Lee Bagwell, but—ah, yes—everything else went to Alice Pate. She's the executor.''

"Alice wanted it all and got it. Perhaps she was trying to relieve *her* conscience by making Theda traipse out here with her little offerings. Now she can start being the grand lady, riding out here in that big car to leave off a little mess for us. Think she'll do that?''

Ruth Anne's voice was rising; in a moment it might be a scream. Mavis bent forward, trying to see Ruth Anne's eyes. "She could of not known. Theda could of made out the will without ever telling her.''

"I won't believe it for a minute. In fact, doesn't that give her a pretty good reason for killing Theda? All that money?''

"Why would she do it now? Theda made the will a long time ago.''

"Things change. Maybe the two of them weren't getting along so well. Theda said she was going to change her will, threatened Alice. I don't know. I suspect there were plenty of reasons.''

Ruth Anne shook her head, her shoulders slumped as if she had been hard at work. "It wouldn't matter now, anyway, even if I got it all. Wouldn't change the past. Life might be a little easier, not so much hand-to-mouth, worrying if the welfare check will last. But I couldn't go back to that house to live. It would haunt me. Let Alice have it, I don't care.''

"Will you sign these papers then?'' Owen Luther pushed them forward. He sounded anxious, no longer looked at ease. Already there was a pen in his hand.

Ruth Anne took it. "I'm trusting you,'' she said. "I don't want to read that mess. Show me where.''

Owen pointed to the bottom sheet. Ruth Anne took the pen, signed and then signed again on another set of papers.

She laughed. "When do I get my five dollars? It'd buy us some pork chops."

Owen did not look up. "It will be a few weeks. It'll come in the mail." He turned toward Mavis. "If you'll just sign, too, Miz Lashley. There." he pointed.

Mavis took the pen, her fingers trembling. She could hardly see the line, her eyes blurred.

"Well, now, I suppose that's all." Owen thrust the papers back into his briefcase, clicked it shut, and started to get up. Mavis fumbled with her purse, ready to follow. Then Ruth Anne touched her on the shoulder, and Mavis sank back down, frightened for no reason she could think of.

"Would you stay a little while?" Ruth Anne's voice was low again, but pleading, a sound Mavis had not heard from her before.

"Why sure, honey. What is it? You feeling sick?"

"No, not that. I want to tell you something." Ruth Anne turned back to Owen who was standing, embarrassed, in the middle of the floor, his head shiny in the light coming from the ceiling fixture. "You'll wait for her, won't you?" Ruth Anne asked, as pleasantly as if she were seeing a guest out the door in some fine house. "We won't be too long."

"Why sure," Owen said, giving Mavis a look, one eyebrow raised. "That all right with you, Miz Lashley?"

Mavis still felt fear like something caught in her throat, but she said, "That'll be just fine. You wait out in the car if you don't mind." She tried to laugh. "Maybe you've got some lawyer work to do while you're waiting."

"Sure, sure, that's a right good idea. You just call if you need me."

He turned and went out quickly, and Mavis wondered what he thought she might need him for. Quickly, Ruth Anne closed the door, and the room was circled again in dimness. She sat where Owen had sat and leaned across the table.

"You ought to know," Ruth Anne said. "Somebody should, and you're better than most. At least you show some caring, and I've known you longer than anybody else around here, even if it was just a glimpse now and then when I was a child."

"Know what?"

"The truth. About what happened. What you've heard before was probably just gossip. But whatever happens now, I want somebody to know the truth. You're going to be it. I don't have any other choice."

"All right," Mavis said, the tightness growing bigger in her throat. "Go ahead."

Ruth Anne bent forward into the lamplight and it circled her head like a halo. Sitting there in that small space, Mavis thought suddenly of a gypsy fortune teller, gazing into a crystal ball. Except that here there was no crystal, just Ruth Anne's fingers working together in front of her on the worn tabletop, and instead of the future, she would be telling of the past.

Chapter Sixteen

She didn't have to send me away. She was just looking for a reason and one came along. If that mess out at Silver Lake hadn't happened, Theda would have found another excuse to get rid of me.

It was all so innocent! Lord, if something like that happened now, nobody'd raise an eyebrow, thankful it wasn't worse. But back then, people got all worked up about such things, and Theda got her excuse.

It was Buck Woodall's idea. He was a little bit older than the rest of us, had a car and was on the football team, and of course anybody he looked at was flattered and couldn't say no to anything he wanted to do. When he drove up that night in front of my house (the car was blue, the color of peacocks, he had a flattop haircut and looked to me like something right out of the movies), I called out to Theda I was going, but didn't even stop to listen whether or not she said anything back. I didn't care, anyway.

We went to the drive-in restaurant, I can't remember who-all. Eula Medlin was there, I know, because she got sick later in the car and ruined my skirt—but the others are just a blur now, though I suppose I thought they were my best friends at the time. Buck drove up and we all ordered hamburgers, mine with mustard and pickles, I still remember, the only way I liked them then. The others laughed, said, "You pregnant?" as soon as I said the words, a standing joke.

The night was hot and nobody mentioned going home

after we ate, couldn't bear the thought. Then Buck said he had an idea—would we like to do it?—and we all yelled out, "Yeah, Buck, sure," before even knowing what it was. He didn't tell all of it, just answered, "Why don't we go out to the state park by the lake for a little while, it'll be cool." Eula or one of the others said, "It's closed after eleven o'clock, they put up a gate." But Buck said, "Well, honey, we can just take it down again, can't we?" and we all laughed like that was the funniest thing we ever heard.

The ride was short, the darkness close around us and the radio blaring. I had such a warm feeling of belonging. I could have ridden on and on into the night. When we turned off onto the side road that led to the park, I wished we would just keep driving; I didn't want that feeling to end.

Sure enough, there was a metal bar across the road to the park, with a sign warning of fines for trespassing, but one of the boys jumped out and pushed it open and we drove right through. "Take home that sign for a souvenir," somebody called out and laughed, and we wondered who would dare. The road narrowed, curved, and suddenly we were in an open space and saw stars gleaming on the water, so pretty, as lovely as anything you'd ever see in a movie. For a moment there was silence—before Buck turned the ignition back on so we could have the radio—and we could hear insects rasping, the sound of night birds.

"Ya'll come on," Buck said, getting out of the car. "I got a surprise."

I couldn't see his face in the darkness, but I knew he would be smirking: He stood in the corridors at school while girls passed him by, and he would have that knowing look. I'd get shivers when he stared at me like that. Going around to the trunk, he opened it, found a flashlight and turned it on three six-packs of beer. A cheer rose up, scaring the birds, and we all reached in and took a can.

At first, we just sat on the edge of a picnic table and drank beer and looked out at the water, brighter now, the moon would soon rise. Again I felt that warm feeling, as if this would never end, or at least I didn't want it to. We could stay here forever, like children in a fairy tale, and never have to

go home again to face whatever unpleasantness hung there
like fog. I almost shivered when I thought of going home
later, Theda calling out to me, asking questions about where
I had been and then not believing even if I told the truth.

Buck had another surprise. Before I even realized, he had
a cigarette lit and was passing it around, the strong, sweet
scent a sudden perfume. I took it with a feeling of daring (it
wasn't my first time to smoke, but it still seemed quite exotic
to me), and I took in a deep breath and let the burn stay there
until I could hold it in no longer. The night became softer,
fuzzier, and I laid my head on the shoulder of whoever sat
beside me, not even caring who it was.

How long we stayed there I couldn't tell you. Hours, it
seemed, but that may have been only my feeling. When Buck
yelled out, it was as if he had awakened me from a dream,
and at first I didn't even understand what he was saying.
Finally, it came: "Hey, y'all, let's go swimming. I bet the
water'd feel real good."

Maybe it was Eula who said, "We don't have our swim-
suits, how can we?"

Everybody laughed at her, the boys stomping around slap-
ping one another. "You got underwear, don't you?" Buck
said. "Or didn't you wear none tonight, hoping you'd get
laid?" There were more snorts of laughter, but the next thing
I knew people all around me were peeling off clothes, and
there was sudden whiteness in the dark, as if bodies were
invisible and the specks of clothing floated around us. "Come
on," Buck called out, and a pair of white shorts plunged
toward the lake and disappeared.

Others followed, and I took off my clothes. I walked carefully over the ground, suddenly cool to my feet, the pine
needles satiny. At the edge, seeing the others in the water, I
waited, not afraid but not ready yet, either, as if something
told me this was a marking point in my life, would mean
change. Then I had no choice because Buck grabbed my
ankles and I plunged down, went beneath the water as if
fathoms down to another world—until I could not breathe
and came up again. Buck disappeared beneath the surface,
and I could feel him trying to get between my legs to raise

me up on his shoulders, but I pushed him away, swimming out toward the middle of the lake, and lost him in the darkness.

Again, I don't know how long it lasted, but finally I heard the others calling out to me, and I could see them on the bank. The moon had risen behind the trees and there was a stronger glow, so that I could see figures bending, turning, getting back into clothes.

"Hey, Ruth Anne," Buck called out. "Let's take your picture." He must have had a camera in the car without telling us. "Show us your stuff." I don't know what made me do it, but I just stood up (near the shore, mud oozed through my toes) and unsnapped my bra and faced him. Maybe it was just the dare. Maybe it was to prove something to Theda (I thought later that I had never seen her breasts, never could imagine I might have nourished there). He snapped the camera, and in the brilliance of the flash, I could see the startled faces of the others on the bank, heard the chortlings of the boys' and girls' intake of breath. I got out then, dressed, and we all piled back into the car, no music now, silence, something broken between us. Buck drove carefully, and dropped us all off—no loud good-byes to wake the neighbors, no screeching tires.

I had forgotten all about that night until I got called to the principal's office at school. My mother was there, my daddy, and the principal with the picture Buck got caught passing around. Silently, the principal showed it to us, and there I was with my poor little tits glistening from the water, a look on my face of almost peace, and the light of stars in the background. My daddy turned away, but Theda gazed like iron.

They found out who the others were; no doubt Buck was only too happy to tell to save his own skin. They expelled us for a week, and that would have been the end of it (except for the snickers of the others at school, but we knew they were a little envious, wondering what else might have gone on there). But it was not the end for me.

Perhaps Theda already had a school picked out, but within a week she announced, as calmly as if she were calling me to come down to supper, "We have found a boarding school for you. You won't be going back to school here. We'll buy clothes next week and Tommie Lee will drive you there."

"Why?" I asked. "I could go back to school on Monday."

Theda's armor was lowered for a moment; anger spilled out from that big breast as if from a wound. "You have to ask? How can I ever hold my head up in this town after this? Exposing yourself like a common slut. And goodness knows what else you did. I should take you to a doctor and have you examined, but I can't bear to do that. You will go away and we'll hear no more about it."

My daddy moped around all the next week, but never said a thing. I knew Theda wouldn't let him; he'd get it worse than I did. "Certainly you take up for her," I could hear Theda say. "Follows right in your footsteps, doesn't she? Another disgrace for me to put up with. I don't know how I have the strength to deal with it all." When he kissed me good-bye, it was with such a long, lingering grasp on my arms (Theda was not there, hidden away somewhere upstairs, unless she looked through the blinds at the window) that I thought later perhaps he sensed somehow it was the last time we would touch, more than just good-bye.

The school wasn't so bad, I suppose. It was one of those places they send girls to who get in trouble of one sort or another and pretend it's some kind of finishing school—where you wear white gloves all the time and learn how to cross your legs at the ankles so boys can't see up your skirt. And in the spring, there was a maypole pageant for parents and friends to attend and refreshments later on the lawn (though, Lord knows, there were a lot around like me who never had a visitor). At first, I made decent enough grades, and there were times of real enjoyment: sitting in a dorm room with a bunch of girls who lay across the beds and smoked forbidden cigarettes with blankets over the windows, talking about boys. Those times, too, I felt a sense of belonging, of being a part of something.

Then my daddy died. All of a sudden it came out of the blue, no word of warning, no knowledge that he had been feeling ill, "going downhill," they said later, ever since I had gone. How would I know? Theda never wrote a single letter, and I suppose my daddy was too scared to call, or he just didn't want me to know how bad he was feeling.

The director of the school called me into her office. I walked there wondering what I might have done. Had someone found out about those innocent nights when we sat and smoked, giggling, until it was nearly dawn? She was sitting behind her desk, very straight, hands folded in front of her on the polished surface, a thin woman, tight as a rubber band, who looked just to the side of your face, as if she feared she might read our thoughts in our eyes (and we *did* have wild fantasies about her, laughing almost till we peed in our pants while we made up stories about her and the big, silent young janitor who stoked the furnace and raked the lawn, visions of churning black-and-white flesh before our eyes).

"Ruth Anne," she said, "I'm just as sorry as I can be, but I have some bad news for you."

I was to be expelled, I was failing a subject.

"We just got a call. Your daddy has passed. He went quick and without suffering as far as anybody knows. His heart. Apparently, he has felt poorly lately."

I suppose I didn't believe her at first. She looked even further away from my eyes and I could not tell whether she was lying. If she had come over to touch me, tried to comfort me, I think I would have hit her. Tears sprang out of my eyes, but I made no sound. The director pointed to a box of Kleenex on her desk, but I did not touch it, let the tears fall.

Finally, she said, to dismiss me, "The car will be here to take you home in a few hours. Why don't you go upstairs and get your things ready? I'll have one of the teachers come help you."

"No, don't do that," I said, and my voice must have startled her.

"Fine," she said, her lips tight. "If you want it that way. You have all our sympathy."

I didn't care what I packed, giving no thought to mourning, dark colors, simple lines. I threw it all in a case and sat out on the front veranda of the big old house that served as a dormitory, while other girls passed by me and stared a little oddly, though they did not come up and speak. I was glad. If they had offered one kind word, had touched my hand, I think I would have begun to scream and would have been unable to stop.

Of course I knew the car, and I ran down the steps and was at the door as soon as Tommie Lee stopped. I opened the door and started to get in, but then pulled back: there was Alice Pate—pale, thin, almost disappearing in the darkness of the backseat except for one of those ugly big hats like Mama always wore.

"Get in, Ruth Anne," she said. Her voice was soft and she held out a gloved hand.

"No!" I said, and started to turn away, ready to run, keep on running until I fell down flat on my face on the country road that led to town from the school.

But Alice said then, "I understand. I know you don't want me here. Theda asked me to come."

And for that one moment I could almost like Alice Pate, knowing what she must be going through, knowing Theda. I realized, too, that Alice was going to be living in that house, perhaps already had her bags packed to move in as soon as they put my daddy in the ground. I think she knew what I expected when I opened the door to the car—my mother there, my last hope of a breast to lean on, arms to comfort— and she knew the utter loneliness I felt then, no one left to love me.

Those next few days were like a bad dream I couldn't wake up from. They dressed me in ugly black clothes that hung on me like bags (Theda, already, had forgotten my size in that short span of time), walked me to the funeral home to view the body, holding me tightly so that I would not fall, faint, collapse on the body and try to kiss the powdered face, finally led me to the church and guided me through the service.

At the cemetery, all I remember is a clear blue sky, the sun fading, and the first rush of dark birds that come near sunset; though they were silent then, their screams would come later, after we had gone. I didn't even go back to the house. Tommie Lee drove me back to the school in Theda's car, not even Alice to accompany me. We arrived late at night, and I went up the stairs to my room and closed the door, and I never discussed what happened with a single soul there. Most of the girls, I think, never knew, and the director asked not one question.

Everything fell apart after that. I didn't care about grades any longer and failed most subjects, sometimes not even bothering to get up to go to class. As time passed, others began to avoid me, I was so unhappy, and I was left out of those late-night sessions in dorm rooms, hearing others' voices drifting down a hallway to where I hunched in bed. When at the end of the year the director called me to her office (for one bleak moment I remembered the other time the world turned dark around me and I almost fell), I simply stared at her while she told me, looking again past my eyes, that they could no longer keep me. I left and no one said good-bye.

From then on, I drifted from one school to another, from one summer camp to another. If I clumped with others, they were girls like myself—lost, on the periphery, strange. We deliberately took on a look that was different and wild, simply to shock and make the others notice us. Instead of giggling in dorm rooms, we smoked dope in bars we weren't even supposed to enter, far too young, and took any pill a hand held out to us. Occasionally, as if suddenly awakened, I would see myself passing by a mirror and would not know myself at first, then quickly turn away, trying to blot out sudden remembrance.

I don't know how we found him. Someone in the group must have heard. We were just tagging around town one spring night (were supposed to be studying for finals in whatever school it was at the time) and met some boys who had beer. We sat under trees at the edge of a park and drank. The townspeople tolerated us as long as we stayed in the background: after all, we spent money. I simply followed along, and when somebody suggested that we ride out to this farm, there was this weird guy there, a guru, they said. I climbed into the car without question.

We drove over bumpy roads. All I could see in the reflection of the headlights were blackberry vines blooming in the deep gullies in the dust at the sides. If the others talked, I did not listen. This was simply another ride, another place to go. What did I care about a man living out at the other end of nowhere, crabbing in the earth?

When we got there, we were welcomed by strange voices, friendly and warm, as if we had returned from a long journey, and though there was no feast prepared, they gave us food—I remember bananas, fresh-baked bread with butter, and sweet cider to drink. I thought, If we had wounds, they would bind them up and care for us until we are rested. They led us through rooms in the old farmhouse (scrubbed clean, if barren) and laid us down on mattresses on the floor, the girls together, the men separate (unless they left, I don't remember seeing them again), and there were no pawings in the night, no one brushing close against my skin, saying, "Here, take a hit," and the sweet smell of smoke.

Three of us stayed, just never went back to school. Perhaps they looked for us, the police and our parents. But what would Theda do? She'd be glad to be rid of me. No more money to spend on fancy schools, no more letters reporting failing grades, unacceptable behavior, expulsion. How she must have breathed a sigh of relief. If we were listed as "Missing," we wanted to be, far away from all that had gone on before.

His name was Hart—that was all he ever called himself, and we, those that loved him, would say, "He is Hart, our Heart, the one to whom we owe our being." As soon as he entered a room (it was several days before we saw him, at one of the services at sunset), you were drawn to him, as if his heart did have some strange pull, radiating outward. I thought of a picture that used to hang in the chapel of one of the schools I attended, a picture of Christ, standing at a doorway, His heart pictured ruby red and pulsing like a light—his was that real to me.

No one knew how he came there, or how long ago. Some said he was once a preacher with a tent and a little organ that a fat woman played while the congregation, poor folks who had no hope of anything better to do on a hot summer night, sang in high, flat voices hymns about redemption by the Blood. When someone offered to give him the farm, he folded his tent (it was still in the barn out back), and he took along those who would come to form his little body of believers, later accepting others as they came. Few stayed. It was no easy life, scratching at the rocky soil to grow vegetables for the group; canning fruit from the rotting orchard that we tried to peddle in town; milking the few cows that had come with the place. But somehow we went on, perhaps with gifts from others who had gone away; perhaps with money those who still stayed on managed to obtain from back home.

No easy life, either, in that house. We were separated, the women from the few men, and Hart decided who was to have who, his choice first. He preached against the sins of the world, TV sex, laxness, magazines of lust, yet we joyed when he came in the night and tapped us on the shoulder and took us away to the room he had for himself at the top of the house (furnished better, a real bed, a place to put clothes), shedding our few garments even before we entered the room and spending sweaty nights upon that bed, exhausted next morning, though we had to do our work with the envious eyes of the others on our backs.

And I loved him! He was gentle, loving, though there could be great anger. If someone disobeyed him, went against his will, his anger would rise like a summer storm and the guilty would be punished. Instead of kisses on our cheeks, there would be bruises, or we would go hungry, bread and water for a week. But we accepted our punishment, relished it, I think, as if we were special for being singled out, even for his wrath. We did not complain, and it was such a joy to be back within the rays of his heart again after the punishment was over, that we might almost seek his displeasure, just to enjoy our redemption more.

'You are my children in the Lord,' he would say as we sat around him on the bare floor of the living room in the house. Outside the sun would set behind the trees, the sky turning dark as a peach pit, purpled, and he would be surrounded by that bright light. 'I will guard you and protect you. Woe be to him that takes what is mine! You have been pursued by enemies, like animals hunted in the night, but now you have found a place to rest, of peace. The Lord has called you here, Jesus has guided you like the little ones, and He has given me the word that I must guide you, punish you if you sin, to save your souls from damnation.'

We swayed our heads from side to side, blinded by the light and our love.

It couldn't last, of course. Times changed, people changed. We had less and less food as floods came or dry seasons. The cows died. People drifted off into other lives; some got jobs in town at the sawmill there, or turned to waitressing at the truck stop. But I did not leave. Where could I go at that point? Back to Theda? No doubt she would welcome me with open arms. "Here I am," I could say, arriving on her doorstep in my ragged blouse and frayed skirt that flared out over my stomach. "Here I am with child, your grandchild, Theda. Will you take us in? Will you care for me as you care for Alice? Will you hold my hand while I deliver this baby?"

He wouldn't have let me go, of course. I was about all he had left—me and one or two others as lost as I was—still trying to stay in his heart's glow. We locked up the house and put what little we could into the truck, along with that old tent (patched up, with a banner sagging across the front saying, *Revival Tonight. Hear Preacher Hart and Get on the Road to Salvation*), and drove down the road, stopping at one small town and then another to pitch the tent in any empty meadow.

If we had enough money to get them printed (from our "free will" offering at the end of the service), we passed out handbills on corners, me getting bigger every day, and that night awaited those who came, out of curiosity, tired of TV, or worn down with sorrow, hoping for a moment's peace. I stood up front and led the singing, saying those strange bloody words so different from the hymns I had sung as a child, and if we got any money it was as much pity for me as for the words of inspiration Hart gave them, his voice rising, falling, like the wind.

Lord, I couldn't tell you how many nights we spent in that

tent. In the winter, it would be freezing, and we would wear coats, the small kerosene heater in the middle aisle glowing but giving no warmth. Summers made it seem like a furnace, and the women who came flapped cardboard fans against their faces, drying sweat and tears. I had another child, and the older one began to take part in the service, singing songs of Jesus in a sweet baby voice. We made more money. But never enough, never enough food or gas or heat. Hart lost his glow, his heart hardened and he watched people turn away and then not even come into the tent. He cursed them at times from the platform, and they ran as if fleeing devils. He turned his heart from us, too, from me, and I bore bruises, purple, like flowers, on my arms, my body, never on my face since they would show.

And then he abused my body more, or forced me to do it. One day he simply said, 'You will go out into the streets and lie with men (reviling me, saying I was worth nothing more). 'I will bring them to you. I demand it.' Still, I did not complain, loving him, feeling that I was unworthy of his regard; at least he still showed some interest in me, unlike Theda who didn't know then whether I was alive or dead and didn't seem to care.

We lived in a cheap hotel, two rooms; I cooked on a hot plate, and the children played in the small space between beds and the TV set. I waited while Hart went out (painted up now, my hair combed, strange to have it so), and when he would return and leave the man in another room down the hall, I would go out wordlessly, leaving the children with Hart, and walk down the darkened hallway, smelling of others' lives, to where the man waited. I did whatever they wanted, dull, blind, as if a button switched off in my head as I entered the door, though there would come the thought, almost pleasing, that while I was lying here with these men, their wives would be waiting at home, tight-lipped, proper, like Theda, long ago waiting for my daddy. Perhaps it was like flashing my breasts in that photograph—I wanted to defy her, say, "This is what I think of you."

After it was over and I cleaned myself off, I would return to our rooms and hand Hart the money, and he would take

it, sometimes with a kiss, heart flaming again for me, and
he would take me there, the children rushed into the small
kitchenette and warned not to open the door.

I don't know how much longer that would have gone on.
Perhaps not long at all. I was losing my looks, breasts sagging after being pulled on by two babies, skin slack; I lost
weight. Once, the man walked away from me when I came
into the room and left. Hart beat me for that, more than
before.

Then he beat the children. Always in the past, when he
was pursued by the demons that seemed to come to him more
and more, they were spared. Now, when I returned, I would
find them locked in the bathroom, crying, red finger marks
on their arms, buttocks. "They were bad," he said, his voice
sounding as if it came from a cave. "They had to be punished." If I argued, said they were too little and didn't know,
he would hit me, and the children would scream in terror,
more upset with my bruises than their own.

For them I decided to leave Hart. For them alone. I still
loved him, still gloried when he took my body and I felt the
warmth of him, his arms. But I could not let him hurt my
children.

I made a plan. There was this massage parlor I worked in,
near the hotel. Hart found the place, made me go there when
it was cold on the streets and he could find no one for me,
and I didn't mind. At least I got out of the hotel, smelled
different air, not so stale—and there were others in the place,
two or three girls, and when no men came, we would sit and
smoke and talk, and I would laugh inside, thinking about the
similar times, when we had talked in the dormitory rooms,
silly girls wondering about boys, a million years ago.

I planned to bring the children there. Paula, the one in
charge, said it would be all right for a few days, till I got
someplace for me to live without Hart and found a baby-
sitter. I could keep working there, she said. I was getting a
few regular customers and that was good money. The other
girls could watch the children while I was in one of the little
rooms doing what I had to do. It was all set.

I remember the night—damp, cold, rain blowing in on

high rushing clouds. I left the massage parlor, warm air all around me for a moment till the door closed, then walked down the street to the hotel, not noticing those few people who passed. I would go in and act like nothing was different, cook the babies' supper, offer to fix something for Hart, though I knew he wouldn't eat with us. He had taken to going out when I returned, took what money I had and left. I didn't know where for and was afraid to ask. Once he was gone, then I would leave. I already had the children's clothes packed in two shopping bags hidden at the back of the closet. I would write him a note.

Partly it worked just as I expected. 'No,' he answered when I asked if he wanted supper. He was putting on his tie by the mirror and I could not see his eyes; his voice told me nothing.

'Will you be late?' I said. I don't know why. It didn't make any difference.

'No, not too late.'

We sat then, the children and I; I fed them. We were silent. They seemed to know something was about to happen, like animals before a storm. When one spilled a glass of milk I almost screamed, expecting Hart to strike him. But all we saw was Hart's dark back, his hand lifting his hat to his head. He did not say good-bye as he went out the door.

I hurried the children through their food, afraid that Hart would come back, though it was usually well after midnight when he returned and we would be asleep or pretending to be. I bundled them up, told them we were going for a little trip, and their faces glowed with excitement; Hart hardly ever let us out. I threw a few things for myself into an old suitcase and got the shopping bags from the closet and turned to leave, all thoughts about Hart pushed way down inside of me—I was afraid I might not go, despite all my resolutions, if I thought of his loving me, of how I would miss him.

I opened the door, saw darkness, then a blinding flash as Hart's fist hit me in the face. Falling back, feeling blood spurt already from my nose, I heard the children screaming, though they hushed as he jerked them aside and slammed the door. I was still holding the shopping bags. 'Bitch!' Hart yelled at me. 'Abomination!' I had memories of him on the platform preaching; the voice was the same. 'Did you think I would not know? The Lord told me of your betrayal, warned me. You belong to *me*, all of you. I will not lose you!'

He beat me then, with his hands, with anything that came to him, dishes, pots. I lay moaning, but did not protect myself, feeling that I deserved it, wondering who had told him at the massage parlor, which girl (because that must have been how he found out; perhaps he was a regular of one of the other girls). I could not see the children, but heard them whimpering in the corner.

Then there was silence, except for the sound of Hart moving around, scratching like a rat in the walls. 'Come on,' I heard him say to the children, and he moved the shopping bags from my hands where I still clutched them. I felt liquid spread over my body, warm, soothing it seemed. With a rush of joy I thought that Hart was binding up my wounds, comforting me. He loved me still. The door was opened and I knew that the children were out in the hallway.

'Let's take something in remembrance,' Hart said (I don't know who to, perhaps the voice inside his head), and I screamed as he jerked the gold loop from my ear, ripping flesh. I heard a scratching sound, saw light, then heard the door close.

Warmth fell upon me, light showered down around me brighter even than the light of Christ's heart in the picture I had seen years before. At the moment I expected peace to come, I felt the fire burning on my back, running down my body like water trickling. I was paralyzed; pain spread, covering me, holding me down. I smelled kerosene from the heater in the apartment and knew what Hart had poured on me. "No!" I screamed out, but there was no one to hear me. And for a moment I did not care, wanted to be dead, but I thought of the children somewhere with Hart, the marks of his fingers on their bodies, and I would not die.

I rolled around, thrashing, unable to stand, and pressed myself into the bed. The smell of burned wool mixed with the smell of my burned flesh, and I knew that I left pieces of my body clinging to the covers as I moved back and forth, mouth open and a scream coming from it still, though it sounded to me like some far-off noise, a machine rasping or an animal, nothing anyway human.

Someone must have heard, finally, or smelled the scent in the hallway. The medics came, and I heard the one word, 'Jesus!' Just before fainting, I thought, He is here, Christ has come to me, His heart open to take me in.

They found him, of course, soon after, Hart and the children, at the bus station. He was buying tickets for Florida with the money I had given him that night, my blood still crusted on his hands. They put the children in a foster home and Hart in jail, and came to me, asking what he had done, what had gone on before. I lay in the hospital bed, my body numb from medication, my mind as white as the bandages that covered my body, the linens of the bed, the white-painted walls of the room, and I did not talk to them, would not help them with their case.

'Why?' they asked. ''Why protect him, after he did this to you?'' (And I wondered if they could see the healing wounds on my back and arms, the grafts upon my legs). Still I did not answer, fingering the fuzz that was just beginning to grow back upon my head, the piece left on my ear. That I did not let them repair, a badge I felt I must wear the rest of my life.

There were newspaper stories, pictures of that ugly hotel room, shadowed and burned. Hart's face stared out, and I hardly knew him, bearded, eyes closed off. The foster parents told how the children screamed in their sleep and would hardly play in the daytime, though people from all over sent toys, money, offers of adoption. Theda sent money to me (in an envelope addressed by Alice), no note but the silent message that I was not to come to her, be quiet. Someone from the hospital must have contacted her. How embarrassed she must have been. Her own flesh and blood involved in such a scandal.

They tried Hart. I was better now, able to sit up and read the papers. I wanted to go to him, to sit by him in the court-room, to hold him. He seemed so alone there, with frowning faces around him. They came to me again and said, ''If you testify, we can put him away for years. Don't you want that? They'll give you the children back right away. Otherwise, it may be a long time. You'll have to get out, get a job, prove you can take care of them again." Still I shook my head and stared at the whiteness, and finally they left me alone.

He was convicted. No surprise to anyone. The nurses peeked at me to see how I was taking it; they knew of my refusal to testify, and though they cared for me, bathed me, emptied bags, said fluttery words of encouragement, I could feel always their astonishment, anger, that I had let such things happen to me and to the children. They did not know about love.

I had to make one last effort. I wrote the judge, asking for leniency. "Remember the Golden Rule," I said. "Forgive him. I have; his children will someday, when they understand. He was good, is good, though that goodness may have sunk out of sight over these hard years. But I know he loves us, and we love him."

Forgive.

Chapter
Seventeen

Mavis got off the bus at the mall on Main Street. Looking around, she saw a bench shaded by a crab apple tree, empty, with no one else nearby who might bother her, so she walked to it slowly, scattering a rush of pigeons looking to be fed, and carefully spread her handkerchief on the rough wood and sat down. She did not want to see Charles Morgan, not yet. That morning, she had waited as long as she could to call him, expecting that he might call her first, and when she heard his tense, expectant voice on the phone, she knew he would press her about the visit to Ruth Anne.

What could she tell him? That whole long, sad story? Mavis wanted to put the horror of it out of her mind. She gave a little shudder now just thinking about it. And what would be accomplished anyway? Nothing would change. Charles Morgan would learn nothing more about Theda Hedrick's death, and repeating Ruth Anne's words would only imprint them more strongly on Mavis's memory, making any attempt at forgetting that much harder.

She would never forget that long afternoon, not really, sitting there in that darkened trailer while Ruth Anne told of her strange love. Love? Would Mavis have called it that? Surely it was not what most people felt when they said that word—warmth, tenderness. But then, Mavis had heard other perversions of love since Theda was murdered; perhaps she shouldn't have been surprised at Ruth Anne's infatuation, madness even, which she called *love*. Even Hart, a devil if there ever was one, he, too, might have chosen the word for what he felt. Who would ever know?

She could not talk to Owen Luther about any of it yesterday after they drove away from the trailer, leaving Ruth Anne still standing in the doorway, a silhouette behind the door screen, and the two children watching them from a place in the sand. Mavis had sat beside Owen in numbed silence in the car, the air-conditioning making her shiver, though she did not ask him to cut it down.

How could you let those things happen? She wanted to turn back and ask Ruth Anne. If the woman had wept, showed shame, regret, Mavis could have taken her in her arms and comforted her—but when Ruth Anne had finished her story, she looked as blank and hard as the tabletop, and Mavis could not move a hand toward her. She got up and simply said good-bye, and Ruth Anne stepped aside to let her pass.

"Take care of yourself," Mavis said. She could think of nothing else to say.

"All right." Ruth Anne's voice was dull, the way it must have been in the hospital when they asked her questions, unrevealing.

Mavis turned and pulled open the door of the trailer, ready to go outside. Something hanging there brushed against her arm, rough to her skin. She looked and saw the sleeve of a jacket, a man's surely, too big for Ruth Anne, a man's tobacco smell on it. Mavis's heart sank even further. Was Ruth Anne involved with another man after all she had been through—*burned*? Mavis jerked her arm away; she couldn't bear it. Hurrying down the steps, not even careful to keep herself from falling, Mavis said no more and hurried to the car and the cool air, afraid she might be unable to breathe if she stayed one second longer in that bleak, open space in front of Ruth Anne's trailer. . . .

"Lady, you got a quarter for something to eat?"

Mavis had not seen the man walk toward her. She looked up at his runny eyes, smelled his many scents, and it was as if the coat on the back of Ruth Anne's door had suddenly come to life in some horrible way. She jumped up, clutching her purse, and quickly walked away, upsetting the pigeons again, the flap of their wings like her frightened heartbeat. She walked quickly away, listening for the footsteps of the man to see if he would follow her.

Gradually, her heart settled down, her head cleared. She looked up at the sky and almost smiled. It was one of those glorious summer days when the temperature fell and the air cleared, so that the sky looked as blue as deep ocean water and you could smell flowers when a breeze came by. People on the street walked a little more spritely, as if a weight had been taken from their shoulders; a man with very white hair smiled at Mavis and tipped his hat when he passed by. Lord, how long had it been since anyone gave her that old, courtly gesture?

The building was cool inside, no need for air-conditioning. Mavis climbed up the stairs to the second floor, the marble balustrade smooth under her fingertips. She would like to have turned around, go back outside into the sunlight, but she knew she had to get this visit over with.

"Well, I was about to give you up." Charles jerked up from his desk when she opened the door to his office and went in without knocking. "Never thought I'd live to see the day when you'd be a second late." He smiled at her.

"Well, things change," Mavis said, her lips feeling tight. "I'm not like you young'uns flying around."

Charles laughed, his face relaxed. "That don't include me. *Young*. Sometimes I feel as old as one of those statues sitting with the pigeons up yonder on the square, like I'm turning solid."

"Wait till you get arthritis in your knees and hurt every step you take. That's when you'll think *old*."

"Maybe," Charles said, his smile fading. Perhaps he was afraid he had hurt her feelings. Just as well, maybe he wouldn't ask her too much. She sat down on the fake leather chair and waited for him to speak.

Charles cleared his throat and pushed aside some papers on his desk. "Owen Luther called this morning. He said you and Ruth Anne had quite a little chat out there in the trailer."

"We talked."

"Owen said he didn't hear a word, sat in the car sweating,

afraid to turn on the air-conditioning and run the battery down.''

"It was women talk, part of the time. He wouldn't have been interested."

"I'm not too sure about *that*. I'm interested. What did Ruth Anne tell you? Come on, Mavis, that's why I sent you out there—to see if you could find out anything that would help us."

"Nothing that will help, I don't think." Mavis sighed and looked down at her purse in her lap. "She's had a hard life, Ruth Anne, no life for anyone, but especially for a girl brought up to have something, the way she was." (Mavis bit her tongue, she was almost about to say, "brought up in a good Christian home," but the words would have gagged her, after what she had learned about Theda Hedrick.) "So much heartbreak, and no end of it in sight. And those children"—Mavis made a little sound with her tongue—"what they have been exposed to. Such a stain on young lives . . . I don't know if it'll ever wash out."

"What, Mavis? What?"

She sighed and sat back and told him, briefly, skipping over the parts she could not talk about; she would have blushed red with embarrassment. But she told him most of it, the horror and the pain. Charles Morgan watched her lips intently, his gaze never wavering, and Mavis could see in his eyes the gradual look of dismay that spread there as she spoke. When she was finished, there was such a silence in the room that it made you want to cry, as if someone, something, had died and they mourned its passing. Lives used up and gone.

"She must have hated Theda," Charles said finally.

Mavis shifted in her chair. "I don't know. Maybe there was hate and love all mixed up together. She waited so long, Ruth Anne . . . waited for Theda to love her. Maybe Theda just couldn't, was one of those people who should never have had children.

"There are plenty of those. They have babies while good people who want children try and try but can't have them. It hardly seems right."

Mavis thought of her own child, gone, but brushed the thought aside. "People say it's the Lord's will, but sometimes that's hard for me to understand."

"Yes, ma'am," Charles said quietly, then looked up in the air as if her thoughts still hung there. "I still think Ruth Anne might of had a right good reason to kill Theda. Just the hate if nothing else. And she couldn't know that she wouldn't get anything from the will. People cling to ideas when it comes to things like that, hoping it will be so."

Mavis shook her head. "I don't believe one word of it. Ruth Anne didn't expect anything from Theda—though she still wanted love. And if she was going to kill her, why wait? Why now? No, it just doesn't make any sense."

Charles leaned back and crossed his legs, clasping his hands behind his head. "That's the problem with all of them," he said. "The ones that might have done it. I guess they all had a pretty good reason—I don't think anybody was too happy with Theda—but why would they kill her now? Why not before? Certainly, they all had the opportunity."

"What do you mean?"

"Well, nobody exactly has an ironclad alibi. Ruth Anne living out there in the woods—who'd know whether she was there or not? She might have just left those children alone and come over to Theda's house. From what you've said, those young'uns probably had been left plenty of times before to scrape for themselves. And she knew the house, probably could guess where everybody would be."

"But Theda had already made arrangements. She had gotten rid of Tommie Lee, let him have the day off."

"Well then, Theda could have met Ruth Anne somewhere. Probably she'd want to keep Ruth Anne out of sight and from coming to the house. She wouldn't want the neighbors to see her and gossip. And anyway, we don't even know if Theda gave Tommie Lee the time off, it's just his say. Who knows whether he was at the movies or not?"

"He doesn't have sense enough to lie, Charles Morgan. You know that."

"Don't take much sense to kill, but I won't argue that now. We checked on Charlene and her boyfriend, too. Can't find much on her—just that time she was arrested at the demonstration—but her boyfriend's got a record."

"What for? What'd he do?"

"Nothing real serious. A few arrests for drugs, possession. Driving under the influence."

"Half this town probably has a record of that. It doesn't prove a thing."

"No, but sometimes if people do one thing and get off, they think they can do another."

"It's a long way from smoking marijuana to killing somebody."

"Maybe they didn't mean to. Maybe they just planned to rob her or something, and Theda resisted and they lost their heads. It's happened."

"I'm sure it has, but not this time. I'm certain of it. Anyway, why would they pick now to do it? Charlene had it pretty good there—a place to sleep, her food, and some little money, enough to go to school on, anyway. Why would she upset things trying to rob Theda? It wasn't like she was a stranger they didn't know."

Charles Morgan shook his head. "I guess I'm just grasping at straws. We don't really have any good evidence for anybody doing it, and no ideas where to look for more. Nothing fits together."

"We have to look harder, that's all. I want to talk to Alice. I thought she was just there in the background, living with Theda all these years, copying her clothes, shopping with her. But she had more to do with what went on, with Ruth Anne, than people suspected. It was Alice Pate that sent Ruth Anne money all along, probably even to buy that dinky trailer way out in the woods after Ruth Anne recovered and got her children back. Who else would do it? Theda never did anything for her before unless it was Alice got her to. Theda would have even less reason for caring for Ruth Anne after she got into all that trouble."

"Do you think you could? Talk with Alice, I mean?"

"Probably, though I don't know with what reason. I never did just pop in there to make a social call, and with the funeral over, I can't think what excuse I could give."

"You'll think of one, Miz Lashley. I know you."

"Just what does *that* mean, Charles Morgan?"

"I didn't mean a thing." Charles laughed. "Just saying you are resourceful."

"Nosy, you mean."

"No, you really care, it seems to me. What happens to those folks. It's not just curiosity, just wanting to gossip."

Mavis got up and straightened out her skirt. "I suppose so. All of them seem to have gone through so much already I hate to see them hurt more. I'll do what I can to help."

Charles gave no reply, and Mavis turned, went out the door, and did not look back as she moved down the shadowed hallway to the stairs.

Chapter
Eighteen

Mavis couldn't sit still that night. After she got home from her visit to Charles Morgan's office, she turned on the sprinkler on the lawn to give the grass a good soaking. Then she washed out a pair of hose and hung them on the shower rod in the bathroom to dry. She watched the six o'clock news on TV, but two minutes later she couldn't have told you a thing they said except the weather, which called for thunderstorms the next day. Even though she wasn't a bit hungry and really couldn't face cooking a meal for herself, she ate a bowl of cereal with peaches cut up on top and managed to get down two cups of coffee, which would probably keep her awake half the night.

"Lord, what is the *matter* with me?" she said out loud, as she thumped down the Sunday school manual she held in her hands (she couldn't keep her mind on that, either). "I'm just like a child with ants in his pants." She felt the way Charles Morgan must feel, frustrated that nothing was happening in relation to Theda's murder. She wanted to talk to Alice Pate again; she was sure there was something Alice could tell her. But how in the world would she approach her? Mavis still hadn't come up with even a halfway reasonable excuse to go up to the house on the corner and knock and invite herself in.

And something else bothered her, too, something that Charles had said. It was at the back of her mind like a name you can't call to your tongue, and try however hard she might, she could not come up with it. She went over all the people

156

they had discussed—Ruth Anne's sordid story, Charlene and her boyfriend with his besmirched background, and poor Tommie Lee Bagwell. To think that Charles could give any serious thought about him being a possible suspect, even though Tommie Lee couldn't come up with anybody who'd seen him at the picture show.

That was it, that's what had been bothering Mavis: Tommie Lee couldn't name names of anybody who saw him there. Well, of course not. It would only be a bunch of young'uns at the show that time of day, the middle of the afternoon, and they wouldn't be interested in Tommie Lee. Just carrying on, drinking sodas and eating popcorn and doing Lord knows what else, not watching a forty-year-old man with his eyes glued to the screen.

But Mavis knew who would have seen him, would have noticed. Althea Lupton sold tickets down at the Capitol Theater, had been there as long as anybody could remember, and she'd know. Althea didn't miss a thing.

Mavis looked up the number in the telephone directory and dialed it. Althea would surely be there. She maintained the ticket booth at the theater as if it were her home—a radio playing low in the background, a stack of *True Romance* magazines on the counter, and a heater next to her feet, which she kept going summer and winter. Sometimes you'd pass by and there would be Althea right up in the window polishing her fingernails as pretty as you please if it was slack time between features. Children were afraid of her. She demanded to see some verification of their ages, and she would bless them out if they tried to trick her.

"Hello, Capitol Theater, may I help you?" That was Althea's put-on voice, talking through her nose. Once, years ago, she probably thought she might end up being a movie star or something, working at the theater, and she had never quite lost her early affectations.

"Althea, this is Mavis Lashley. How're you, honey?"

Althea's voice came back to normal. "Just fine, Mavis. I haven't seen you in Lord-knows-when. You never come to the picture show anymore."

"I stopped long ago, haven't set foot in one since *The*

Sound of Music. From what I can tell, there hasn't been a decent picture since. Just blood and things people used not to talk about."

"Well, they're not all like that." (Mavis knew that Althea got to see each new feature free, so if somebody called up and wanted to know what the picture was about, she could tell them.) "They have things for children sometimes about animals."

"Not for me. I'll sit home and read a good mystery."

Althea gave a little sniff, audible over the phone. "Well, I'm sure they have just a speck of violence in them, and some other things, too, if you know what I mean."

"Yes, but you can use your imagination just how much or how little you want to. It's not spread out in technicolor for all to see."

"Well, I reckon."

Mavis cleared her throat to change the subject. "I know you're busy, Althea, so I won't keep you but just a minute. I had a question I wanted to ask you."

"What's that?" Mavis could almost see Althea perk up, shoving her magazine aside.

"I can't be too specific right now, but it's real important. I'll tell you more when I can."

"Goodness, is it some kind of secret?"

"No, not really, but I just can't explain it in detail. All right?"

"I guess it will have to be. What is it?"

"Do you know Tommie Lee Bagwell?"

"Why sure I do. Theda Hedrick's chauf-*feur*." Althea tried to make it sound French; she must have heard it in the pictures. "He's down here once a week regular as clockwork. Don't seem to matter to him what's on; I doubt he even looks. He puts down his money without a glance at me and takes the ticket when it pops up. Sometimes I almost give him change, like he was one of the children and only pays half price. Big as he is, he still looks like a little boy in the face."

"Did he come in last week? The day Theda was murdered?"

"Well, let me think. It would have been real unusual if he had. His regular time is on Saturday, when all the kids are there. Like I said, he seems just like one of them."

"Think real hard, Althea. It's important."

"I am, Mavis. I don't keep no record, but I've got as good a memory as anybody else, and I'd say no, Tommie Lee Bagwell didn't come in at a different time. He was there on Saturday, like usual. In fact I wondered if he wasn't needed back home since it was right after the funeral. Seems like there would have been things for him to do around the house."

"You worked all week? Nobody else was selling tickets?"

"Mavis, you know better than that." Althea sounded as if she were swelling up. "I pride myself on my regularity. I was here every day. I only get relief on Sunday, which is no real relief since I have to spend half of Monday straightening things up again."

Mavis could think of no more questions. She paused, hoping that Althea might have a sudden recollection, but there was silence. "I guess that's about all," she said finally. "If you think of anything else, call me."

"All right, honey. And you call *me* when the secret's out."

Mavis hung up the phone. When *would* the secret be out? When would they know what had happened? And a more important question: when would she tell Charles Morgan that Tommie Lee wasn't at the movies when he said he was?

And where had Tommie Lee gone the day Theda died?

Chapter
Nineteen

As it turned out, Mavis didn't have to invent an excuse to go up to Alice Pate's to talk. Bright and early the next morning—before she was dressed, curlers still in her hair—the doorbell rang. Lord, it's Dale, she thought, a thrill of pleasure rushing all the way down to her fingertips. She had so much to tell him. Wouldn't he be surprised?

She hurried to the door, opened it, her mouth already half shaped to say, "Well, aren't you a sight for sore eyes?" when she saw that it wasn't Dale standing there smiling at her. "What do you want?" she asked, her voice rough and low, not like her at all. She almost slammed the door shut again, even though the screen was locked, half afraid.

Tommie Lee jumped backward, as if she had struck him. His eyes were wide, and he brushed back his white hair, shining now in the morning sun, with a nervous little gesture. "Miz Lashley?" he finally said. "It's me, Tommie Lee. You okay?"

"Bless my soul," Mavis said, her voice back to its normal level. She opened the door; it was hard to be afraid of Tommie Lee, even though he had lied about where he had been the day Theda was killed. "You scared me," she said to Tommie Lee. "I wasn't expecting anybody."

"I'm sorry, ma'am, I didn't mean no harm."

"Don't you worry," Mavis said, ashamed. "It's all right. I'm sorry if I hollered. You come on in."

"I shouldn't stay," Tommie Lee said, but came in nevertheless. Mavis stood aside, pulling her robe closer to her neck with both hands. "I got a message."

"Message? Who from?" Mavis walked into the living room and motioned for Tommie Lee to follow her. He sat down tentatively on the edge of the recliner.

"From Miss Alice."

"What does *she* want?"

"She wants you to come up and see her. To talk."

"Well, I declare," Mavis said. "And I was wanting to talk to *her*. When?"

"Tonight, later on. She said about nine o'clock."

"Why so late? I don't like wandering around after dark, even in this neighborhood."

"I don't know, ma'am. She just told me."

Mavis shrugged her shoulders. "I guess the Lord will protect me. You tell her I'll be there."

"That's all," Tommie Lee said. "She didn't say nothing else." He stood up and the recliner bounced back and forth with a squawking sound. Tommie Lee jumped away and looked behind him. Mavis wondered if she should have given him a tip; she always did when he carried groceries for her. But she didn't have any change in the pocket of her robe, and she certainly wasn't going to leave Tommie Lee there in her living room and go get her pocketbook.

"Thank you for coming to tell me," she said. "I appreciate it."

Tommie Lee shrugged, turned, and started back toward the front door. Then, scaring him all over, Mavis said very loudly, "Tommie Lee Bagwell, you come right back here. I want to know the truth about something."

Mavis had just remembered her conversation the night before with Althea Lupton down at the Capitol Theater. When Tommie Lee had come to the door, she had been so surprised to see him there, and then to get the message from Alice Pate, that she had forgotten all about his lie. He hadn't been at the moving pictures at all, and she was determined to find out where he was.

"Yes'm?" Tommie Lee asked, only half turned. He looked

as if he might bolt at any moment, like a child caught in some misdeed.

"I said I want to talk to you."

"Miss Alice, she might be mad if I stayed."

"Never you mind. If you get in any trouble, I'll explain."

Tommie Lee turned then and walked slowly back to where Mavis stood, eyes to the floor. She moved back and sat on the sofa again, and pointed toward the recliner for Tommie Lee to sit down. "You remember when the policeman talked to you? About the day Miz Theda died?"

"Oh, yes, ma'am. I was out in the garage." Tommie Lee looked suddenly excited, maybe relieved. "He asked me about the car."

"What else did you tell him?"

Tommie Lee looked puzzled. "Nothing. Nothing I can remember."

"What about where you were the afternoon Miz Theda died?"

Tommie Lee looked as if he were straining to remember. Then he looked down. "You mean at the picture show?"

"That's right. What did you tell him?"

Shrugging, Tommie Lee still did not look up. "Just that I went down to the show after Miz Theda give me the day off. I tole him about the picture, what it was and all." Tommie Lee looked up, eyes filled with hope.

"I know that's what you told him, but that wasn't the truth. You saw that picture on Saturday, didn't you, your regular day? It was on all week."

Tommie Lee's mouth went into a big O shape. "Oh, no, ma'am, I didn't do that."

Mavis's voice became very stern. "Tommie Lee, you know it's a sin to tell a lie, particularly about something as important as this. I talked to Althea Lupton—she's the one that sells you your ticket every time you go—and she told me you never set foot in the Capitol Theater on Wednesday, and there's no way you could have snuck in. Now I want the truth."

Slowly, Tommie Lee raised his head; tears dribbled from his eyes, and Mavis had a pang of guilt over making him feel so bad. "You'll feel better if you tell," she said. "Then you won't have a bad conscience anymore."

"You won't tell nobody else?"

"Not if it isn't important. The policeman, maybe, no one else."

Tommie Lee's head fell down again, his neck grew red under the white hair. "No, ma'am, I didn't go to the show that afternoon." His voice was very low. "It was to a bad place. I try not to go there, but I can't help myself sometimes."

"What sort of place can it be?" Mavis tried to think what in the world he was talking about. Surely, Tommie Lee hadn't taken to drink and gone to some bar.

"To the bookstore." Tommie Lee's head almost disappeared between his legs.

"Well, what's so awful about that? Nothing wrong with looking at books." Then a thought came into Mavis's head, and she blushed almost as brightly as Tommie Lee. "What bookstore?" she asked, her voice hard again.

"Down by the bus station. You know."

And of course she did know, that little hole-in-the-wall place all boarded up so there were no windows to see through, and a sign on the door saying, YOU MUST BE 21 TO ENTER, ADULTS ONLY. If Mavis or any of the ladies passed by they would certainly look away, and Mavis herself had signed a petition some people got up to close the place, but the owners (a gang of foreigners from up North, she was sure) must have paid somebody off, and they stayed open, selling Lord knows what kind of smut. And to somebody like Tommie Lee—it might as well have been to a child.

"Why, Tommie Lee Bagwell, I'm surprised at you."

Snuffling, Tommie Lee raised his face; his eyes were red-rimmed. "I'm sorry, Miz Lashley. I couldn't help myself, hard as I might try."

"Pray," Mavis said, though she wasn't sure that would help Tommie Lee when he had a need for such things. She thought of him up in that little room over the garage, looking at pictures of naked ladies, and blushed again; how foolish she had been those years ago when she was selling magazines, thinking that Tommie might be interested in a subscription to *Sports Illustrated*.

"I'll try, Miz Lashley, real hard," Tommie Lee said. Mavis fished around in her pocket and found a tissue, more or less clean, and handed it to Tommie Lee.

"Blow your nose," she said. "Go on home. But don't let me hear anything else about you hanging out around that place again. It's not fit for a single soul."

As if the recliner had thrust him, Tommie Lee jumped upward. "I won't, Miz Lashley. You won't ever catch me there again." With that, he turned, and, before Mavis could say another word, he was out the door. By the time she went over to lock the screen and close the door, Tommie Lee was out of sight, only a limb on a bush at the edge of the yard swinging too swiftly for it to be wind giving any sign that Tommie Lee had rushed on by.

Chapter
Twenty

Mavis was ready long before it was time to go. All day she had tried to make the time pass swiftly, but it dragged on, slow as a yawn. She cleaned out the medicine chest in the bathroom and found bottles with just a few pills left, whatever illness they were prescribed for long forgotten. Only the aspirin for her arthritis pain remained when she was finished, along with the one cleansing cream she had used each night as long as she could remember. ("Never get me to use all that mess," she would say when the ladies showed her magazine advertisements for special lotions, and she knew they secretly envied her soft, smooth skin that showed not one blemish.)

It was the same for the kitchen drawer where she kept rubber bands and plastic bags only slightly used, and a whole bunch of coupons long out of date. She hated to throw anything out—you never knew when you might need that very thing—but she made a clean sweep, and when she was through, the drawer was empty except for a new roll of Baggies, and one each of different sizes of rubber bands.

Then she worked in the yard. The day changed, clouds came up, darkening in the west, and there was a slight breeze that would provide some coolness; she did not like to stay in the sun. Near the back fence, she weeded a long row of chrysanthemums and pinched off the buds so that they would hold their bloom till fall, then raked up the wilted stalks of crabgrass that she had pulled up.

Still, it wasn't time to get ready to go to see Alice Pate.

She chided herself for being so excited. Alice probably wouldn't say a thing that was important, yet Mavis felt that part of the mystery might unravel that evening, and she yearned to know what would come. Then she had a thought: What if it was dangerous, going up there late at night, without anybody else around? What if Alice Pate did kill Theda and had found out that Mavis had been poking around? Surely Ruth Anne wouldn't tell her, and Tommie Lee would be too ashamed to reveal anything about their conversation that morning. And Charlene—well, she had come to Mavis all on her own and wouldn't have any reason to inform Alice. In her mind, Mavis went back and forth, arguing to herself (though it did pass the time, and finally she could eat and then get ready). While she was finishing up a bowl of ice cream (a special treat, a new carton from the drugstore), she decided at least to call Dale and tell him where she'd be.

"How are you, Aunt Mavis," he said, answering before the second ring.

"My goodness, you must have been sitting on the phone."

"Well, I *was* expecting a call."

"I can call back later," Mavis said, though she knew she would be going out.

"No you won't. We'll talk right now. If somebody calls, they can wait."

"It won't take long. I just needed to tell somebody where I'm going."

"Where's that?"

"Up to Alice Pate's—she asked me to. Sent Tommie Lee down this morning to tell me."

"What in the world does she want?"

"Now how would I know if I haven't seen her?"

Dale did not answer her question. "You be careful now, you hear me?"

Mavis's own arguments came back into her head. "You really think there's some danger?"

"You never can tell. I mean, she gets the money, the house. What better reason?"

"Maybe, but I just don't believe it. She could have killed Theda before now. That will was made a long time ago."

"Yes, but there's probably a lot we don't know."

"And we never will unless I go up to talk to her." Mavis's desire to make the visit won out in her arguments. "Surely she wouldn't do anything, even if she did kill Theda. Sending Tommie Lee down like she did in broad daylight. And she certainly wouldn't know whether I told anybody about it or not. Murderers aren't *that* careless."

"Some are—that's why they get caught right away. But I suppose you're right. I'm curious, too, wondering what she's going to let out of the bag. But Mavis, you be careful," he said again. "Call me the minute you get home."

"What if it's late?"

"I don't care. You call."

She dressed carefully after she hung up the phone, excited, reminded of that time years ago when she had gone to the Hedrick house to sell magazine subscriptions. She arranged her hair and freshened a handkerchief with toilet water—even splashed a little at the base of her neck—and tucked it under the edge of her sleeve. Even then, it still wasn't quite time to go and she went to sit in the living room, carefully arranging her skirt about her so that it would not wrinkle.

Then she heard the thunder outside. "Now it's going to rain," she moaned out loud. "Wouldn't you know?" Looking out the window, she saw the last light fading behind clouds; lightning danced along the top, outlining them as if they were bound in shiny satin. She decided she couldn't wear her good shoes in such threatening weather, so she went into the bedroom to change. Was it an omen, this storm (though it was predicted, she heard the weather report on the six o'clock news)? "I'm just being silly," she said aloud again, "thinking in such a way." Resolutely, she got up, went to the front coat closet, and took out her umbrella with no more thought of fear. The Lord would protect her. Moving quickly, she turned on the porch light and locked the door.

Rarely was she out alone at this time of night, and she had not realized how dark the sidewalk would be, the thick summer leaves trembling now in the sudden wind, another sign of storm. The light from the streetlamps hardly penetrated.

Years ago, when she and John first moved here, people sat out on their porches on summer evenings, rocking and fanning with Japanese fans if there were no breeze, and you could hear voices calling out in greeting when someone passed by. Now, they were all inside, watching TV no doubt, and the porches were empty, chairs turned up against the wall to protect them from rain.

Mavis walked quickly, a brush of fear returning—all the time you could read in the paper about somebody being robbed or worse, though so far, nothing had happened in her neighborhood. (But then, it suddenly occurred to her, Theda might have been murdered in the very house Mavis was hurrying to . . . and taken away right under all their noses in broad daylight.) She gave a little shudder and hurried on.

Around the corner, it was brighter, the trees further apart and the pink glow of the streetlights hitting the sidewalk. The porch light was on at the Hedrick house. Mavis turned up the walk, then almost stopped when there was a bright streak of lightning quite near, followed almost immediately by thunder. A sudden gust of wind fanned down the shrubs around the base of the house, and overhead, trees swayed. Just as Mavis reached the porch, dark drops of rain, heavy as sodden leaves, plopped all around her, and she pressed the bell quickly, hoping she could get inside before the storm came.

The door was open; she hadn't noticed at first—strange, what with so much meanness going on these days. Time was when no one ever bothered to lock a door when they left home, visitors always welcome to come in and leave a note or rest a while, but those days were gone now. Surely, the screen door was locked, but when she pushed on it, the door swung open with just a small scraping sound where the bottom stuck momentarily, metal against wood. All Mavis's doubts returned. Should she really go in (though if she turned back now, she would probably be soaked to the skin, the rain getting harder every minute)? She jammed her purse more tightly under her arm. I've gone this far, she said to herself, I might as well go on in. She pushed the screen wide open and stepped inside the darkened hallway.

Lightning and another roar of thunder shuddered the house, but the sound of the rain outside was softened, and once the rattling of windowpanes stopped, the house was very quiet. "Hello?" Mavis called out and waited, but she got no answer. She felt like a fool standing there in an empty-seeming hallway yahooing at the top of her lungs, but she called out again, "Anybody home?"

Still there was no answer, and now Mavis felt a little fist of anger inside her chest. It just wasn't good manners to give someone a special invitation and then not be there when they came. Certainly, Alice Pate knew better; Theda Hedrick would never have done such a thing. Mavis decided that she would wait just five minutes more and then march out the door, even if she did get drenched on the way home. She had on her second-best shoes, so it wouldn't matter a whole lot if they got wet.

She walked into the living room, where a single light burned at the far end, giving the room a soft glow. Although the furniture was the same, the same summer slipcovers covering it, there was something different about the place, a change since the day of the funeral. Looking around, Mavis tried to decide what seemed strange. Then it occurred to her: the tabletops were bare of the fancy china figurines—pale shepherdesses and ladies with bouffant hairdos—that had stood there before. And the dainty cups and saucers lined up rigidly on the mantel in their gold wire holders that Mavis remembered from before were gone. Even the vase of flowers that stood on the table where the lamp burned seemed different, carelessly arranged, as if someone had gone about the yard, cutting blooms with no particular plan, just pleasure, and then filled a pretty vase. Before, the flowers looked as if they had been carefully placed in sharp pin holders, each one separate and distinct, unmoveable, as if they had been made of metal. Such small changes, but now the room seemed less formal, friendlier, and for the first time, Mavis could see how people might sit there, relaxed, perhaps with their feet up on a hassock, and talk, even laugh, without feeling that a frown would come for disturbing the arrangement.

Mavis sat down, forgetting her upset for the moment, protected from the rain that washed against the windows. Whatever happened to all those things? she wondered. Alice must have disposed of them—items that so much reflected Theda's taste—hardly before her body was cold in the ground. Such haste, Mavis thought, surprised.

"I've changed things a bit. I wanted the place to look simpler."

Mavis nearly jumped off her chair. Sitting there, her mind occupied, she had heard no sound from the front hallway; Lord knows how long Alice Pate had been standing there, watching her. She turned, ready to say something like, "Why, I think it looks real nice," but then she stopped, and before she knew it, her hand jerked up beside her mouth as if to restrain a cry.

"I've changed, too," Alice Pate said, her voice tentative, as if she were ready to take the words back if Mavis somehow did not approve.

Mavis simply stared. Yes, indeed, Alice had changed. Not the hair; it was always cut short, a gray-flecked cap, like a boy's; nor the face, though the skin that clung tightly to the cheekbones was shiny now, no longer covered with makeup; the lips were pale. But the clothing was startling, or perhaps the absence of it: Mavis would have expected some outlandish dress, draped and tied, in strange dark colors like overripe fruit. Instead, Alice wore a simple soft shirt, the sleeves rolled up to show her thin wrists, no jewelry on the fingers, and straight long pants that fell against her legs, outlining their slimness. The shoes were plain dark brown.

"Well, I declare," Mavis finally said. "You do look different." She peered through the low light and added, almost without thinking—because it was true—"I think I like you better this way. Not so much like Theda."

Alice laughed and came into the room and sat down across from Mavis. Crossing her legs, she took a cigarette from the leather case she carried and lit it with a lighter from the table in front of her. Mavis had never seen her smoke before.

"Not like Theda, that's for sure." She laughed again, her voice light, almost girl-like, and said, "Theda would have a fit if she saw me like this. She went to such lengths to keep things proper, picked out all those clothes for me to wear." Alice blew out a stream of smoke and sat back. "I'll take them all down to the Mission next week and leave them there, though I can't imagine some poor woman walking in there and deliberately choosing one of those drab dresses."

"If you're poor, you don't notice, I guess." Mavis frowned slightly, feeling somehow Alice shouldn't joke about such things.

Alice must have seen her lips. "Excuse me acting this way," she said, leaning toward Mavis. "It's just such a relief. I feel like I've been playacting all these years and now I don't have to anymore. That's partly why I asked you to come up here, just to see me like this and react. Before I went out in public, I wanted to see if you'd faint dead away at the sight of me. It's been so long since I just walked along a sidewalk with other folks and said something as simple as 'Good morning' as we passed, that I guess I'm a little afraid now. I wonder if they'll turn around and stare, like I was some freak or something."

Mavis made a dismissive gesture with her hand. "People don't notice things much anymore, dress outlandish as anything. You go on out. You've been cooped up here in this house too long."

Alice shook her head in agreement. "Lord knows, much too long, but still I'm a little afraid. I know what people will say: 'Killed Theda Hedrick to get her money, now she's living in that house like Miss Got-Rocks.' I know the police suspect me. Others are bound to talk."

"Talk doesn't really hurt. People probably talked before."

Alice shook her head again, a little more slowly. Her lightness faded. "I know. It was all pretend, but Theda wanted it that way, and I went along. I suppose I didn't have any choice if I wanted to stay."

"Did you? Want to stay, I mean." Mavis was surprised at the directness of her own question.

Alice bent closer and peered through the gloom into Mavis's eyes.

"Yes," she said quietly. "In the beginning. It was different then; things turned bad later.'' She was quiet for a moment, then leaned back again in her chair. Smoke from the cigarette curled about her face.

''I never expected any of this to happen, not in my wildest dreams. I only barely knew Theda at first, working down at the office for Dr. Hedrick. Back then, I thought I was the luckiest thing alive just to have that job. I barely had enough money to scrape through high school. My daddy couldn't do much after he got injured working in the mill, and my mama did whatever odd jobs she could find—sewing, doing laundry—to stretch the little bit of pension he got. When others at school talked about college, I just shut my ears, knowing I couldn't go.''

''A shame,'' Mavis murmured, though Alice seemed not to hear her.

''After I graduated, I clerked in the dime store for a while and that helped out a little bit at home. Then I got a job salesclerking in Wilson's Department Store, in the basement, selling men's clothes. Dr. Hedrick came in there to buy everyday things—his good clothes came from one of the expensive men's shops on Main Street; in public he was always dressed up, a flower in his buttonhole—and I would wait on him. He'd just stand if I was busy until I finished. One day he said, 'Miss Alice'—we knew each other's name by then— he asked, 'I need someone to work in my office; the girl I've had up and got in the family way and now she's leaving. You think you might handle the job? I perceive you are a right fine person, always nice to people here in the store. That's the kind of person I'd like in my office.' ''

''Well, wasn't that nice?'' Mavis said, more to herself than to Alice. Seeing Alice the way she was now, the strange clothes gone, her face plain, she could understand why Dr. Hedrick would have been drawn to Alice. She seemed down-to-earth, friendly, and would put people at ease.

''Well, needless to say, I was tickled pink. Right away I said, 'I'd be real thrilled to work for you. You just say when you want me to start.'

''So, that's how it all began, just chance. I loved the job; it was hardly like working, keeping records and making appointments, and the patients seemed to like me, too. They'd sit in the office and tell me all sorts of things, more than to the doctor I thought sometimes. Some sent me postcards when they went on vacations, or a birthday note. My daddy died, and it made me cry—I hadn't before—when a lot of those people showed up at the funeral home.

"I never had any problem with Dr. Hedrick. You know what I mean?"

"Yes," Mavis said, and the vision of Dr. Hedrick and Charlene's mother entwined upon the sofa came before her eyes.

"He was always a gentleman. With my daddy gone, I guess he kind of took his place, though he wasn't all that older than me, just graying a little around the temples and protruding in the middle. Of course I knew about him and that colored woman. Charlene's mother. Did you know?" She looked quizzically at Mavis.

Mavis shook her head.

"I guess a lot of folks knew about that, too, and talked, though the two of them tried to keep it hidden. I was green as grass at first, didn't suspect a thing, though I wondered why he stayed late so many nights in the office. Far as I knew he didn't have all that much work to do, but he'd murmur something about having to read up on things when I would comment on him working too hard, and I must of thought that was reasonable.

"Then one night—it was fall, just turning cooler, rain drizzling—I left the office without my umbrella. I got all the way downstairs and to the bus stop before I realized I didn't bring it, so I thought I'd better turn back, it might be raining hard by the time I got off the bus. I went inside the building. The elevator operator teased me, 'Can't keep you away from here,' and I laughed as I got off at our floor. Dr. Hedrick was still there, no surprise, the light still on. I went in quietly, not wanting to disturb him.

"I had my own key, so I opened the door and went to my desk. I was already bending over to open the bottom drawer when I heard the voices—low, indistinct. Now, who in the world would he be seeing at this hour? I said to myself, wondering if it was some kind of emergency. I couldn't help but peek in—the office door was cracked—and then I saw them, all twisted up on that red sofa, him as white as biscuit dough, fat belly hanging, and her dusky skin; they gleamed with sweat. I ran out then, forgot my umbrella, and sure enough, I got drenched after I got off the bus. 'What in the world is the matter?' my mama asked when I walked in the door. I must have looked like a witch.''

''That must have been a real shock,'' Mavis said. Again that vision, made more vivid by Alice's words, swam before her eyes.

''Lord yes. I respected him so, he had been so good to me. But I couldn't show I knew a thing. I needed that job. For the first time in my life, I had a little money put aside, and I could buy a new dress without feeling guilty. My mama couldn't work anymore, so she depended on me. I had to pretend like nothing happened, and I did, too. I walked in next morning and opened up and took Dr. Hedrick his mail, saying 'Good day' as pretty as you please, though it was weeks before I could look at the sofa in his office without seeing the two of them twitching there. Some old lady would come in and sit down in that spot, and I'd almost get a fit of giggles, thinking what if she knew what happened there the night before.''

Mavis blushed, thinking that she was glad Dr. Hedrick had not been her doctor.

''In those days, Theda didn't come to the office very much. I had never seen her around town before. Lord knows, I'd of remembered if I did. Even then, she dressed in those strange, foreign-looking clothes, and walked as if there was some invisible line around her that no one could cross. I expect she thought Dr. Hedrick was carrying on with me at first; she was cold as ice, hardly even looked my way when she would come in and announce, 'Miz Hedrick to see the doctor.'

'' 'Yes, ma'am,' I would say, and buzz him on the intercom, and he'd rush out if he didn't have a patient, take her arm, and escort her into the office with all the care in the world. Sometimes through the door, I would hear their voices rise, angry, but I would type on the typewriter loud as I could so as not to hear their words.

"I felt sorry for her, Theda. All that money, clothes, a fine car to ride around in—I would peek out the window when she'd leave and watch Tommie Lee help her in—and yet here she was, with her husband carrying on with the colored woman who cleaned his office. I don't know how she found out, but she knew. She knew."

"Most likely," Mavis said. "Those things get out."

"Maybe that's what started it all, my feeling of concern for her. Maybe she felt it when she came in and we talked. Because she did start coming around more regularly after a while, and her whole way of talking changed. No more, 'Miz Hedrick to see the doctor' kind of thing. She'd come in the door, all done up, gloves and hat, and give me a little smile, like a doll's somehow. Theda had little teeth and they gleamed through her lips. 'How're you?' she'd ask, and sit down in the chair that was at the edge of my desk.

" 'Just fine,' I'd answer, slightly embarrassed, included now in that space around Theda. And she would ask me questions—about my mama, about home, what I did when I wasn't at the office, did I have a boyfriend—and I'd find myself answering back, no longer so ill at ease, talking as if we'd been friends a long time. I had never thought of it before, but I must have been lonely. The girls I went to high school with all were married, had babies, and we lost touch, and I never did date very much. I began to look forward to Theda's visits, could predict the days, and I would dress special those times. 'You got a boyfriend?' my mother would tease. 'No,' I'd answer back, afraid my face was red."

Alice looked away from Mavis for a moment. Mavis smiled at her, hoping to reassure her. Surprisingly, she felt no embarrassment. A warm feeling flowed from her, imbued with a kind of sadness, for the two lonely women who had found some comfort in each other. Alice went on.

"Theda invited me out a few times. 'Why don't we go to lunch?' she asked one day, trying to make it sound real casual. 'I'll pick you up downstairs in the car. You can get

away, can't you? Don't tell the doctor; it'll be our little secret.'

"I could go, of course. Dr. Hedrick never checked up on
me. Sometimes, he went out with other men to lunch and
stayed two hours if he didn't have a patient, coming back
with the scent of cigar smoke hanging on his clothes. I bought
a new dress special for that occasion, and I was already
downstairs in front of the building waiting when that big car
came along. I climbed in, feeling that I entered a new and
strange world, my heart fluttering. At lunch—in the dining
room of the Marshburn Hotel, only ladies lunched there and
we wouldn't see Dr. Hedrick—I could hardly eat a thing, and
I felt the glances of the other women in the room and guessed
there would be whispers afterward.

"I can't even remember now how long things went on like
that—lunches, a ride in the dark backseat of the car, nothing
more. A year or two perhaps. Then Ruth Anne did that silly
thing out in the state park, and it all changed.

"It was funny. Theda asked me all about myself, but she
never told me about her. I could have asked, of course, but
even though I was now inside that barrier Theda kept around
herself, there was still some space between us, and I knew I
risked anger if I intruded. But that time, she poured it all out
to me: the ride in the night, the drinking and the dope, the
picture the principal had held up in his office in broad daylight with Ruth Anne in it bare-chested. 'He thinks it's nothing at all,' Theda cried out about Dr. Hedrick. 'Says she'll
settle down, I shouldn't be so upset. But people will know,
they will talk about me. I can't stand that.' Theda cried. It
was the only time I ever saw her shed a tear. We were in the
car and I took her in my arms. . . . She shook on my shoulder like a child. That's when I knew that I loved her."

Alice sighed, drew back and sat watching Mavis; except
for the ticking of a clock somewhere out in the hallway, a
great silence fell upon the room. When Mavis finally spoke,
her voice was very soft, held out as a comfort. "Love," she
said, thinking how many times she had heard that word in
the past week, used so many ways to convey such different
feelings, "we have to find it where we can. It's never easy. I

suppose the only easy love is the Lord's, and sometimes even that is hard to see. But you have to believe in it, love I mean, look for it. There isn't much else.''

"Then, it was wonderful. Like finding something you only half knew existed, just hope for, though maybe I should have picked up on signs then, little things that would have told me what was to come. I didn't think what Ruth Anne did was so awful. I had seen her only a few times when she would come to the office with Theda, a plain girl, strange in the ugly clothes Theda bought for her, and silent, with eyes that I felt somehow disapproved of me. It sounded just sad, nothing else, her exposing herself that way and being shown around to a bunch of boys in the bathroom at school. But Theda was insistent. 'She has to go away so it'll all die down,' and back then, I wasn't about to contradict a word Theda said.

"Within a week, Ruth Anne was gone, and I could see right away the change in Dr. Hedrick. He had never talked about her or Theda before, but now he would look through his mail eagerly each morning, hoping, I knew, that he might have a letter from Ruth Anne. He sent her money; I mailed the envelopes off myself and could see the tint of green or blue of the checks inside. I don't know if Ruth Anne ever got them . . . maybe she wasn't allowed to at school. But he never got a letter far as I knew. He lost weight, I'm sure of that; his clothes hung. And though I never crept back at night when he stayed late to work, I knew he wasn't messing around with anybody at the office anymore. If he sat there after dark, it was to avoid going home alone to Theda.''

"Such a shame," Mavis said. "People do foolish things."

"Maybe I did, too, but then I didn't care. With Ruth Anne gone, I saw more of Theda. She would invite me to the house, here, on a Saturday afternoon when Dr. Hedrick would be out playing golf. I would wander through these rooms, so silent that it scared me at times, like being in a tomb. But Theda would follow me, talking away, laughing— because she seemed quite happy then, opening her small mouth wide in joy—and we would sit close and talk, though what about I can't remember, until it was time for me to go, a sudden pang in my heart at having to leave.

"I would have been satisfied with that, so much more than I ever had before, but then, all of a sudden, Dr. Hedrick died, a heart attack, and there seemed the chance for so much more. Right after the funeral, Theda, veiled, black as shadows, said, 'You'll move in now, of course. I'll need a companion. People will understand.' It never occurred to me to say no. I packed what few things I wanted to take and put my mama in a nursing home, and moved into this house. I've been here ever since, closed off more each succeeding year."

"Why? Why did things change?"

"I don't know that I can tell. Just small things over time. Theda was still so bitter about Ruth Anne. She always wanted to show off her daughter, but everything she tried—dancing lessons, piano lessons, the special clothes that only made her seem ridiculous to other children—all that failed. Ruth Anne had no grace, no ear for music. 'She took after his side of the family, country clods,' Theda would say about Dr. Hedrick. Probably, if Ruth Anne had been a beauty, the homecoming queen, the best student in the class, Theda would never have sent her away, no matter what she had done."

"Poor girl. If only Theda had given her another chance."

"Yes, but Theda wanted respectability above all, wanted her position as 'The Doctor's Wife,' hated whispers. She must have just closed off a part of her head inside when she let me move in, knowing there would be gossip. After a while I'd tell her I thought she should do more for Ruth Anne, have her here for visits—though I knew Ruth Anne would look daggers through me every minute she was in the house. Theda would glare at me for days, not speaking, but sometimes later she would hand me a check and I would send it off to Ruth Anne. Though I know she hates me, Ruth Anne has me to thank for that trailer she lives in, that piece of land. When Theda found out about the trial and all that had gone on— somebody sent her a newspaper clipping, we never knew who—she was unforgiving, afraid people here would find out. But she let me send the money, and later I finally persuaded her to take out a few gifts now and then, to make some effort.

"But it wasn't just Ruth Anne. It was me. Theda had to rule me the same way she tried to do Ruth Anne. Those clothes. I always hated them, never felt comfortable, and the shopping trips in the car were like torture, people staring. I put out a picture of my mama and daddy in my bedroom, and Theda made me put it away. 'Tacky,' she said, and I didn't argue. After Charlene came and Theda accepted her, afraid not to, afraid Charlene might tell who her daddy was, she seemed to be jealous of the two of us. We'd just be talking in the kitchen—I helped Charlene with the food sometimes, got to feeling so idle sitting around that I could almost scream—and Theda would sneak in like she was going to catch us doing something and make some ugly remark: 'Well, are you two having *fun*?' I could understand then why Dr. Hedrick might have sought out someone who wouldn't tell him to keep his elbows off the table and forbid him to sit in the living room because he would wrinkle the slipcovers.

"Gradually, whatever there was between me and Theda wore away. Like water on a rock, little by little. But I stayed on. Where else would I go?"

Mavis spoke quickly. "You could have found a job, someplace to live."

"It wouldn't be that easy. I was older, had no skills really. I couldn't compete in an office with those young girls. Theda paid for everything—she never gave me money—and I used up what little I had saved paying for my mama before she died in the nursing home. And you get used to things, good things. In the end, I suppose I was just lazy." Alice looked down at her hands. "And maybe I still felt something for Theda. In quiet moments, she could still be loving, before bitterness came. I clung to that, too."

"I understand," Mavis said, though she couldn't say more to comfort Alice. She stirred in her chair; her foot was half-asleep.

Alice moved, too, straining out toward Mavis. "I didn't kill her, you know. I had no reason to. Theda and I had gone on the same way for years and nothing changed. The will was old. She made it soon after I moved in here and she never threatened change. We could have gone on the same way till we were old and doddery.''

Standing, Mavis moved her toes, hoping her foot would not fail her. She knew it was time to go. ''I know you didn't, honey,'' she said. ''I've known all along. Don't you worry. I have a feeling we'll find out soon who it was. Then you won't have to worry.'' Mavis took a step toward the door to the hallway.

''It's funny,'' Alice said. ''You were about our only visitor in all those years. That night a long time ago, when you came to sell magazine subscriptions. We were still reasonably happy then, Theda and I, and when you left, she said, 'What a nice woman. You could probably trust her with anything.' It was surprising, Theda never said much good about anybody. But I remembered that. It's the other reason I asked you to come up. I wanted you to know.''

Mavis did not answer, but smiled and put her arm briefly around Alice's shoulder, as if she had been an unhappy child. Alice touched Mavis's hand, but did not follow her to the door. Mavis let herself out, firmly shutting the door behind her, feeling almost as if she were shutting up Alice in the tomb the woman had imagined.

The rain had stopped, though low-hanging leaves still dripped with a heavy sound. The air had cooled. Mavis shivered and pressed her arms around her body. She walked quickly down the street.

Chapter Twenty-one

Mavis had to return her library books; another day and there would be a fine, and she hated to pay the extra money for what would seem like laziness on her part. Sometimes, when she stood at the desk and saw others put out a dollar or two for books that should have been returned a week before, she gave them a hard look, wondering if they were embarrassed.

"Lovely day," Mrs. Hedgpeth from across the street called out to Mavis as she closed the door and started down the walkway. Mrs. Hedgpeth always was out early of a morning to work in her flowers, which flourished more lavishly than any on the block. Mavis took care of whatever came up in her yard, but she didn't have the patience to spend half the day digging, and besides, her knees couldn't stand all the bending and squatting; she'd be paralyzed.

"It sure is," Mavis answered back, and waved. She clutched the books and her purse in her other arm.

"We needed the rain. My flowers just soaked it up."

Mavis smiled again, but said no more, and turned up the street toward the bus stop. Mrs. Hedgpeth would talk half the day if she had the chance.

It *had* been nice this morning. She was up earlier than usual, having slept soundly all night, not up even once for a trip to the bathroom. Far from upsetting her, the talk with Alice Pate had put a kind of resolution to all she had heard about Theda and Ruth Anne and all that had gone on before. While some small spot in her heart urged her to condemn

Alice and Theda, she did not allow that feeling to spread. They had suffered enough already; Mavis could not press upon them, upon Alice now, any more bitterness. The rain last night had washed everything fresh, and the clean air and morning sunshine, sparkling rather than steamy hot, gave promise of other seasons, better times to come. Mavis walked faster than usual, and the books seemed hardly a weight in her arms.

The library faced the main town square, and Mavis stepped off the bus almost in front of the door. The library had always been there, growing over the years, taking over one space, then another above Morton's Drugstore, and finally spreading out into an office building next door, so that it seemed almost a rambling old house, up a few steps here, down a few there. If you didn't know your way, you'd almost need a map, and even Mavis, who had gone there as long as she could remember, sometimes had to get help to find exactly what she wanted.

She went every week and took away her mysteries. Olivia Raines, the librarian, set the new ones aside for her, though sometimes the gangly teenage boy with unlaced tennis shoes, who worked at the desk, gave them away without knowing, and Mavis would be upset; she liked to see her name on the first line of the new blank tag in the back of the book. Usually, she would be finished with all the books days before they were due, but this week she had been so busy that she had been able to get through only three of the four, and she would have to renew.

The stairs upward were steep, dark, and Mavis stopped midway to catch her breath. There was talk of a new library in the city council, and Mavis hoped that if they did build one, it would be all on the first floor. She hated the thought of change, however, and knew that any new building would be a cold, impersonal place, like some office, rather than the comfortable rooms that had come to seem almost like her own home.

"How're you today, honey?" Mavis said to the small woman who stood behind the desk just inside the door.

Olivia Raines looked up. Older than Mavis by years, she

had a tight, pinched face with two livid spots of rouge on each cheek, her only gesture to makeup. She wore half-glasses, but seemed always to be looking over the top of them, and her lips were constantly pursed, as if she were about to *shush* people for talking any moment. "Fine," she said, but her expression did not change. Mavis laid the books down on the desk.

"I've got to renew this one," she said, pointing. Olivia slightly raised her eyebrows; Mavis never renewed. "I've been busy," Mavis added, surprised at even that small change in Olivia's face. Olivia opened the back of the book, then very carefully took a stamp from the rack where others dangled, perfectly aligned, and touched the paper slip inside the back cover. "Only a week's renewal," she said, as if Mavis didn't know. "There are others waiting."

"You have anything new that's good?" It was a ritual question. Olivia always had Mavis's books beneath the counter, waiting.

"Sure enough. I'll have them ready when you leave." Olivia turned away.

That was part of the ritual, too. Mavis never just went up the library stairs, returned her old books and picked up the new ones and left; instead, she went to sit in the large main room where there were soft leather sofas, so old that the covering was dappled dark, like forest leaves, colors merging. On racks by the side were newspapers from other towns and cities, even places up North; and there were magazines, too, the ones that Mavis sold years ago but could never afford to buy. She flicked through them, looking at the beautiful clothes, houses, and let her mind drift, half dreaming that she moved in such places, almost able to feel soft silk against her back, the heaviness of jewels on her fingers. It was silly, she knew, but she enjoyed that brief escape. "My visits are like going to the picture show," she told Dale once when he came to pick her up at the library and found her half-asleep, and teased her about her daydreaming. "I can make the story any way I want," she said, "don't have to see the ugliness they show nowadays on the screen. No harm in that, is there?"

A few others occupied the seating area this morning. Most Mavis knew, regular patrons like her, who had their own routines, favorite periodicals, and would be quite upset if someone else took the magazine or paper they automatically reached for when they sat down. Nodding to them (because no one spoke there, with Olivia's sharp eyes upon them), Mavis sat down on a low sofa that gave out a faint sigh with her weight. She sat a moment, admiring the bowl of bright zinnias in the center of the table in front of her, Olivia's work. Flowers, it would seem, were her only pleasure; she provided them from early spring till frost.

Mavis reached for a newspaper first. Not the local one. She got that every evening and read it after supper, noting deaths, divorces, transfers of land. Here, she read the city papers that gave the national news, at least as much as she was interested in—that, and what was on the nightly news on TV (she turned up the sound then and watched), was all she needed, all she could stand. With the world in such a shape, you didn't really want to be aware of everything that went on.

MURDER. The word caught her eye in a headline. For a while she had forgotten Theda's death, all that she had learned in the past few days. The word pressed down on her and took away some of the joy of the day. But then, there were always such stories in the paper, death and killing; she couldn't escape them.

It was then that the idea came—why hadn't she thought of it before? The newspapers. The ones from the city, they would have carried stories about Ruth Anne and what happened with Hart those years before. Alice had mentioned the clippings Theda had received. If only Mavis could see them, perhaps they would tell her something, provide a clue that would help solve Theda's death.

Pushing herself up, she dropped the paper, and the wooden rod that held it clattered against the table. A man across from her jumped as if struck and looked at her with anxious eyes. Mavis did not even apologize, but replaced the paper on the rack and went over to Olivia's desk. Ignoring Olivia's frown, she said, "I want to look at some old newspapers, Olivia. How can I do that?"

Olivia looked at Mavis as if she had lost her mind. "What kind of old papers? What for?"

"The *Journal*." Mavis pointed to the center of the room where she had been sitting, as if Olivia should know. "Years ago. Something I want to look up."

"They're on microfilm," Olivia said, her voice prideful. "We usually reserve them for scholars."

Mavis did not back down. "I've paid taxes in this town for I don't know how long, and I guess I've got as much right as any *scholar* to look at what you've got here."

"Now don't go getting on your high horse, Mavis Lashley. I reckon you can see the films. Just a minute."

Olivia fumbled in a drawer and found a key, motioned for Mavis to follow her. Quickly, she walked through several rooms with Mavis hurrying behind her, until she arrived at a rear door which said PRIVATE, PERSONNEL ONLY. Olivia stopped and inserted the key into the lock. When the door opened, Mavis took a step back, surprised by the row of gray machines lined up there under fluorescent lights like a band of strange animals. There were no windows, and this bleak, airless room was so unlike the rest of the library (homey there, like your own living room) that she could hardly believe she was in the same place. "My goodness," she said, "I didn't know this part of the library even existed."

"We're not just backwoods," Olivia said, making a snuffling sound through her nose. "Now just what year do you want? The files are over there." She pointed to shelves, each one filled with small boxes neatly labeled on the side.

Mavis had not thought of that: How in the world would she know when everything happened? Standing there in the middle of the floor, she felt foolish; any minute now, Olivia would start tapping her foot. Already she was saying, "I haven't got all day. That young'un out there'll give away half the library if I'm not there to stand over him. What year?"

Quickly, Mavis tried to calculate. From what Ruth Anne said, her girl was no more than a baby when she tried to leave Hart and he tried to kill her. Now she must be six years old or thereabouts. Mavis subtracted a year and came up with a date and blurted it out to Olivia. Without a word, the woman turned and went to the shelves and pulled out a box. While Mavis watched, she went to one of the machines, switched it on and inserted the film. "There," Olivia said. "You just turn this knob forward or backward, whichever way you want to go. Don't mess with the film when you get through. I'll put it back on the shelf later. Turn off the machine and the lights." Olivia pointed overhead, and before Mavis could ask one question, she turned and went out the door.

Mavis hurried to the machine, sat, and put her head inside the boxlike cover and started spinning the knob. Excited, she scanned the headlines and felt as if she moved in some space machine back through time. She would stop, read part of a story, then realize this had nothing to do with her search, and start again, moving the film forward. But then once more, something entirely irrelevant would catch her eye and she would pause and begin to read. My, how things had changed in just a little while, she thought. Five, six years, you never would have thought it.

The spool of film ran down, and she began to get discouraged. Perhaps she had been wrong about that child; children grew bigger these days, and Mavis never was around them very much anymore. She had stopped helping out with the nursery at church on Sunday mornings because the crying bothered her. Perhaps Ruth Anne had been mistaken about the time; she had gone through so much, who could blame her? She sighed. If she wanted to look at another year, she would have to call Olivia, who would make Mavis feel like a fool. This probably was just another wild goose chase.

Then she saw the word FIRE in heavy black type. She jerked the film to a halt and could read the full headline: WOMAN SET ON FIRE BY JEALOUS MATE. Her heart almost stopped beating at the sight of it. Before, while Ruth Anne was describing what had happened to her, Mavis had listened, understood, but the words had little reality for her; now, seeing them in black and white, in the paper, all the horror of it descended upon her, as if she witnessed the scenes herself. She bent closer to read.

The story repeated Ruth Anne's words, telling how she had been planning to leave Hart, a former preacher who had made her prostitute herself on the street. When she had gone back for her children, he had attacked her, set fire to her and left her for dead, and if it hadn't been for Ruth Anne's quick thinking, she wouldn't have survived. As it was, she was in serious condition at the hospital, with burns on a good part of her body; if she recovered there would be scars. Her children had been placed in a foster home by the Department of Children's Services. Hart was in jail.

That was only the first story. Others appeared in later editions, reporting Ruth Anne's condition, her gradual recovery, the plastic surgery that was done. They were waiting on her to try Hart, who still remained in jail. Somebody managed to get hold of the foster mother, and she told how the children cringed at first every time she spoke to them and cried out in the night with terrible nightmares. Mavis skipped forward eagerly and found the account of the trial.

And that part was brief. Ruth Anne wouldn't testify. She had been mute in the hospital on the subject and they hadn't really pushed her. Now, even though she had to walk bent over with a cane, recovering from skin grafts, she just shook her head when they asked her to testify against Hart. Finally came the letter pleading with the judge (because they went ahead and tried him even without Ruth Anne's testimony, and he was convicted) to forgive him.

Mavis sighed at the sadness of it all, thinking that Ruth Anne had changed very little, still talking of love after so much hate. She started to switch off the light and go back out into the homelike atmosphere of the library. This cold room, the harsh light shining down, depressed her, and she wanted to sit again on the soft cushions of the sofa out by the magazine rack, relaxed. Then she noticed at the bottom of the column the words "continued on page 14," and, casually, she turned the knob until she found the page. There, staring at her, were pictures. Old ones, must be, of Ruth Anne, which they had not released before (still hoping, perhaps, she might testify; now they didn't care), her face bruised, swollen so that Mavis would not have recognized her, her ear bandaged where she wouldn't let them fix it, a permanent badge of the degradation she had suffered. And even a brief glimpse of the children being herded into a car, a woman trying to shield them from cameras. Down at the bottom of the page was a picture of Hart taken stark full face, with numbers beneath his chin, eyes haunting, his beard scruffy, all shape gone.

And at that moment Mavis knew what had happened, recognized what she had not seen before, plain as the nose on her face. She knew who killed Theda. How in the world would she ever prove it?

Chapter
Twenty-two

The dedication of the Mission was to be that afternoon at two o'clock. Getting ready, putting on a thin dress with a flower design and her one strand of good pearls, a gift from John years ago, Mavis was glad she had not volunteered to help.

"But honey," Zeena Campbell had protested. "It's just going to be the grandest thing." During the week, Zeena and some of the other ladies volunteered in the Mission kitchen to help with the evening meal for the homeless, and nobody was a bit surprised when she took over and organized the refreshments for the dedication. "There'll be a representative from the mayor's office, and probably one of those TV trucks from Channel Five, and I'm sure the paper will want photographs. We're serving frozen Kool-Aid with ginger ale poured over it, and one of the ladies is making cheese-straws—there'll be finger sandwiches of all sorts. Now don't you want to help?"

Zeena had caught Mavis in the foyer just before she was going into church a few Sundays before, and Mavis wanted to turn away, embarrassed by Zeena's shrill voice. "Not this time," she said, and tried to smile. "I'll come, but I'll just stay in the background. I have my job there, but it's not very important. You go on and get somebody else to help." Zeena gave a little pout and then turned away.

When Mavis arrived, she noticed a white-painted TV van, with the equipment on top, parked in the driveway next to the Mission. Zeena had been right. Well, maybe this was sort of special. The Mission certainly had grown in just a few years under Reverend Simms's direction. Out of nothing, he had built it up to where everybody recognized what a great service it was to the poor people around town. He got a lot of contributions to remodel the old church building and to provide food, and there was talk of buying a farm somewhere outside of town and using it as a place where alcoholics could go and get off that poison, so that they could return to society again.

Mavis entered the foyer near the office, but instead of taking her usual route to the back room where the clothes were stored, she entered the main sanctuary. Already, a large group was gathered there, some of them as finely dressed as folks you might see at the country club, Reverend Simms's big contributors, she supposed. Mavis wondered what they would think of Zeena's Kool-Aid punch and soggy finger sandwiches. On the side, people from the TV station strung cords, running around with earphones on their heads, and in the rear, on the platform, stood four men in matching cream-colored suits with bright blue bow ties that Mavis knew had to be the gospel quartet that was going to sing as a part of the dedication service.

Then Mavis saw Reverend Simms right in the middle of that bunch of people, like a dark bird, dressed in a brand-new suit. (Usually he wore a shiny one, so old you expected his elbows to go through the sleeves any minute). He talked and moved his arms, more animated than Mavis had ever seen him, though she had to admit she had never heard him preach and wondered whether he might easily get worked up when he was preaching to the winos and shout like a revivalist. At his side, hands clasped and eyes turned down, but with a look of utter delight on her face, stood Sue Dillon, released from her duties in the Mission office and shining now in Reverend Simms's reflected glory. Lordy, she looks almost pretty, Mavis thought, dressed in a pink cotton pique dress with white banding on the collar and cuffs. There was a sparkle of gold at her neck, and Mavis guessed it was a cross, some gift from her childhood that the people out at the Bible college probably wouldn't have condoned had they seen it around her neck.

"Hey there, Mavis!" It was Zeena. Mavis looked to the far corner of the sanctuary, behind one of the cameramen, and saw the refreshment table. Zeena stood there and waved, dressed bright as a rainbow. Weakly, Mavis raised her arm and waved back. Several people turned to stare at her, startled by Zeena's voice. For a moment, Reverend Simms also stopped talking and looked at Mavis, but then he turned away.

Well, she might as well get it over with—go over and get a cup of that pale-looking punch and eat a cheesestraw; at least they might taste good and, hopefully, there wouldn't be anything too foreign in them. With all the excitement going on, Zeena and the others would forget her, and Mavis could go about her search, the real reason she had come here this afternoon.

"Mavis, I've always liked that dress." Zeena touched Mavis on the arm. Mavis noticed pink lipstick on her front teeth. "It looks just as cool as can be."

"Thank you, Zeena." Mavis knew she should pay some compliment, but she couldn't get out the words.

"Let me get you some punch." Zeena pulled a little on Mavis's arm. "It's real cold, though I'm worried all the Kool-Aid will melt before the service is over."

"What are they going to do?" Mavis bit into a cheesestraw and decided it wasn't too bad.

"Well, now is the open house part with the refreshments. Then there will be some hymns by the Four Harmoniers—that's the quartet—they performed on the 'Old Fashion Revival Hour' once on TV and are in great demand. The mayor's assistant will make a little speech, and then Reverend Simms will lead us all in prayer and make a few remarks. If there's anything left to eat, people can have more refreshments when it's over."

"I may not be able to stay the whole time," Mavis said. If she disappeared she didn't want anyone looking for her.

"That'd be a shame," Zeena said. "I'm sure it'll be inspirational."

Just then, one of the other women came in from the kitchen

with more frozen Kool-Aid, and Zeena turned to help her put it in the punch bowl. Red dots splashed out on the yellow paper tablecloth. Mavis turned away, looking back toward the center of the room, which seemed brighter now; perhaps they had installed additional lights for the cameras. Reverend Simms and Sue Dillon still stood in the middle of a little circle, both talking almost animatedly. A strange sound came from the back of the platform, rather like a pig squealing, and for a moment everyone stopped talking and stared. It was the Harmoniers warming up with a few notes. People laughed and started talking again. Soon the program would start, Mavis thought. Now would be a good time to get away. Zeena seemed to have gone back to the kitchen, and no one would notice that Mavis had departed.

She set down her plastic punch cup on the table and smiled at the two ladies who stood there with ladles in their hands. "More?" one asked, just moving her lips to shape the words. Mavis shook her head no and turned around. More people were coming in. A woman in a perky suit entered with two identical-looking young men behind her, paused a minute, then pointed to the front and hurried forward as if she had just been let loose from somewhere. The mayor's representative, Mavis knew, hoping to get votes and glad, no doubt, the city didn't have to pay for the food the Mission gave out to all those winos.

Mavis walked quickly down the side aisle to the back of the sanctuary, then across and out to the foyer again. Cooler air struck her, and she paused a minute in the pale light and put her handkerchief to her lips; the scent was refreshing. For the first time, here alone, even though there were dozens of people quite nearby, she felt afraid. Was it because she, of all those people, had murder on her mind instead of a simple service dedicating a building that attempted to serve the needs of the poor? She shook her head.

Quickly, Mavis moved into the corridor where the offices were located. There was sudden quiet, no buzz of excited voices. She walked down the hallway and could hear her footsteps. The front office was empty—Sue was away from her desk, out enjoying the limelight for what must be the first time in her life—and Reverend Simms's door was closed. The clothing room was never locked. Mavis pushed open the door and the old smell of clothes filled her nostrils despite the cologne on her handkerchief. She looked around. Everything was the same, yet she felt that something new awaited her here, some revelation. Perhaps the Lord was guiding her. Putting down her purse, she bent over the bags of clothing, some new but unremarkable, others there still unsorted from her last visit when she had no time to finish. Nothing unusual as far as she could see.

She was about to turn away, thinking that she was just being foolish, she had read too many detective stories, when she thought about the closet at the rear of the room. There she stored the completely unuseable clothes, rags really, that people should be ashamed of sending anywhere, just looking for a tax deduction. Mavis piled up the junk in the closet, and when it became too much, she got Sam Jones, the janitor, to come in and take the whole mess out to the trash in back.

Picking her way through the shopping bags and boxes of clothing, Mavis approached the door. She had to move several bags, but she was finally able to open it. The musty scent became even stronger. Standing back, she looked at the items discarded there. Again, nothing unusual caught her eye. Lord knows what she expected to find. A clue? Probably she was just fooling herself.

She was about to close the door when she noticed a piece of fabric that seemed familiar, though she couldn't say why. She could have tossed it there herself, yet why would it stand out? Bending, almost losing her balance, she reached out for the material: a dress, she realized, when she finally pulled it from beneath the other cast-off clothing that nearly covered it. Brown, with a pattern of tiny leaves, an old woman's dress from another time, but not ragged at all, bright jet buttons running down the front. Certainly, Mavis hadn't put it there. The dress would have done quite nicely for some older lady, and they'd snap it up at an antique store for those young people that got themselves up in old clothes as if they were children raiding their parents' closet for dress up.

The dress seemed to be caught on something; Mavis tugged. It gave a little, and she pulled some more, trying not to rip the material. When it came loose, she almost fell backward, only then realizing what had held the dress in the closet: a hat, big and round, like a cartwheel, a dark muddy color.

Of course, Mavis knew whose it was. Theda's. Who else would wear a hat like that, except maybe some ladies up North where fashions were different. At first, Mavis wondered if Theda had left it that day when Tommie Lee drove her to the Mission. But why was it stuffed way back in the closet? Who would have done such a thing? And, surely, that brown dress, so old-timey, was not one of Theda's. She wouldn't have been caught dead in it.

Mavis caught her breath. She recognized the cloth, the sturdy brown material with leaves running through it. She had seen the pattern in the picture Dale had showed her of Theda laid in the morgue, the sash around her neck like a vine, strangling her. That belt came from the dress Mavis held now in her hands. It was what killed Theda, the belt—and the hands that held it so tightly.

"Did you find what you were looking for?"

The voice came from the doorway. Mavis had heard no one in the hall, intent upon her discovery in the closet. She remained kneeling and turned her head. Reverend Simms stood there, smiling at her.

Mavis tried to stuff the hat between two bags of clothing. "I was just straightening up a few things." She tried to laugh. "I'm not much one for ceremonies, so I didn't stay in there for the speeches."

"Yes, I saw you. I saw you leave. That's why I came out."

"Well, you didn't have to do that. You go right back out there and take your place on the podium. They must be about ready for you." Mavis wanted to stand up straight; her knees were throbbing. But she remained half kneeling, with her body bent over the concealing bags.

"I will," he said. "But I have to take care of something here first."

"What's that?"

Reverend Simms continued to smile, but his voice sounded

very solemn. "You know what I mean." He reached back and pulled the door closed behind him, still looking at Mavis.

"Yes, I suppose I do." Mavis stood up, no longer attempting to hide the dress, the hat.

"You know, don't you?"

Mavis sighed. "Guess, maybe, is more like it. It was hard to believe."

"How?"

"The papers. Newspapers. I looked them up in the library."

Reverend Simms laughed, throwing back his head. "The same way as Theda. She said someone sent them to her in the mail. Don't you think I've changed?"

"Some," Mavis said. "No beard. But the eyes don't change. I would know them anywhere."

He stared intently at her. "You didn't guess before?"

"I should have. The children look like you. They reminded me of somebody the first day I saw them, but I never could say who. Now I know." She stared back at him, saw his eyes darken and become the demented eyes of Hart in the newspaper. "Why did you kill her? Theda? What could she do to you?"

"What could she *do*?" Reverend Simms's voice was a shout. "Everything! Ruin me. Take all this away." He gestured vaguely toward the auditorium, past the doorway. He moved forward, leaning just slightly. Mavis had nowhere to go.

"Do you know what it's like in prison? Did you ever eat mush with bugs in it, sleep on a filthy mattress with no cover to keep you warm? I couldn't even be with other people. They threatened to kill me, said I wasn't worth letting live." Little drops of spittle had formed at the corners of Reverend Simms's mouth—Hart's mouth—and threatened to run down. Mavis wanted to turn her head away, but she continued to stare at him.

"But I got out. They couldn't give me much time in jail when Ruth Anne wouldn't testify against me, and I behaved. What else could I do? The guards didn't like me any better than the prisoners, so I didn't give them a chance to beat me, mess me up. And all that time, I thought how I would get out and nothing would stop me then. I would not be hungry or cold or afraid again, no matter what it took.''

Hart moved still closer, but Mavis could see no further than the surface of his eyes, as if, beneath, he looked somewhere else, at scenes unknown to her.

''I knew where Ruth Anne was. She kept in touch, even visited a few times, with all the other prisoners watching and making catcalls, wondering why she still loved me.''

Mavis jumped at the word ''love'' as if she had been slapped. Hart must have seen her, because he laughed. ''Yes, *loved me*, she always had. She was the only one. Ever. And I loved her, too, as best I could. I needed her. Without her, there would be no one.''

''What about the children? Did you love them?''

Hart pulled back. He wiped his mouth and appeared to be thinking. ''Sometimes, when they behaved, when they weren't too much trouble. I planned to raise them up right, to fear the Lord, and if that required a belting once in a while, I didn't see no harm.''

Mavis thought of the dark smudge on the girl's cheek when she had seen her out by Ruth Anne's trailer and shuddered to herself. ''Why did you come back here?'' she asked. She didn't want to talk about the children any longer.

''Where else could I go? Ruth Anne's was the only place. And I thought no one around here would know. They all read the local papers, who died and who got married. They wouldn't recognize me without the beard, wearing decent clothes, even if they did see pictures.

''Then that bitch came here!'' Hart almost spat out the words. He picked up a scarf from one of the bags of clothing in front of him and began twisting it around his hands. ''Came prancing in here in those fine clothes of hers to demand a receipt for the finery she brought in for the poor and needy. I was as nice as can be to her—I didn't know Theda, Ruth Anne never had a picture—and then she recognized me, just as you did. I knew it right away. I could tell from her eyes.

"She didn't hide it. 'Write down my name on the receipt,' she said to me . . . and then gave it: *Theda Hedrick*. 'You must know how to spell it,' she said. I still didn't let on anything then, wrote out the receipt the way I would have for anyone, and she took it as if she were grasping a piece of garbage, afraid to cover her fingerprints with mine on that little piece of paper, and I hated her with all my heart."

He paused then, wiped his brow and swallowed. Mavis watched him, thinking of tales she had heard as a child. Look at a snake and it won't strike. She couldn't turn away from his eyes.

"She came back, of course, a few days later—called first and said she wanted to see me. She marched in like she owned the place and sat down in my office. She had on that hat"—he pointed to the bags and the hat sprung up between them—"had her face painted up bright as a harlot's. And began to tell me what I'd have to do. *Her* tell *me*! After I had built up this place, gone from a filthy storefront with three drunks listening to my preaching to a real church—no tent, no winds rolling through the dust and country folks shouting on summer nights. Who are they waiting for out there to hear speak, thanking folks for their donations and support? Reverend Lonnie Simms. You know, you saw. Cameras and someone the mayor sent.

"Do you think I would let her take that away? Because that's what she wanted, what she *demanded*. Sitting there as polite as if she were sipping tea in some rich lady's living room, she said, 'You will have to leave, of course. I can't run the risk of people finding out. You're getting to be known. I read in the paper about the dedication coming up. You know how those reporters are, always digging. They might find out what happened, and then it would be all over the front page. I can't risk that. Not that embarrassment. I prayed every night while the trial was going on that no one hereabouts would find out, and only took a relaxed breath when they put you in prison. That's the end of it, I thought. Ruth Anne will go away—I even gave her money to leave that city—and she will never see him again.

" 'But I was wrong, I suspect. She must be the one that

got you here, suggested that you could start up the religious business again. I wouldn't put it past her. Maybe it was her way of getting even with me. I don't know anymore. I don't care. You must leave.'

"I did try to reason with her. I pointed out the good, real good, we were doing. I wasn't greedy, wasn't taking much from what was given. Ruth Anne wouldn't accept it, even if I tried to make us rich. But Theda didn't hear me. Just sat there with her little mouth screwed up in a half-smile, as if I were something she wouldn't walk on.

"She got up to go. 'I'll give you a week,' she said. 'Just leave and nobody will be the wiser. But if you don't I'll go to the police and tell them about you, talk to others in important places, and they'll see to it that this place is closed down. In spite of your dedication, there must be violations, permits. My name still means something in this town. You'd better do as I say.'

"She walked slowly, not even turning around to see whether or not I followed her. I knew then what I had to do, so I ran here to this room—the door was open—and grabbed the first thing I saw, the belt from that dress you were holding, and then I went after Theda. She hadn't even reached the foyer. I put it around her neck from behind, and even then I think she didn't believe what was happening; a little shiver went through her body. She really didn't struggle very much, too fat, I thought, too satisfied, sure that someone would rescue her. Only her hat fell off and rolled around on the floor before it flopped down. I dropped Theda beside it.

"Then I had to decide what to do. I could see that big car outside, but no driver in it. I thought no one would notice for a while; it was late in the afternoon and I could wait till near dark. I dragged Theda back here and just left her; she looked like another bundle of clothing. Later, I pulled the car up nearer the door and it wasn't too hard getting her inside. Nobody saw. There aren't too many people around here after dark—too afraid. After that, it was easy. I decided just to dump her somewhere, and I wanted to get rid of that car as soon as I could in case I was seen. Nobody would expect the likes of me to be driving such a fancy car.

"Any place would do, so I stopped the car by the cornfield and dragged her into the rows, and I left her. Left the car, too, and came back to town. It's not far. When I got back here it was late, but that's when I discovered the hat, Theda's, still lying on the floor in the foyer. I bundled the dress around it and threw them both in the closet. I really had forgotten about them until I saw you holding them in your hands."

Hart sighed. His eyes looked tired to Mavis. "I suppose there will have to be another body dropped off somewhere." He began to wind the scarf that he had picked up tighter around his fists. "You'll tell, won't you? You'll ruin it all."

Mavis felt no fear. It was as if she talked to someone who was very ill and needed to see a doctor. "That doesn't matter now. Why don't you give it all up, tell? Maybe they'll understand. Theda was at fault, threatening you that way."

"No!" he almost screamed. "I will not go back to that prison, any prison. I'd rather die. But I'll kill you before that happens. You should have stayed out of all this, kept away from Ruth Anne. We had a sort of life out there in the woods, nearly happiness at times. Women sticking their noses into things—it always gets them in trouble."

Hart moved closer, the scarf—bright blue with crimson triangles, silk—held taut in front of him. His eyes were glazed, as if he could not see. Mavis tried to draw back, but her legs were held by the bags and boxes around her. She didn't think to scream.

Then she had a thought. Bending, she grabbed the dress and hat she had been holding and, with all her might, flung them at Hart. The brown fabric covered his head and the hat hit his arms. "Bitch," he screamed at her, fumbling at the cloth that clung to him. With a bound, Mavis jumped over the boxes and rushed past him, shoving him so that he lost his balance and, with a great roar (surely a sound a devil might make), sprawled over the clothing onto the floor.

Mavis pulled at the door and for a moment was terrified that it was locked . . . she couldn't budge it, the wood was swollen by the humid weather. Then she pulled again and it opened, and she ran through, slamming the door behind her. She turned left and ran down the hallway toward the rear of the building where there was a door opening onto the pulpit. The crowd would be there, waiting for Hart to give his message—the photographers, the TV cameramen—and surely he could not hurt her in front of all those people. For all his blind fury, Hart would not follow her out onto the stage in front of them. But she had to hurry. Already she could hear him pulling on the stuck door just behind her.

Oh, dear Jesus! The doors to the pulpit were locked, heavy metal double doors, locked to prevent any interruption in the ceremony. Mavis banged on them and opened her mouth to scream, but just then she heard the whine of the portable organ and the sound of shrill voices singing in close harmony:

> There is a fountain filled with blood,
> Drawn from Emmanuel's veins. . . .

No one would hear her over the noise. What in the world could she do? She couldn't turn back: Hart was there, already scrambling through the door of the clothing room. She would have to go on.

She rarely had gone down this hallway before, but remembered that there was a door to the kitchen on the other side of the building. Half running, her knees watery, she moved down the hallway toward the door, shadowy, at the end. The scent of food hit her, the tuna salad that Zeena had spread on dry little rounds of bread for the refreshments, the old smell of cabbage they must have served to the needy week after week; she almost vomited. She pushed on the door and tried to turn the handle, and then began to cry: it, too, was locked. They wouldn't hear her; the kitchen would be empty now, all the ladies out front listening to the Harmoniers and waiting for Reverend Simms to come make his speech.

Only one other possibility remained. Another door opened off just to her left. She could hear Hart breathing around the corner, standing in front of the clothing room trying to decide which way she had run. She tried the door, praying aloud, "Dear Jesus, make him go the other way. Let him think I ran outside." Sudden coolness hit her, and the even older smell of food, as the door opened. In the vague light from below she could see steps going down.

With not another thought, she quickly slipped through the door and pushed it closed, hoping the hinges would not squeak. For just a moment she felt safe, enclosed; perhaps Hart did not know of this old cellar door, would not think of it. But then she thought, he knows every inch of this place; it is his. Her only hope was that he would think she had run the other way and would go in pursuit of her outside the building. In the meantime, if she waited for a few minutes to be sure he didn't follow her, she could go back out into the hallway, scurry around to the sanctuary, and find safety there.

Slowly, she pushed her foot across the step, felt the edge, went down. The stale smell became stronger. Surely this was the old cellar, used to store food years ago. Perhaps the furnace was there, too, though everything was covered in dust, as if no one had passed by in ages. She continued down, able to see a little more. The windows, filmed with cobwebs, were at ground level, but must have been behind low-growing shrubbery since the little light that came in was hazy, watery green, like something at the bottom of the sea. Mavis held tightly to the rail and moved to the bottom of the stairs.

What was that noise? A flickering somewhere in a corner. Mavis shuddered. A rat—she knew it. Well, there were worse things, and she could stand it for a few minutes. She looked around. A few pieces of old furniture were scattered about: a sofa and a chair, stained stuffing spilling out of them. There was a long church pew in one corner and a kitchen table, ghostly white. Behind her, past the stairs, she saw only darkness; the windows ended.

Then she heard another noise, fainter even than the rat's scrambling; surely nothing more than the squeak of this old building swelling with summer dampness. She looked around her, but realized that the sound came from above. Perhaps she was under the kitchen and someone had come back there to bring in an empty platter, even though the ceremonies were going on. Mavis shook her head. No use scaring herself to death; there was silence now. Still, she realized suddenly, that despite the coolness there were rings of dampness beneath her arms.

Again the sound came, a scraping, two surfaces rubbed together. She looked up once more and, this time, she saw a crack of light. The door had opened, was being shut again. The line of light had disappeared.

Oh, dear Jesus! He was up there, waiting at the top of the stairs. Waiting for his eyes to become accustomed to the darkness. Then he would start coming down the stairs. Mavis moved quickly, back into the rear of the cellar. Her own eyes had adjusted, and she could see vague shapes, shelves behind the stairs. She tried not to slide her feet over the cement, hoping that if she made a slight sound Hart would think it was a rat (though her heart was pounding so hard that she felt he would surely hear it). Moving further, she held out her hand, found rough wood, and little by little, let her fingers reach out onto the shelf, praying for a weapon, knowing there could be little there.

Hart's step was light on the stairs, but she could not mistake it. No creaky building sounds, no scurrying animal; it was slow, deliberate. He seemed to know that he had time, there was no way out for her. Now she could see his feet, the steps open in front of her. His white socks shone brighter than the porcelain tabletop in the corner, and his sharply pointed shoes were darker than the shadows. He continued his slow descent.

"I know you're here."

She expected the words, almost holding her breath until they came. She breathed out and it was like a sigh of relief.

"You were a fool. We locked the back doors to keep people from coming in and interrupting. Wouldn't that have been entertaining"—Hart gave a low laugh—"all those folks standing around out there waiting for a speech and you coming in like a crazy woman with me behind you? Now that would be a fine picture for the paper."

Hart was at the bottom of the stairs now. He waited. Mavis could see the outline of his dark body and it looked relaxed, like that of someone casually waiting for a friend on a street corner, nothing else in mind.

"Let's not carry this on any longer." Hart turned, and Mavis could see the bright scarf in his hands, though the rest of him remained a silhouette. "I will try to make this as painless as possible. Don't you believe in the Lord? I thought all you church folks were so eager to get up yonder with Jesus. I'm only doing you a favor." He laughed again, louder, and the sound made a small echo in the corners of the cellar.

Mavis tried to pull back further, but the shelves blocked her. Still, her fingers searched behind her. She touched something moist, so that she almost jerked them away, but then she felt deeper. For just a moment she turned to look behind her, trying to peer into the darkness, but she could see nothing, and when she turned back again, Hart had already come nearer to her. She could hear his breathing.

"I know you're there. You can't go anywhere. There's just the furnace room, but the door's in the other corner. And even if you could get to it, it would only be another dead end."

Mavis gave one last lunge, no longer caring about any noise; Hart could probably see her outline now, anyway. Her fingers struck something, far back in the corner of the shelf. Glass, a jar, probably an old canning jar that someone left there years ago. Her fingers grasped the rim and she pulled it out, ready to fling it at Hart. "Go away," she said, knowing how foolish that must sound. "They'll find out, they'll know. You can't get away with this."

"I'll take my chances." Hart was directly in front of her now. She could smell his breath, peppermint covering up a fetid scent. "You couldn't have told anyone. You didn't know till just a few minutes ago. They'll find you in another field, just as they did Theda."

As he reached for her, Mavis brought down the jar, aiming for Hart's head. But her arms stopped, were held rigid; Hart's fingers on her wrists tightening. The jar dropped on the floor with a great sound, and she could feel prickles of glass piercing her hose.

Then the fingers relaxed, and she waited for the feeling of cool silk around her neck, choking, and then blackness. The blackness came, but not before she heard a great roar, the cry of a wounded animal, and saw a spray of crimson fly across the pale light of the cellar like fireworks in a summer sky.

Chapter
Twenty-three

"Am I in Heaven yet?"

Later, when Dale would tease her about saying such a thing, Mavis would declare that she was dead serious, not trying to fool folks at all.

"No, I guess not. If you were, I probably wouldn't be here." She opened her eyes and saw Dale's own staring intently at her, filled with concern, though he tried to put a little smile on his lips. "You okay?" he asked, and stroked her hand.

"Well, I guess so." Mavis felt around with her other hand, expecting blood, perhaps, or broken bones. She touched her neck and felt nothing more than the pearls she had fastened on earlier in the afternoon. How long ago that seemed now.

"What are *you* doing here?" Mavis raised her head up and looked sharply at Dale.

"The paper sent me at the last minute. One of the other photographers was supposed to cover the dedication, but her baby-sitter didn't show up, so they called me. I was out there in the sanctuary when we heard the cry."

Oh, Lord, Mavis thought; she had almost forgotten Hart and that terrible scene in the basement. She struggled to sit up, with Dale helping her, though she wanted to tell him to stop, she could do it herself. But then she relaxed against his arms, realizing she still felt a little faint. "Well, I declare," she said, looking around. She was in Reverend Simms's—Hart's—office, lying on a small sofa there. She had never actually come into this room, just passed by as she was going to the clothing room and said "Howdy" to him as she passed. It was like a cell, she realized, no windows and just that plain sofa and a desk and chair and bookcase behind them, one picture on the wall of Jesus knocking at the gate.

"You want something to drink?" Dale stood up from his kneeling position in front of her. "I can go out to the kitchen and get something from the ladies. They're real worried about you, wanted to come in here, but Charles Morgan said you weren't to be disturbed."

"No, I'm all right." Mavis sat up straighter, putting her feet down on the floor. Her head no longer swam. "What is Charles Morgan doing here?"

"What do you think he's doing here? With all that commotion, didn't you think they'd call the police?"

"I don't rightly know. Last thing I remember, Reverend Simms was coming down those stairs after me . . . and was about to strangle me the same way he did Theda. Did you know that?"

"Yes, we do now."

"Why didn't he do the job? We were all alone, he was ready." Then she remembered the splash of red and almost cried out.

"Not quite alone," Dale said. He went behind the desk and pulled out the chair, set it in front of Mavis, sat down. "Somebody else followed you down into the cellar."

"Who? I didn't see a soul."

"No, I'm not surprised. You had all you could do dealing with just Reverend Simms. But somebody else was listening at the top of those stairs and then followed him down, while you were talking I guess." Dale made a gesture toward the doorway, as if someone stood there. "Sue Dillon, she was the one—the girl who worked here at the Mission."

"Well, I declare, that poor thing. She must have been scared to death."

"Maybe, but she saved your life."

"How? What do you mean?"

"She stabbed him. Reverend Simms. Stabbed him in the back with a letter opener she must have picked up in the office. She slipped out of the sanctuary after Reverend Simms disappeared, but nobody thought anything about it at first, thinking they were just going out to take care of some last-minute business. The program started, and just when the quartet was finished singing, ugly as it was, we all heard this great bellow coming from somewhere deep in the building. Folks probably thought the Devil had got loose in the basement. Some people on stage unlocked the doors at the back and ran outside to the hallway, and by then they could hear Sue Dillon screaming regular as clockwork. They followed the noise down into the cellar. Reverend Simms was there, covered in blood, with Sue still screaming and holding the letter opener. You had fainted dead away.''

"Oh, my Lord," Mavis said, remembering too vividly now Hart's dark shadow in the pale light, his arms upraised, and the crash of the broken jar. "That poor girl. I want to see her."

Mavis stood up suddenly, and darkness jumped before her eyes. Putting down her hand on the edge of the sofa, she tried to steady herself, and Dale grabbed her other arm.

"Don't you think you'd better take it easy a little while longer?" The darkness cleared and she could see Dale's eyes, worried again, intent upon her face. "Charles Morgan may not want you to see her anyway."

"Well, you just let him try to stop me. Come on."

Mavis pulled her arm away from Dale's hand and started toward the door, into the hallway. Just then, there was a wail, and Mavis recognized Sue's voice. In the hallway, there seemed to be a commotion all of a sudden, and when Mavis looked, she saw two men coming along, walking heavily, with a black canvas bag swinging between them. Her heart almost stopped. Hart, surely, was in that bag. Dale hadn't said he was dead, but she must have known all along. Despite all that had happened, she thought, What a pity it was; he had tried so hard, wanted so much, only he didn't know how to go after it in a decent way. And he had hurt so many people trying.

The body passed on; the men went outside through the foyer, and in the brief moment of the door opening, Mavis glimpsed the crowd outside, people jostling one another to see, the white TV truck in the background and young kids making V-signs before the cameras. Tonight they would run home to see themselves on the six o'clock news, hardly even aware of the tragedy that had gone on right in front of their eyes.

Moving out into the hallway, with Dale just behind her, Mavis walked the few feet to Sue Dillon's office. After the cry, there was silence, and Mavis saw the girl now, sitting weeping in a chair in the corner. Charles Morgan stood in front of her, his big arms loose at his sides, his hands clenched as if he wanted to do something but didn't know what. Another man sat off to one side with a pad of paper in his hands, a pencil ready to write.

"Sue, honey?" Mavis's voice broke the silence. It seemed to bring calm into the room.

Sue Dillon looked up, her face swollen and splotched, her hair, all done up before, fallen and limp. The pink dress Mavis had thought so pretty when she had seen Sue up in the front of the sanctuary was splotched with drying blood, like dark flowers. When Sue saw Mavis standing in the doorway and, with a cry, covered her face, Mavis noticed that there were dark rings of blood underneath her fingernails.

"Now you just calm down, honey." Mavis moved toward Sue. Charles Morgan drew back to let her pass. Mavis touched Sue on her head and, all of a sudden, the girl grabbed Mavis's hand, clinging, it seemed, for dear life.

"I loved him so much," Sue Dillon cried out.

"Yes, I guess you did." Mavis shook her head from side to side. "I suppose anybody could see that if they just looked hard when they came in here. But people let things like that pass by and don't notice."

"He said it was all right." Sue was hiccuping now, her words coming quickly in short little bursts. "Said we were married in the eyes of the Lord. We couldn't let it out because people would talk. He said we would go to Africa together and set up a mission just like this one—for the natives—after I finished out at the Bible college." Sue closed her eyes and a great wave of pain passed across her face. "I'm going to have his baby!'' she cried out again. "What in the world am I going to do?"

Oh, Lord, Mavis thought, I didn't reckon it could get any worse. Just like before, with Ruth Anne. Him leading innocent girls astray with his promises and fancy words. That man was the Devil himself. Poor Sue Dillon, she didn't have a chance, working there in the office near him. Mavis could just see him—Hart prancing in, those black eyes shining, silky words on his lips—seducing Sue before she even knew what was going on. How many others had he done that to? Lord only knew, and even after they learned all about him, they still spoke of love. But why had Sue killed him, if she loved him, even to save Mavis?

"I didn't know about *her*." Sue almost spit out the word. "The one in the trailer with the children. Reverend Simms never talked about where he came from, what happened in the past. And I only saw him here. He said he lived out in the country, just a little place, not a fit place for me to go to. I never suspected, never questioned him. Not till today."

Sue pulled her fingers away from her face and sat up straighter in the chair, staring at Mavis. "I was listening to what he said while he was back there with you in the clothing room. I never expected to. When he left the sanctuary, I thought he was just coming out to take care of something, and when he didn't come back right away, I went out to see if I could help.

"Then I heard you two talking, him saying all those awful things, and I knew then how he had fooled me. I wanted to hate him. I picked up that letter opener from my desk without even thinking, and followed him when he took out after you down the hall to the cellar stairs. Still, I didn't know what I would do. I just came down the stairs quietly and walked behind him—and stuck the letter opener in his back when he tried to strangle you. It was so awful. I couldn't go through it all again."

Sue suddenly put her hand over her mouth and her eyes showed fear for the first time. There was silence in the little room.

"Again?" Mavis asked. And then, of course, she knew.

Sue would have been at the Mission that day when Theda came back all alone to see Hart; she was probably just a few feet away when it all happened. "It *was* 'again,' wasn't it, honey?" Mavis's voice was very soft. "You helped him the first time. How did he make you do it?"

Rocking, her face covered with her trembling, stained fingers, Sue began to wail once more. "I didn't *want* to!" she cried out. "He came into the office and told me I must do something, no questions asked. He said the Devil had sent somebody to torment him, to ruin his work here, and he had to get rid of her. I didn't know then he had killed her. I'd been busy, the door was closed, and I nearly fainted when he took me out into the hallway and there was Miz Hedrick spread out on the floor, her eyes staring, and that belt around her neck.

"We put her in a plastic garbage bag I got from the kitchen, just stuffed her in like a pile of old clothing. That's what I tried to think it was—nobody real a-tall. I had seen Miz Hedrick only once before, anyway.

"When it was dark, he pulled the car up right to the door, and we dragged her outside and put her in the backseat. I followed after him in that old truck he drives, so scared I thought I'd have a wreck and everything would be ruined. When we got out of town, we waited on the road, but nobody came by and we dragged her out into the cornfield. Reverend Simms opened the bag and let her slide out. Her arm flopped and hit my leg, and I ran back to the road, screaming. Reverend Simms hit me to make me be quiet. That was the only time I was afraid of him."

Sue had calmed, her voice quietened. She spoke almost as if she were talking to herself, a child reliving a bad dream hoping it will pass. Mavis wondered if it would, if Sue Dillon, like Ruth Anne, would forget all the horror, all the things she had done for that demon of a man because of what they still called love. She'd never know. Such a waste of lives, it seemed to her, but who could have protected those two girls? Theda, perhaps, had tried in her own way, and Sue Dillon must have a mother—sitting out in some pokey country house with snake plants and begonias on the front porch—who would have to bear the knowledge of her daughter's sins for the rest of her life. Perhaps no one was safe in this world. Even her own daughter, she thought with horror, might have had a similar fate had she lived. At least Mavis had that, the perfect memory of her own child unsullied, untainted with another's blood.

All of a sudden Mavis was very tired. She looked at Charles Morgan and he straightened up, unclasped his hands. "You take care of her," she said to him, pointing to Sue Dillon. "She's been through a lot."

He shook his head. "I'll do that, Miz Lashley. You go on home now and get some rest. I'll call you tomorrow if I need to talk to you more."

"Yes," she said, turning to take Dale's arm. "I'll do that thing."

Dale led her outside. The crowd waited still, but became a blur through the sudden tears that flooded Mavis's eyes.

Chapter
Twenty-four

"You certainly *will* stay for supper. I won't take any ifs, ands, or buts about it." Mavis shook her finger at Dale, who sat in the recliner across from her. The light was low in the living room, but still slanted in bright rays across the yard outside.

"Mavis, you've been through a lot today. I don't think you need to cook for any extra company." Dale leaned toward her, that concerned look in his eyes again.

"I have to eat, don't I? It won't make a bit of difference whether I cook for one or two. One extra plate to wash won't kill me." Mavis fingered the crocheted doily on the arm of the sofa and smoothed it out; she had made it so long ago, with her mother's strong fingers guiding Mavis's own until she could do it by herself. She had kept this piece of handiwork all these years.

"You aren't afraid, are you?"

"What in the world would I be afraid of now? There's nobody to come after me."

"I thought maybe you were still thinking about all that happened."

Mavis breathed out loudly, took her fingers away from the doily and held them in her lap. The dark scene in the basement flashed briefly before her eyes, then the tiny office where Sue Dillon gave her sad confession.

"Maybe," she said, "but I wasn't feeling fear."

"Now don't tell me you weren't afraid when Reverend

Simms—or whatever his name is—came after you in the basement."

"Of course I was. Who wouldn't be? But I was praying. I trusted in the Lord." Dale did not answer her and looked away from her eyes. "I just wish I could have prevented it all. I should have guessed sooner than I did what was going on, should have known what Reverend Simms was up to. I never liked his eyes. They were just mean, and I think I tried to forget that, thinking he was of the Lord. If nothing else, I should have seen his looks in those poor young'uns' faces . . . did, in fact, though I couldn't put my finger on it."

"Don't go blaming yourself," Dale said, looking back at her. "Nobody else knew it, either. The police would still be in the dark if it wasn't for you. They should give you an award."

"Oh, shoot. I'd be too embarrassed." She brushed the air with her hand, dismissing the thought. "No, I just want a little peace and quiet for a few days."

"What do you reckon will happen to them?"

"Who?"

"Those children, Ruth Anne."

"Why, nothing I expect. The authorities will probably investigate and fuss at Ruth Anne for exposing those poor little things to that man, but they won't take them away. No, I expect Ruth Anne will just sit on in her little trailer, more closed off than ever. If they're lucky, the children may grow up without knowing too much about their daddy, though I wouldn't put it past Ruth Anne to tell the whole story to them, still loving him and all. Now that he's dead, she'll probably make him a saint or something."

Dale took out a cigarette and lit it. Mavis didn't like for him to smoke in the house (it took hours to get the scent out again), but she did not frown at him this time, glad for his company. "Funny how they loved that preacher," she said. "Ruth Anne and Sue Dillon both. He sure must have had a way about him." She shook her head.

"They were searching, I guess. Needed somebody strong like that, someone to tell them what to do."

"Yes, maybe so. I wonder who'll tell Sue Dillon what to do now. You don't think they'll put her in jail, do you?"

"Not a chance," Dale said, looking around for an ashtray. He found one on the table next to his chair. "That Bible college will take over, send her off somewhere far away."

"You think they'll still have her back after all this mess is in the paper?"

"Sure they will. They'll forgive and forget. There will be a big church service and she'll weep and wail and carry on, and they'll say it was just the work of the Devil and then forgive."

Mavis shook her finger at Dale once again. "Now don't you scoff. Hart *was* like the Devil in a way, seducing and perverting their love."

Dale blew smoke in the air and let his eyes follow it upward. "Strange, isn't it? Love. Seems to come in so many shapes and sizes. Half the time you would think it was just the opposite."

Mavis joined her hands, looking down at them. "Yes, I know. It's all so sad. I still think about Theda and Alice Pate all those years, things going sour between them, hiding. And now just Alice all alone."

"Think she'll stay?"

"Why sure, where else would she go? She's got Charlene and Tommie Lee to take care of her. Who else would do it?"

"Won't she be wondering about the neighbors, the gossip?"

"No, that was Theda's worry. I don't think Alice will mind. And things are different now. People overlook things."

Dale crushed his cigarette out in the ashtray and started to reply, but just then, there was a large thump on the porch outside.

"Lord, is it that time already? It's the paper." Mavis started to get up from the sofa, pushing on the arm to help her rise. She stood, but then she stopped. "I think I'll just let it rest for now. No doubt everything that happened will be all over the front page, and I don't want to see it just yet." She smiled at Dale. "You come on," she said, motioning toward the back of the house. "I'm going to fix us some supper. You can sit and keep me company."

She turned and began to walk away. "You know what?" she said, as she opened the kitchen door. "I think I have some apples. I could make my special apple dish. You know, you've had it before. People say it's the best thing they ever put in their mouth."

About the Author

Robert Nordan was born in Raleigh, North Carolina, and attended Duke University. After working as a sales promotion copywriter in New York, he completed graduate studies in psychology at the University of Chicago and is now employed as a clinical child psychologist in an urban medical center in Chicago.